LOVE___
PRIVATE INVESTIGATORS

IN

The
Martian Falcon

ALAN K. BAKER

SNOWBOOKS

Proudly Published by Snowbooks in 2015

Snowbooks Ltd.
Tel: 0207 837 6482
email: info@snowbooks.com
www.snowbooks.com

Paperback ISBN 9781909679481
Ebook ISBN 9781782068877

Printed in Denmark by Nørhaven

*Dedicated to the memories of
Richard S. Shaver and Raymond Palmer,
creators of the Dero and other perils
of the Inner Earth*

There were gods who were old when Mars was a green planet...
– C. L. Moore, 'Dust of Gods'

From the New York Times
23rd June, 1925

MARTIAN FALCON STOLEN

PRICELESS ARTEFACT SEIZED FROM METROPOLITAN MUSEUM OF ART

TWO SECURITY GUARDS DEAD, ANOTHER SERIOUSLY INJURED

POLICE SUSPECT ZOMBIE MOB INVOLVEMENT

The ancient artefact known as the Martian Falcon was stolen last night from the Metropolitan Museum of Art in a raid which police have condemned as 'violent' and 'outrageous.'

According to a security guard who survived the raid, at about 10.30pm he and two colleagues heard suspicious sounds coming from the Martian Exhibit Hall and went to investigate, whereupon they were attacked by three zombies.

Two of the guards were killed and partially eaten, and the third badly injured; however, from his hospital bed the survivor was able to give police a description of his attackers, which has left them in no doubt that the Martian Falcon was stolen by the walking dead.

Lieutenant John Carter of the New York Police Department, who is leading the investigation, told reporters: 'We are unsure of the reason for the theft, since the perpetrators would be unable to sell the Falcon on the open art market. However, we cannot rule out the possibility that they were commissioned by an unknown collector who will keep his new acquisition secret.'

When asked why the zombies would have left one of their victims alive, Lieutenant Carter replied: 'No comment.'

CHAPTER 1
A Hell of a Town

Coming to New York had been a bad mistake.

Howard Phillips Lovecraft reflected on this sad fact as he walked along Clinton Street from his apartment to the small drugstore on the corner with Atlantic Avenue, where he could procure a small but satisfying breakfast of sausage, biscuits and coffee for small change.

Which was convenient, since small change was all he ever had in his pocket.

What was less convenient – although equally sad – was that his financial circumstances were in such a parlous state that this would be his only meal of the day.

The haze of diesel fumes which usually obscured the sky and watered down the sunlight, even in summer, had cleared thanks to a strong easterly wind from the Atlantic, but as Lovecraft looked up into the bright blue firmament, he felt there was precious little to be cheerful about. Even the multitudes of diesel-engined skycrawlers, which had so enthralled him on his arrival six months ago, had lost their technological allure. The aircraft, some of which were merely the size of buses, while the cargo carriers were like floating freight trains, had taken on the aspect of huge, ungainly thrumming insects in his imagination; he briefly contemplated the notion that there were no human beings onboard, that the skycrawlers were independent creatures from some distant world that had descended upon Earth for dark and incomprehensible purposes…

Lovecraft chuckled to himself. *There's a story in there somewhere*, he thought, and his step quickened as he reached the corner of Atlantic. The traffic was brisk against a backdrop of steel, glass and concrete skyscrapers which rose like an alien forest into the cloudless sky, and Lovecraft hesitated for a moment as the realisation came to him that this was not Earth – at least, not the Earth he knew and loved. The floating mechanical beasts had not left their world at all: *this* was their world, and Howard Phillips Lovecraft was the alien visitor.

Providence, he thought. *Oh Providence! Why did I leave you?*

He walked along the sidewalk, passed noisily by growling heaps of steel and chrome which honked angrily at each other, and lamented the lost peace and tranquillity of his hometown, where the gentility of the eighteenth century could still be felt in the elegant colonial architecture and gently winding streets.

How long must I linger here in this frightful city, he wondered, *before common sense overcomes pride, and I can return to my beloved Providence?*

He paused before entering the drugstore to buy a copy of the *New York Times* from a street vendor. The machine stirred to life at his approach, and when he asked for the paper, a mechanical arm, whining on exposed servos, dipped into a steel basket, selected the correct title and held it out to him.

Lovecraft fished a dime from the pocket of his embarrassingly threadbare trousers and dropped it into the slot on the front of the vendor. 'Thank you,' he said, as the mechanical hand released the paper.

Two young men who were passing glanced at him in surprise and burst out laughing. 'He's talkin' to the vendor!' said one to the other. 'What a chump!'

Lovecraft briefly considered remonstrating with them, reminding them that politeness cost nothing, and for some people it was a habit which could not be broken, no matter who or what one was addressing. Their bearing, however, not to mention the size of the muscles bulging beneath their shirts, suggested that this would not be the wisest course of action.

'*Daaaaannnnkuuuuussssirrrrrr!*' exclaimed the mechanical voice of the vendor.

Lovecraft winced at the ugliness of the sound, shoved the newspaper under his arm, and went into the drugstore.

There were several free seats at the counter. He took one next to a tall, slightly overweight bespectacled man with a large, bushy moustache that formed a shallow inverted V over his mouth. He gave his order to the sad-faced girl who was mopping up some spilled coffee with a cloth that looked like it was no stranger to such duty, and opened the paper to the classified ads section.

'G'mornin', Mr Lovecraft!' shouted the short-order cook, a Bavarian kobold whose name was Hans, through the large serving hatch leading to the kitchen.

'Good morning to you,' Lovecraft replied.

Hans leaned through the hatch and gave a smile which appeared to be at least six inches too wide for his pale blue face, revealing teeth that were all fangs, while he regarded Lovecraft with his huge black eyes. His long, slender, pointed ears, which extended horizontally from his round head, twitched and turned like a cat's.

'How about I add a side order of meatloaf to your usual, huh? Made a batch fresh this mornin' – and this is the only day this week I'll be able to say that without bein' a liar – not that that'll stop me, *nicht wahr?*'

Lovecraft's mouth started to water, but his lack of funds forbade such an indulgence, and so he replied: 'No, thank you. The usual will suffice.'

'Ach! Have it your own way,' said Hans. 'But you're missin' a treat, lemme tell you that!'

'I dare say,' Lovecraft muttered, as his eyes scanned the 'Situations Wanted - Male' category of the classified ads, eventually finding his own.

WRITER AND REVISER, free-lance, desires regular and permanent salaried connection with any responsible enterprise requiring literary services; exceptionally thorough experience in preparing correct and fluent text on subjects assigned, and in meeting the most difficult, intricate and extensive

> problems of rewriting and constructive revision, prose or verse; would also consider situation dealing with such proofreading as demands rapid and discriminating perception, orthographical accuracy, stylistic fastidiousness and a keenly developed sense of the niceties of English usage; good typist; age 34; has for seven years handled all the prose and verse of a leading American public speaker and editor. Y 2292 Times Annex.

Lovecraft's friend Frank Long had chuckled when he'd shown him the copy. 'A bit wordy for a classified ad, isn't it?' he'd said. 'On the contrary,' Lovecraft had countered. 'I believe it to be concise, well-structured and to the point. It will convey to any prospective clients the undeniable fact that I am no mere charlatan or *poseur* in the field of literary revision, but a genuinely conscientious and knowledgeable practitioner of the English tongue.'

The ad had cost nearly forty dollars, the equivalent of a month's rent in his shabby one-room apartment on Clinton Street; it had been Sonia's gift to him before she moved to Cleveland to take up an offer of employment.

In all honesty, Lovecraft could not say that he missed her.

Getting married had been as big a mistake as moving to New York, and both Lovecraft and Sonia had realised it within a few months. So when Sonia's hat shop on Fifth Avenue was forced to close and the Cleveland job offer appeared, both had seen it as a convenient point at which to part company.

Lovecraft read the ad once again, gave a satisfied 'hmm', and then turned to the front page. The main headline was depressing in its reinforcement of his belief that New York was a den of irredeemable iniquity, a stinking cesspool of vice, violence and squalor where all human decency was subsumed in the animalistic desire for dominance over one's fellows.

'Martian Falcon stolen,' he muttered to himself. 'Oh dear, that's so sad.'

He had seen the Falcon several times during his frequent visits to the Metropolitan Museum of Art, and had marvelled at its strange beauty; each time he had seen it, standing there aloof and inscrutable in its metal case with a single small window set into the front, he had wondered at the nature of the long-vanished civilisation that had created it. Had they been anything like humans?

Lovecraft hoped not.

His fascinated musings had led him to write several short stories about ancient Mars and its people, only one of which he had managed to sell. *Weird Tales* had bought it for a hundred dollars – a king's ransom to the cash-strapped Lovecraft – although it had not been granted the honour of the cover illustration, as he'd hoped.

Where the Falcon was now was anyone's guess, although the police theory that it had been stolen to order struck Lovecraft as plausible. It was, in all probability, now in the home of some private collector with more money than morals – or perhaps on its way out of the country...

His thoughts were interrupted by the harsh clatter of breaking crockery. He looked up suddenly, along with everyone else at the counter, towards the serving hatch, where he could see Hans gesticulating wildly before his hotplate, a spatula in one hand and a wooden spoon in the other.

'*Scheisse!*' the kobold shouted. 'Hey you! Get the hell outa here! Go on! No poltergeists allowed! This is a high-class place, you ectoplasmic son of a bitch!'

In response to this entreaty, another stack of plates toppled from a shelf and crashed upon the floor, eliciting a howl of rage from Hans.

'God*damnit!* What's your problem, *dummkopf?* Why you botherin' me like this? What have I done to you, huh?'

The pages of Lovecraft's paper fluttered in a sudden breeze which seemed to come out of nowhere. He glanced over his shoulder at the door to the drugstore, which remained closed, and then back through the serving hatch in time to see one of the eggs frying on the hotplate lift into the air and hit Hans square in the face. The kobold responded by flailing wildly with his powerful, muscular arms, scything the air with his spatula and spoon.

'I'd kick your ass if you had one, so help me God I would!' he screamed. 'I pay good money for protection from assholes like you! Good money!'

A long link of sausages rose up like an angry cobra from a tray beside the hotplate and flew at Hans, wrapping itself around his neck and then flopping down over his chest. He sighed, threw down his cooking implements and stood with his hands on his hips, like some flapper who had just taken possession of an unusual boa.

'I'm gonna talk to Johnny about this – ya hear that? I'm gonna go talk to Johnny Sanguine about what you're doin'! And then you'll be sorry.'

This threat seemed to have the desired effect, for at that moment a faint, ethereal scream filled the air, the breeze vanished, and the food and crockery in the kitchen lay still. Hans took his none-too-clean cook's cloth from his belt, wiped the egg yolk from his face and looked around the kitchen, a satisfied smile gradually spreading across his features.

'That did it,' he said, winking at Lovecraft. 'That son of a bitch won't be back in a hurry!'

Lovecraft was not surprised. If Hans was paying protection money to Johnny Sanguine, the Vampire King of Brooklyn, the poltergeist had made a serious mistake in showing up in the first place.

He shook his head and returned his attention to the paper. 'Police suspect zombie mob involvement.' He tutted. 'Oh, good lord!'

He caught a movement out of the corner of his eye and glanced at the chubby man with the moustache sitting next to him. The man had taken what looked like a library index card from his coat pocket. The card was blank. He took out a fountain pen and began to write, rapidly filling the card with a tiny, precise script.

'Always takin' notes, eh, Charlie?' said Hans as he banged a plate containing Lovecraft's breakfast on the shelf of the serving hatch and tapped the bell. 'Order up!'

The chubby man merely nodded and gave a good-natured smile as he blew on the card to dry the ink and placed it back in his pocket.

The sad-faced girl picked up the plate and laid it before Lovecraft. 'More coffee, hon?' she said.

'Yes, please,' Lovecraft replied as the aroma of sausage and biscuits drifted up from the plate. His stomach grumbled loudly in response, and he dropped his eyes from the girl's in embarrassment – although she didn't seem to notice as she slopped coffee which was so weak it looked more like tea into his mug.

'Yeah, always takin' notes,' Hans continued as he flipped a couple of eggs on the hotplate. 'You workin' on a case right now, Charlie?'

'Not right now, Hans,' the chubby man replied.

'Ach! Too bad. Whaddya think about that goddamned poltergeist, huh? What a nerve!'

'Have you ever had a problem with poltergeists before?' asked the man.

'Nah. Like I said, I pay good money to keep this place safe. Supernaturals know to stay away.'

'I think you spoke too soon, Hans,' said the man, as he jerked a thumb over his shoulder.

Lovecraft turned to see three zombies coming in through the door. Like everyone else at the counter, he felt his heart rate quicken and the hairs on the back of his neck rise. As the zombies approached the counter, Lovecraft looked down at his plate and saw patches of mould appearing on his biscuits, while the smell of the sausages changed from delicious to stomach-churning as the meat went rancid in the space of a few seconds. He glanced at the zombies' black neckties, noting the symbols of the Enochian alphabet which were stitched into the silk in hair-fine gold thread, and which glowed very faintly. *Their power source*, he thought grimly. *The occult means by which their post-mortem existence is maintained.*

Hans reappeared at the serving hatch, took one look at the zombies, whose immaculate black suits only served to intensify the decay on their grey, lifeless faces, and threw up his hands in exasperation.

'God*damn* it! First a poltergeist, now zombies! What a way to start the day! Whaddya want, huh? I run a high-class joint, and I pay good money to keep it safe, and you're makin' all my food go bad!'

'Relax, kobold,' said one of the zombies, in a voice that made Lovecraft want to cough. The creature placed a rotting hand on the chubby man's shoulder. 'Mr Fort. Come with us.'

'Why?' asked the man, his voice level yet tinged with resignation.

'Someone wants to talk to you. Someone very important.'

'And what if I don't want to talk to them?'

The zombie shrugged, producing a sound that was a mixture of the squelching of semi-liquefied flesh and the cracking of bones that should have been at rest. 'We'll stick around until all the kobold's food goes bad. He'll have to shut up shop, get the place steam-cleaned and then order in new stock. Inconvenient, no?'

The chubby man sighed, took some change from his pocket and placed it on the counter, then stood up and put on his hat. 'See you around, Hans,' he said.

'You take care of yourself, Charlie,' said Hans, his gaze flitting between the zombies. 'And thanks for not stickin' around.'

'Don't mention it.'

Flanked by the zombies, the chubby man left the drugstore.

Lovecraft turned and looked though the plate-glass window. A black Studebaker stretch limousine was parked at the kerb, all sweeping lines and polished menace. The chubby man climbed in, followed by the zombies, and the Studebaker swept away into the growling, honking traffic.

CHAPTER 2
The Diesel-Powered Gangster

Charles Hoy Fort settled into the back seat of the Studebaker and looked out through the side window at the traffic on Atlantic Avenue. He was sitting between two of the zombies, while the third sat on the rear-facing seat in front of him. The stench of their dead flesh was made worse by the thick, cloying scent of their expensive cologne.

'So,' said Fort. 'Who wants to see me?'

The zombie opposite replied: 'Like I said, someone very important.'

'Capone?'

The zombie did not respond, merely gazed at him with his eyes the colour of half-cooked egg white.

Fort glanced to either side, at each of the once-living, now undead men who flanked him. 'Come on, fellas! You might as well tell me: I'm going to be seeing him in the next few minutes, anyway.'

But it was no use; the zombies had clearly been instructed to divulge nothing, probably as a tactic to maximise Fort's fear and unease. They needn't have bothered: Fort already felt fearful and uneasy. He glanced over the shoulder of the zombie facing him, at the cracked, flaking skin on the back of the driver's head. It wasn't easy to teach a zombie how to drive: they tended to floor the accelerator and go in a straight line, directly into whatever obstacle happened to be in their way. Self-preservation was not high on your average zombie's list of priorities – the phrase 'nothing to lose' could have been invented for them.

There was only one man (*scratch that*, thought Fort, *one mobster*) with the magical know-how to teach a zombie to drive properly.

Alphonse Gabriel Capone, the Diesel-Powered Gangster.

Fort sighed and tried to relax as the limousine weaved through the Brooklyn traffic, but it was no use. The lifeless eyes of the zombies, combined with the stench of their decaying bodies and the unknown (and almost certainly unpleasant) reason for his summons, told him that it had been a mistake to get out of bed that morning. As a private investigator specialising in the occult and supernatural, Fort was no stranger to the mob, although, like any other sane person who enjoyed being alive and in good health, he tried to keep his contacts with the criminal fraternity to a minimum.

What the hell does Capone want with me? Fort wondered. *Have I done anything recently to draw attention to myself?*

His last case had been routine enough: a widow out in Coney Island whose dead husband had been convinced that she was having an affair, and had decided to return from the Other Side to make her pay for her infidelity, apparently not caring that the fact that he was dead kind of released her from that particular marital responsibility. Fort had tried to exorcise the spirit himself, but the man's jealousy had proved too powerful an anchor in the physical world. In the end, he had had to bring in his old friend Father O'Malley to perform a banishing. Case closed, client invoiced, no mob involvement. Done and dusted.

I haven't done anything to annoy the wrong people, Fort told himself in desperation. *So why am I here, in a limo full of zombies, trying to breathe through my mouth?*

A thought suddenly occurred to him: a possible explanation which didn't make him feel any better. In fact, it made him feel a whole lot worse.

What if Capone wants to hire me...?

*

The car moved swiftly across the East River on the Williamsburg Bridge, then glided onto Delancey Street and turned north into Midtown. As Fort had more than half expected, they finally came to a halt outside the imposing facade of the Algonquin Hotel on West 44th Street, where Capone maintained his New York residence.

The zombie to Fort's right opened the door and stepped out. Fort heaved a sigh that was part resignation and part relief at getting away from the stench that filled the limo, and followed. The other two zombies quickly climbed from the car and flanked him on the street, doubtless to make him think twice about making a run for it. Fort had no intention of doing so: he wanted to get this over and done with as quickly as possible; in any event, Capone could have him picked up again whenever he chose, and he strongly suspected that next time the gangster's goons wouldn't be so polite.

Feeling a little like a gangster himself, Fort entered the hotel's plush foyer with his new and unwanted entourage and headed for the bank of elevators at the rear, the gilded bars of their doors reminding him uncomfortably of a prison cell. The people milling around cast furtive and uneasy glances at the new arrivals, and those in front of them got out of their way in a hurry.

Fort didn't blame them.

The elevator boy looked like he wanted nothing more than to get out of their way as well, but he had no choice in the matter. With a nervous little nod to Fort, he slid the gilded gate shut as the lead zombie said: 'Penthouse.'

The elevator car ascended – far too slowly for Fort and the elevator boy, who took each breath in a quick, shallow gasp. Not for the first time, Fort wondered if zombies were embarrassed by the miasmal reek that emanated from their reanimated bodies. He had never had the heart to ask one – or the guts, for that matter.

Finally, they reached the twelfth floor, and the elevator boy breathed an audible sigh of relief as he yanked open the gate and squawked: 'Penthouse, sir!'

The zombies ignored him, so Fort gave him a smile and replied: 'Thanks, kid.'

'Follow me,' said the lead zombie. Fort followed him along a wide corridor, past several dark-suited goons who looked him up and down with undisguised contempt. Capone had permanently reserved the entire penthouse level of the hotel for himself and his entourage, and Fort experienced the uncomfortable certainty that he would be here until Capone told him he could leave.

The zombie came to a halt before a set of double doors and knocked.

From the other side, a harsh voice barked: 'Yeah!'

The zombie opened the doors and unceremoniously shoved Fort into a large and beautifully furnished room.

'Charlie boy!' said the man behind the vast antique oak desk which dominated one half of the room. 'Glad you could make it. Come on in!'

'I wouldn't have missed it, Mr Capone,' Fort replied.

Like I had any choice, you son of a bitch.

Capone stood up, and Fort took an involuntary step back. Everyone knew what Capone had done to himself – or rather, what he'd *had* done to himself, by a neuromechanic who preferred to remain anonymous. People saw him on the streets, here in New York and in Chicago; they saw his pictures in the papers, they knew exactly what he looked like; but no amount of familiarity with his image could prepare one for being this close to him.

His fat, brutal face was intact; his hard eyes shone from beneath his thick, bushy eyebrows while his prominent, almost sensual lips curled in a smile that was far from benign. That, however, was where his resemblance to a human being ended. His body was gone ('ditched like last year's Cadillac,' he was fond of saying), replaced by a steel exoskeleton whose powerful pistons served as muscles. His heart (if he could ever have been said to possess one) had been replaced by a small but highly efficient diesel engine, its exhaust gases captured by two large circular filters where his shoulder blades had once been.

Al Capone, the Diesel-Powered Gangster, indicated an overstuffed leather wingchair in front of his desk with a hand whose fingers were the shape of .50 calibre shells, and said: 'Have a seat, Charlie. Take a load off.'

Fort forced himself to step forward and sit down.

'My boys take care of you?'

Fort shrugged. 'They got me here without taking any bites out of me, so yeah, I guess they did.'

Capone gave a loud, throaty laugh as he stomped over on hissing, piston-powered legs, to a large and well-stocked bar. 'Let's have a drink, Charlie.'

'It's a little early for me,' Fort replied.

'I'm sorry, Charlie, I don't think I heard you,' said Capone, all traces of humour suddenly vanishing from his voice.

'Er, I'll take a small bourbon.'

'Sure, Charlie boy, sure!' Capone grabbed a crystal decanter and poured. 'Rocks? Soda?'

'Just ice.'

'You got it.'

Capone handed him a glass, clanked back to his chair and sat down heavily. He slurped his bourbon loudly.

'I didn't know you could drink,' said Fort, fascinated in spite of himself.

'Oh yeah, I can drink. Eat, too. It goes into a receptacle here…' Capone thumped his mechanical torso just below the sternum. 'Course, I don't *need* to, but I still like the taste of good food and good booze. When the receptacle's full up, I just take it out and empty it. Good system. Means I don't have to waste time on the crapper.'

'Sounds perfect,' Fort nodded, taking a sip of his drink. 'So, Mr Capone, may I ask why you… invited me here?'

Capone grinned like a hyena that had just found a fresh carcass to chew on. 'Straight down to business. I like that. Okay, lemme ask you a question.' He indicated his powerful mechanical body. 'Why do you think I got myself kitted out like this?'

Fort shrugged. 'Is it tax deductible?'

'As it happens, yeah – but that ain't the reason. I ditched my old body and got a new one so that no one would fuck with me.'

'I'd have thought that was pretty unlikely *before* you... ditched your old body.'

'Unlikely, yeah, but it still happened. It happened way too often, Charlie. But not anymore – at least until now.'

Fort took another sip of his drink. He didn't like where this conversation was headed, although he had to admit that that was inevitable.

'You read the papers this mornin', Charlie?' Capone continued.

'Yes.'

'Then you know about the Martian Falcon.'

'I know it was stolen from the Metropolitan Museum.'

Capone slammed his glass down onto the desk. It shattered with an ugly crinkle of sound. 'And someone's tryin' to make it look like I'm behind the heist!' he thundered, his face suddenly twisted into a fantastically ugly mask of rage and hatred.

Fort's breath caught in his throat. When Al Capone got mad, you'd better watch out, even of it wasn't your fault. 'I'm very sorry to hear that, Mr Capone,' he said.

'Not as sorry as I am, buddy! And not as sorry as the son of a bitch who's responsible, when I get my hands on him!'

I believe you, you crazy mechanical bastard.

'Do you have any idea who's behind it?' Fort asked.

'Oh yeah, I got a pretty good idea. Johnny Sanguine.'

'The Vampire King of Brooklyn?'

'King, my cast-iron ass! He's nothin' but a two-bit hustler. A cock-suckin' nightwalker who got lucky.'

'According to the reports, the Falcon was stolen by zombies, and you're well known for using them. So you're saying that Sanguine used them so that suspicion would automatically fall on you.'

'Got it in one,' Capone snapped.

'Sounds like he's moving against you,' mused Fort. 'But why bother? You control Chicago; your interests in New York are minimal. What could he hope to gain by taking you out – assuming he's stupid enough to try?'

22

'Oh he's stupid enough,' Capone replied. 'And talkin' of "stupid", I'm disappointed in you, Charlie.'

'I'm sorry to hear that,' Fort said, meaning it.

'It looks like Sanguine is lookin' to make a move on my turf, on Chicago. He'll need to get me out of the picture before he tries it. This is a pretty good start, no?'

'I guess… if that's what he's really doing.'

Capone fixed Fort with his dangerous gaze. 'If? What're you talkin' about?'

Damn, thought Fort. *Shouldn't have said that.*

'Come on, Charlie, spit it out!'

Fort sighed. 'How much do you know about the Martian Falcon, Mr Capone?'

'Not much – apart from it's from Mars and it's pretty goddamn valuable.'

'More than valuable; it's priceless. It was discovered during the US expedition to Mars two years ago, in the ruins of what we assume is an ancient temple.'

'Yeah… so what?'

'Well, I'm curious about life on other worlds – even extinct life, like on Mars – and I've been keeping track of the expedition and its aftermath. Did you know, for instance, that the crew of Rocketship X-M have all suffered psychological problems since they returned to Earth?'

'Who gives a shit?'

Fort shrugged. 'A lot of people, actually – not least the National Committee on Planetary Exploration, and the families of the spacecraftsmen.'

'Okay, so they went gaga. What's that got to do with me and that bastard Johnny Sanguine?'

'I'm not sure it's got anything to do with you. But there have been rumours floating around the scientific community ever since the X-M returned and its crew started to experience mental problems…'

'Rumours?'

'Yes. Some people think that the Falcon might be responsible.'

Capone sat forward suddenly. 'How so?'

'No one really knows. The expedition brought a lot of stuff back: artefacts of all kinds. Following analysis, it was all transferred to the newly-established Martian Exhibit Hall at the Metropolitan Museum of Art. The Falcon was the only artefact to be placed in a lead-lined case, and was only viewable through a small window. The curators explained this as an extra security measure, given the Falcon's apparent uniqueness and pristine condition – don't forget, it's more than five million years old. But...'

'But you think there's another reason,' said Capone.

'Possibly.'

'You think that if anyone gets too close to the Falcon, they go nuts.'

'Without adequate shielding... maybe. Chemical analysis revealed it to be made of obsidian, and x-ray photography showed that it has no internal structure to speak of. It's apparently just a statue, and nothing more. If you ask the NCPE, that's the answer you'll get. I know: I've asked them. As far as they're concerned, there's no correlation between what happened to the crew of the X-M and the Martian Falcon. And they also play down the crew's psychological problems – at least publically; they say they're just experiencing the disorientating effects of such a long space flight. I guess that makes sense: after all, they travelled further than any human being has ever travelled. But I can't help thinking there's more to it than that...'

'You think the NCPE has swept it under the rug.'

'Precisely. For them, it's a piece of damned data.'

'A what?'

Fort smiled. 'By "damned" I mean *excluded*. It's something they can't explain with current scientific methods, so they exclude it from their consideration. It's a familiar phenomenon in science, Mr Capone.'

'Yeah, well, I don't give a fuck about science, Charlie. I want out of the frame for this caper, and I want out *quick*. That's where you come in.'

'Me?'

'Yeah, you.'

'I don't understand,' said Fort, shifting uncomfortably in his seat. 'What can *I* do?'

'Let me explain it to you, Charlie,' said Capone, in the manner of a teacher addressing a particularly dense student. 'Normally, I'd take care of somethin' like this by takin' out the opposition. Normally, I'd just whack Johnny Sanguine…'

'Whack him?'

'Give him the big toothpick, *stake* him – you know what I'm talkin' about.'

Of course I know what you're talking about, for Christ's sake! thought Fort. *But whacking a vampire? My God…*

'You're not… by any chance… suggesting that *I* stake him… are you?'

Capone laughed long and hard at this. 'Oh, Charlie boy!' he said, shaking his head. 'That's what I like about you: you got a great sense of humour. No, I ain't suggesting you stake him. You don't got what it takes to kill Sanguine.'

'Then what do you want from me?' Fort asked, deciding that it was way too early to feel relieved.

Capone leaned forward and placed his angular metal elbows on the desk. 'I want you to find out if that son of a bitch really has the Martian Falcon. And if he does, I want you to find a way of provin' it. I'm gettin' out of the frame for this, Charlie, and you're gonna help me!'

CHAPTER 3
Memories of Cydonia

There was a letter waiting for Lovecraft in the dingy lobby of his apartment building. The return address on the envelope was that of *Weird Tales*. Unable to wait, he thrust his newspaper under his arm and tore the envelope open right there and then. The first line told him everything he needed to know.

'Another rejection,' he whispered, shaking his head and scowling at the signature of the magazine's editor, Farnsworth Wright. 'You're a buffoon, Wright,' he said. 'You can't understand what I'm trying to do, even when I explain it to you.'

He trudged forlornly up the stairs to the third floor (the elevator didn't work, of course) and along the corridor, trying to ignore the troglodytic shouts that emanated from several apartments – some of which actually contained troglodytes.

The door to his own apartment was ajar, the wood around the lock cracked and splintered.

Oh no, he thought. *Oh dear Lord!*

Lovecraft pushed open the door a few inches and peeked into the apartment, grateful for once that it consisted of only one room, the entirety of which he could see from his vantage point. It was empty; whoever had broken in had clearly come and gone. Lovecraft's books had been yanked from their shelves and scattered across the floor; the threadbare sofa had been overturned, and the closet doors were open. The two spare suits that had hung there were gone, along with his overcoat.

You took my suits and my coat? Lovecraft thought with a heavy sigh. He looked down at the light summer suit he was wearing. *This will be less than serviceable come winter... assuming I'm still here in this rat hole of a city.*

There was a payphone in the lobby downstairs. Lovecraft turned and trudged back along the corridor. Once he had called the police, he would return to the apartment and see what else, if anything, had been stolen.

He thought again of the ad he had placed in the *New York Times* and wondered if it would lead to any paid work. *Who am I kidding?* he asked himself miserably. There was clearly nothing else for it: he would have to consult the paper again, this time to search the situations vacant section.

Once again, he would have to try to get a regular job.

*

It was a little after ten o'clock when Fort got back to his office. His secretary, Penny Malone, stood up from her desk in the outer office as soon as she saw him: the expression on his face told her that something was wrong.

'What is it, Charlie?' she asked, her frown echoing that of her employer, darkening her normally bright features.

Fort looked into her cobalt-blue eyes and tried to smile, with limited success. 'Nothing, sweetheart, nothing.'

Penny placed her hands on her slim hips, dark red varnish camouflaging her nails against the deep crimson of her dress. Her frown deepened. 'Charlie...'

'Everything's fine,' he lied. 'I got a new case.'

'Really?'

'Yeah.'

'What kind of case?'

'A customer wants me to track down a stolen item.'

Penny regarded him with unblinking eyes for a few seconds. 'What customer?'

Fort sighed. 'Al Capone.'

Penny gasped. '*What?*'

Fort sat on the edge of the desk, his shoulders hunched. 'And he wants me to track down the Martian Falcon.'

Penny sat down slowly in her chair. 'Tell me this is a joke, Charlie,' she said, very quietly.

'I wish I could, Pen. But it isn't. Capone's goons grabbed me this morning...'

'I thought you smelled funny.'

'... and took me to the Algonquin. He's catching some heat for the heist, but says he wasn't behind it. He reckons it's down to Johnny Sanguine, and he wants me to prove it.'

'Oh *Jesus*. The Diesel-Powered Gangster wants you to go up against the Vampire King of Brooklyn?'

'Talk about a rock and a hard place,' Fort chuckled mirthlessly.

Penny shook her head. 'You said it, hon. So... what are you going to do?'

Fort ran a twitchy hand through his thick dark hair. 'Not a whole lot I *can* do... except take the case. I can't say no to Capone – I'm very attached to my kneecaps, and I want it to stay that way.'

'And what if you manage to pin the theft on Sanguine? What do you think *he's* going to do?'

'I'll just have to make damned sure he doesn't find out it's me.'

Penny shook her head again, more emphatically this time. 'You can't do it, Charlie, you just *can't!*'

'Like I said, angel,' Fort sighed. 'I've got no choice.' He looked at his secretary for a long moment. 'You know, Pen, it occurs to me that you haven't had a vacation in quite a while. Why don't you take a couple of weeks off?'

'Oh no you don't, Charlie Fort!' cried Penny, jumping to her feet, hugging him and placing a kiss on his cheek. 'You don't get rid of me that easily...'

'I'm not trying to get rid of you,' Fort replied, taking out his handkerchief and fussily wiping her lipstick off his cheek.

'Yes you are! You're worried about this case, and you want me out of harm's way. Tell me it isn't so!'

Fort held up his hands. 'Okay, okay! Look, things may get ugly, and I don't want you here if they do.'

Penny shook her head. 'You're such a hon, Charlie, but I'm not going anywhere.'

They looked at each other for a long moment.

'I'm not going anywhere,' Penny repeated, her voice quiet and intense, denying even the possibility of further argument.

Fort lowered his eyes. 'What would I do without you, Pen?'

'Now, don't go getting all maudlin on me, Charlie,' she admonished.

Fort looked at the lipstick smeared on his handkerchief, folded it carefully and placed it back in his pocket. 'Any messages?' he asked.

'Yeah. I took a couple of calls from people answering your ad for an assistant in the *Times*.'

'And?'

'One sounds promising. He's not from New York. Sounds like he's from New England, kind of cultured-sounding, actually. I set up an interview.' She glanced at her watch. 'He should be here in an hour.'

'Good. What's his name?'

'Howard Lovecraft.'

*

Fort closed the door to the inner office, went to his desk and sat down heavily. He found himself thinking about Penny, and her late husband, Archer Malone, who had been his partner. When Archer had been killed during their investigation of a Cavorite smuggling ring in the Bronx two years ago, Fort had been there to comfort Penny. It had been a rough time for them both – as rough as times come – but Fort had done all he could to see her through it.

When Archer was alive, Penny had sometimes joked with Fort that he was the only other man she could ever have seen herself with; there had been a time, maybe a year or so after his death, when she and Fort might have got together. But something stopped them, something which neither of them could define:

maybe it was the memory of Archer and the grief which still hovered in the back of Penny's mind, or maybe it was the nature of Fort's work and the dangers it involved, and the fear felt by both of them that one day she might find herself alone all over again.

Whatever the reason, the moments had come and gone until, perhaps taking the hint, they stopped coming altogether.

Fort looked at the hazy figure moving behind the frosted glass of his office door. He sighed. 'The road not taken,' he said very quietly to himself. 'Had to be that way... had to.'

He swivelled back and forth in his chair for a minute or so, like a clerk who'd been given some onerous task and was reluctant to buckle down and get started. He checked his watch, even though he knew the time, and gave another sigh, heavy and miserable.

Suddenly recalling the events of earlier that morning, he took the library index card from his pocket and quickly read the notes he had written following the poltergeist visitation at the drugstore, then stood up and went over to the enormous bank of file cabinets which covered one entire wall of his office. He opened the drawer marked P and placed the index card inside, then opened a larger drawer and withdrew a thick folder, which he carried back to his desk.

With an hour to go until this Lovecraft character showed up for his interview, Fort decided that the best thing would be to re-familiarise himself with the details of the X-M expedition. The folder contained press cuttings, magazine articles, public information from the National Committee on Planetary Exploration and photographs of Rocketship X-M and its ill-fated crew, along with stunning images of the surface of Mars.

Fort took a leather pouch of Bull Durham tobacco and brown papers from his jacket pocket and rolled himself a cigarette. He lit it, inhaled, blew out a thin stream of smoke, and began to read.

The ship had blasted off from the rocket complex at Cabo Cañaveral on Florida's Atlantic coast on April 16th, 1920. Powered by the latest atomic motors, the X-M had made the flight to Mars in a little under three months – itself a triumph of human ingenuity and endurance. The onboard electro-telescopes provided a huge amount of astronomical data, including the discovery of the strange dark bodies drifting through the plane of the ecliptic between the planets, for which science had yet to come up with an explanation.

It was on Mars itself, however, that Captain Thorne Smith and his crew made their greatest discovery. From high orbit, they detected peculiar regularities amongst the mountains, plains and impact craters which covered the planet's surface. When the ship's telescopes were directed at these features, they were revealed to be the time-worn remains of buildings. Fort remembered the excitement that had spread across the world when the newsreels reported the X-M's discovery of the relics of a long-vanished civilisation on the Red Planet; he remembered waiting, along with millions of others, for news of each new radio dispatch from the expedition. Even now, two years after the X-M's triumphant return, he still felt the same excitement at the thought that there had once been another civilisation out there in the vast interplanetary night.

The ship had landed in the region called Cydonia by astronomers, after the ancient city-state on the island of Crete. She came to rest on a flat, level plain a few miles from one of the larger collections of squares, circles, triangles and pentagons which were scattered across the landscape. It quickly became apparent to the crew that these curious shapes were actually the roofs of large structures which had been buried millennia ago by the constantly-shifting sands of Mars. When the astrogator, Felix Bukowski, discovered a means of entry into one of the structures, Captain Smith immediately decided that the expedition program should be altered so that their planned month-long stay on Mars could be devoted entirely to the exploration of the ruins' interiors.

That the city had been dead for millennia, perhaps millions of years, there could be no doubt. The alien necropolis was vast in extent, and the crew of the X-M had little doubt that their exploration was barely scratching the surface of what had once been a sophisticated planetary civilisation.

For the next four weeks, the crew explored the ruined city, naming it Cydonia after the region in which it lay, mapping it, taking the most interesting-looking artefacts and storing them carefully on the rocketship.

It was in a gigantic vault several hundred feet below the surface that the artefact which came to be known as the Martian Falcon was discovered, sitting serene and inscrutable upon a cylinder of black basalt. With no thought as to the consequences – for what consequences could there have been in that aeon-dead place? – Captain Smith ordered the artefact to be taken back to the X-M, for they saw nothing else like it during their necessarily brief stay, and Smith thought that the way it was displayed implied that it was unique – or at least of extreme importance to the beings who had fashioned it.

The world listened breathlessly to each excited dispatch from the Red Planet; and everyone agreed with Captain Smith when he said that what they had discovered on Mars would keep scientists, anthropologists and archaeologists busy for decades to come.

No one gave any thought to the fact that they were, in effect, vandalising the most important archaeological site ever discovered.

At least, no one human…

Of course, Rocketship X-M's homecoming hadn't turned out to be quite as triumphant as the world had thought. Not that there weren't celebrations and ticker-tape parades through the streets of every major American city, radio and magazine interviews and congratulatory messages from pretty much every government on Earth. There was all of that, naturally, at first.

And then… then something strange happened. The public appearances by the X-M's crew dropped off suddenly, and requests for interviews were declined – always with the same excuse: that Captain Smith and his crew were busy planning the next expedition to Mars, and could no longer spare the time to talk to journalists. The excuse was logical enough: Smith and the others were spacecraftsmen, and their job took priority over their inevitable celebrity; but the suddenness and completeness of this turn-around was perplexing to many. They were no longer seen in public at all, and even their families became disinclined to speak to anyone outside the rarefied community of the National Committee on Planetary Exploration.

That was when the rumours started, with some journalists working for the less reputable papers suggesting that something strange might have happened to the X-M's crew while on Mars, while others noted that the Falcon was the only Martian artefact to be sealed within a lead-lined casket prior to its transfer to the Metropolitan Museum...

Fort leaned forward over his desk, examining a photograph of the Falcon – although he knew every line and feature of its beautifully-sculpted form. It was about fifteen inches tall, its wings folded behind it, its head facing forward, its eyes of obsidian so highly polished that they looked real... looked like they were actually observing you.

'Where are you?' Fort whispered. 'Are you with Sanguine? Is it really that simple?'

He rolled another cigarette, his eyes never leaving the photograph as he did so. 'Where are you?' he repeated. 'And *what* are you?'

CHAPTER 4
The Science of Anomalistics

There was a knock at the door.

'Come in,' Fort muttered distractedly.

Penny Malone opened the door and leaned in. 'Mr Lovecraft is here, Mr Fort,' she said.

Fort smiled at the formality. 'Shoo him in, sweetheart,' he said. 'Shoo him in.'

The man who walked into the inner office was tall, a shade over six feet, and thin in an awkward, gangly sort of way. His suit, while clean and pressed, had clearly seen better days, and his expression as he clutched his Homburg in both hands against his chest reminded Fort of a child who had grabbed a bag of candy and was refusing to let it go. His face was long, thin-lipped and a little gaunt, and there was a slight sallowness to the skin, which suggested that he hadn't had a decent meal in quite a while. But the man's eyes were quick and intelligent, and Fort detected a kind of decency in his bearing.

A good guy who's fallen on hard times, he concluded. *But where have I seen him before?*

The answer came to him almost immediately. Of course – he was the fellow who had sat next to him in the drugstore that morning.

'Come in, Mr Lovecraft,' he said, standing.

'Thank you, sir,' Lovecraft replied, stepping forward as Penny closed the door behind him. He offered Fort his hand, which

Fort shook while he noted the look of recognition on Lovecraft's face. 'And thank you for agreeing to this interview.'

'Miss Malone arranged the interview, not me. But still… have a seat.'

Lovecraft sat in the high-backed wooden chair which faced the desk. Fort noted that he was still fiddling with his hat, and gestured for him to put it on the desk. Penny was right, he thought: his accent was that of a New Englander.

'Sorry about your breakfast,' he said.

Lovecraft gave a small, diffident smile. 'It was hardly your fault. And in any event, I wasn't particularly hungry.'

Fort doubted that. He rolled himself another cigarette, and offered the pouch to Lovecraft, who shook his head. 'I neither smoke nor drink, Mr Fort,' he said, a note of pride in his voice.

'Good for you,' Fort said.

'I… er… that business with the zombies… I do hope it was nothing… unpleasant.'

'Much as I appreciate the sentiment,' Fort replied with a humourless grin, 'did you ever hear of any business to do with zombies that *wasn't* unpleasant?'

Lovecraft lowered his eyes. 'Ah… I suppose not.'

'So… what made you reply to my ad?'

Lovecraft looked up again, clearly relieved at Fort's reluctance to discuss the morning's events, and replied: 'I believe that we find ourselves at a fortuitous confluence of circumstances, sir.'

Fort paused in the lighting of his cigarette, the match held halfway to his mouth. He raised his eyebrows. *A fortuitous confluence of circumstances?*

'That's quite a turn of phrase you've got there.'

Lovecraft gave a quick, embarrassed laugh. 'I'm a writer… an amateur, to be sure, but a writer nonetheless.'

'What kind of stuff do you write?'

'I have written many travelogues and a great deal of journalism – I am an active member of the United Amateur Press Association,' (Fort smiled at the renewed pride in Lovecraft's voice) 'but my greatest love is for the weird and the fantastic…'

'You're in the right town for that,' said Fort.

Lovecraft's mouth twitched, and a slight frown crept across his brow as he continued: 'In any event, I consider the weird tale to be my primary mode of artistic expression.'

Fort nodded. 'Published anything?'

'I've had the good fortune to see my work in print on occasion.'

'Really?' said Fort, who had never heard of Howard Lovecraft. 'Books? Magazines?'

'Er… *Weird Tales*, mostly…'

'Ah, the pulps, eh?'

Lovecraft lowered his eyes and gave a brief nod.

'I've seen *Weird Tales* on the newsstands. Can't say I've ever read it. Real life is weird enough.'

'Indeed,' Lovecraft replied quietly.

A pulp writer who can't make enough to live on with a typewriter, thought Fort. *So he's come looking for a job with me. Yeah, real life is weird enough.*

'So… let's talk about this "fortuitous confluence of circumstances" you mentioned. What do you think they are?'

Lovecraft replied: 'Your advertisement stated the following: "Charles H. Fort, Private Investigator, requires research assistant to aid in the investigation of criminal and other cases of a supernatural or otherwise paranormal nature. Long and irregular hours guaranteed, but pay highly competitive. Only those with an in-depth knowledge of such matters need apply".'

'Good memory,' said Fort.

'Thank you.'

'And you think you're the man for the job.'

Lovecraft glanced at his hat, and Fort guessed that he'd have liked to fiddle with it some more. 'A bit nervous, aren't you, Mr Lovecraft?'

'My apologies, sir, but I am not exactly in my element. I am descended from a New England family of means… although the world of business and finance has not been particularly kind to us. I have been able to survive in modest comfort on the residue of earlier successes, but…'

'But your funds are running out,' nodded Fort. 'Yeah, I understand. So tell me, what qualifies you for this job?'

'In order to create a genuinely terrifying and convincing weird tale,' Lovecraft replied, 'one must first acquaint oneself with all manner of research into both scientific fact and occult lore. Only then will one possess the tools necessary for the composition of fiction which is both shuddersome in its implications and authentic in its background.'

Oh, Jesus, thought Fort.

'For this reason, for the sake of my art, if you will forgive the presumptuousness, I have made just such studies over many years.'

'Is that a fact?' said Fort, taking off his glasses and polishing them with his handkerchief. In spite of his caution, a tiny smudge of Penny's lipstick found its way onto one of the lenses. He tutted and polished anew.

'Yes, Mr Fort, it is. In fact, I would have to say that I believe myself to be just the man for whom you are looking…'

'Do you always speak the way you write?'

'I… I'm not sure I understand.'

'Never mind.'

In spite of the man's awkwardness, Fort found himself warming to Howard Lovecraft. He seemed so completely and utterly… *inoffensive*, not to mention polite; and politeness in New York City was about as rare as a plutonium sandwich.

Fort finally got the lipstick off his glasses, put them back on and saw that Lovecraft was gazing in unabashed curiosity at the enormous bank of file cabinets. He glanced at his host and gave a quick, nervous smile.

'Do they pertain to your cases, Mr Fort?'

'Some. Most are what you might call private research.'

'May I enquire along what lines?'

'The same as my professional work: unexplained events, strange phenomena… *weird* stuff, if you like.'

'Really?'

Fort nodded. 'In my spare time, I collect accounts of such things…'

'Which things in particular?' asked Lovecraft, leaning forward a little.

'I've made a careful examination of pretty much every field of human enquiry – astronomy, biology, chemistry, sociology, psychology, history, geography, exploration, you name it – looking for the phenomena that don't fit…'

'That don't fit?' echoed Lovecraft. 'That don't fit into what?'

'Our view of the way the world works – or *should* work. Put it this way: we *know* that the supernatural exists; we see it every day. Ghosts, zombies, vampires, demonic entities, angelic entities, spontaneous teleportation, strange lights in the sky, all the things that shouldn't exist according to the rules of science, but exist nevertheless. Science is unable to explain them, so it ignores them. I believe that's a narrow-minded approach.'

'I would have to agree,' said Lovecraft, 'although science has been struggling towards a unified theory of the supernatural for two hundred years…'

'And it's come up with doodly-squat so far. It's like Einstein and the unified field theory. You can talk about quantum mechanics, and you can talk about gravity, but you can't talk about them together. It's the same with the natural world and the supernatural world: no one can find a way to make them fit together. There's a new paradigm of reality out there somewhere, waiting to be discovered, and science has given up on finding it.'

'But you haven't,' said Lovecraft.

Fort looked at the bank of file cabinets. 'No… at least, not yet. But sometimes I wonder if I'm wasting my time. I've spent half my life in the world's greatest libraries, collecting data from newspapers and scientific periodicals, not to mention the notes I've made on the phenomena I encounter in my day-to-day work. I call it the "science of anomalistics", when I'm in a good mood.'

'And when you're not in a good mood?'

'I call it damned data.'

'Damned?'

'Excluded. Ignored. A procession of the damned: livid and rotten. Battalions of the accursed, you might say. Things that don't fit. Phenomena that shouldn't exist, but do.'

'But is it entirely true that science ignores such phenomena?' countered Lovecraft. 'Many universities have supernatural faculties: Harvard, Princeton, Miskatonic here in America; Oxford and Cambridge in England; the Sorbonne in Paris; the University of Buenos Aires in Argentina. There *is* work being done on the problem of the paranormal.'

'Yeah, but like you said, that work's been going on for the last two hundred years, and what have we got to show for it?'

Lovecraft smiled. 'I admire your ambition, sir. Perhaps you should write up your research in a book.'

'I am, in my spare time. I call it the *Book of the Damned*.'

Fort took in the smile and realised that he'd told Lovecraft more about himself than he'd intended. Suddenly, he felt like he was the one being interviewed. He should have been annoyed, but somehow he wasn't.

'What do you know about Mars, Mr Lovecraft – and the Martian Falcon in particular?'

Lovecraft raised his eyebrows in surprise at the sudden change of direction. 'Well… I know it was stolen last night.'

'Yeah, you and the rest of the country. What else?'

'It's an artefact created by the civilisation that once existed on Mars, about five million years ago. We believe that the Martians became extinct as a result of catastrophic changes in the climate of their world – at least, that's the conclusion drawn by the NCPE following their examination of the data gathered by the X-M expedition… although I have to say I've wondered about that, in view of the problems suffered by the crew upon their return.'

Fort nodded. 'Yeah, I've wondered about that myself.'

'And then there are the rumours concerning the hieroglyphs…'

Fort regarded Lovecraft in silence for a moment. 'Go on,' he said.

'As a member of the United Amateur Press Association, I am in contact with a great many correspondents, from all walks of life – including those of academia. Many have commented on the failure to translate the hieroglyphs discovered in Cydonia…'

'It's understandable enough, though, isn't it?' said Fort. 'There's no Rosetta Stone on Mars – at least, none that was discovered by the crew of the X-M.'

'Ah!' said Lovecraft, leaning forward again, a sudden look of excitement animating his gaunt face. 'That's where the rumours come in. Some of my correspondents have speculated that the expedition may indeed have discovered something like the Rosetta Stone – or at least something which allowed the NCPE to begin proper translation work on the hieroglyphs found in the city... and *especially* those found in the chamber where the Falcon was discovered.'

'Interesting,' said Fort slowly. 'And you're suggesting that the NCPE doesn't like what the hieroglyphs say and have suppressed that information, right?'

'Not me – my correspondents.'

'But you think there might be some truth to the rumours.'

Lovecraft shrugged. 'One is forced to wonder why the crew of the X-M dropped out of the public eye so suddenly, amid suggestions that they were suffering from mental difficulties, and why the Falcon was the only artefact brought back from Mars that was placed within a lead-lined receptacle prior to its transfer to the Metropolitan Museum... not to mention why it was stolen. Now, I admit that there is no link between those questions and my correspondents' speculations on the possible translation of the Martian hieroglyphs...'

Fort held up a hand. 'Okay, I accept that... but it's intriguing nevertheless. Who are these correspondents of yours? What are their credentials?'

'Their credentials are impeccable, I assure you,' said Lovecraft, and Fort marvelled at his ability to convey simultaneously both enthusiasm and mild offense. 'George Angell is Professor Emeritus of Semitic Languages at Brown University in Providence, Rhode Island – my hometown, incidentally – and Dr Albert Wilmarth teaches history and folklore at Miskatonic.'

'They sound like an impressive enough pair,' conceded Fort, 'but what makes them think that the NCPE has secretly managed to translate the Martian hieroglyphs?'

'There's one intriguing thing which set their speculations in motion; not exactly evidence, I must admit, but…'

'What's that?'

'I take it you listened with fascination to the dispatches from Mars during the expedition.'

'Of course I did, along with half the world.'

'Do you recall Captain Smith's statement that they had retrieved nine samples of hieroglyphs from the city – the so-called rock books – and that they would be bringing them back to Earth?'

Fort nodded, his fingers tapping impatiently on the desk blotter.

Lovecraft leaned forward a little further on his chair. 'And do you also recall how many rock books were transferred to the Metropolitan Museum for display to the public?'

Fort's fingers stopped tapping. 'Eight.'

'The question is, Mr Fort: what happened to the ninth book?'

'The NCPE must still have it.'

'Indeed. And why did they see fit to keep it?'

'That's another question.'

'A question to which it may be worth seeking an answer, don't you think?'

'Mr Lovecraft…'

'Yes, Mr Fort?'

'Call me Charles. You've got yourself a job.'

CHAPTER 5
The Big Toothpick

Johnny Sanguine adjusted his black silk necktie in the mirror and smoothed his eyebrows with his tongue. He regarded the pale, lean, handsome face, the broad forehead, the finely-chiselled alabaster cheekbones, the deep brown-blackness of the almond-shaped eyes above the perfectly-proportioned nose, and smiled. His crimson lips parted to reveal glistening, pearl-white fangs.

While it was true that to human eyes, vampires cast no reflection in mirrors, vampires could see themselves perfectly clearly.

And Johnny Sanguine liked what he saw.

His tongue, long, thin and ten times more prehensile than a human tongue, inched outward again and curved back to caress his fangs; slowly running down the length of them, taking in the smooth, graceful curves and pausing at the needle-sharp points.

'Admiring yourself again, Johnny?' said a female voice behind him, low and sensual, like ambergris-scented smoke.

Sanguine's smile faded slowly, tongue withdrawing, red lips closing over fangs, sheathing them once more. 'What's not to admire?' he asked quietly, his eyes finding hers in the mirror.

While Sanguine's eyes were nearly black, those of Rusty Links were almost luminous in their tawny magnificence, and the deep red of her long hair complemented them the way a sunset complements late-autumn leaves.

She joined him at the mirror, looked squarely at his reflection, and reached with her left hand to stroke the back of his head. 'Not much.'

He gazed at her reflection for a long moment. She wore a white blouse beneath a charcoal-grey jacket and skirt and high heels. Her black silk stockings made her long legs shimmer like quicksilver.

'What do you want, Rusty?' said Johnny Sanguine.

'It's here,' she replied.

'The Falcon?'

'The Falcon.'

Johnny Sanguine turned suddenly from the mirror and glided to the centre of the drawing room. When he turned to regard Rusty Links once more, the feral smile had returned to his lips. 'Finally!' he said.

Rusty looked around the room at the fine antique furnishings, the heavy velvet drapes flanking the windows, the crystal chandelier that hung like a thousand frozen dewdrops from the gilded ceiling rose, and said: 'It's going to look great in here, Johnny.'

'More than that, sister,' Sanguine replied, his grin growing yet wilder. 'It's going to get that diesel-powered bastard thrown in jail. With him out of the picture, I can expand into Chicago. Nothing can stop me. You wanna come along for the ride?'

Rusty returned his grin. 'You know I do, Johnny.'

There was a knock at the door.

'Bring it in!' Sanguine shouted.

The door opened, and a male vampire entered, carrying an object which had been carefully wrapped in pale chamois leather. Sanguine indicated a Regency writing table between the two tall sash windows. 'Thanks, Carmine,' he said. 'Put it there.'

'You got it, boss,' Carmine said, and placed the object on the table. 'You need anything else, boss?'

'Nah. Beat it.'

Carmine nodded and left the room.

Sanguine approached the object and slowly unwrapped the chamois, revealing the statue.

The obsidian from which it had been fashioned five million years ago glinted and glistened with a strange mineral life, as if the light playing upon the folded wings and the feathered breast and the great, beaked head were sliding down to the table top instead of reflecting the way light should.

Johnny Sanguine and Rusty Links looked in silence at the Martian Falcon. The Falcon looked back at them.

'So beautiful,' whispered Rusty.

Sanguine ran a long-nailed finger from the top of the statue's head, along its beak to the exquisitely-carved feathers upon the breast. 'It almost looks alive,' he said. 'Look at the eyes, how they shine... like there's something behind them.'

He leaned over and peered more closely into the Falcon's obsidian eyes. As he did so, Rusty took a couple of slow paces back towards one of the sash windows. Without looking behind her, she placed a hand on the latch, undid it, and slowly and silently raised the window. A breeze, warm and slight, entered the drawing room.

Sanguine did not notice.

'Have the zombies been taken care of?' he asked, his gaze still held by the Falcon's.

'Yeah. They've been deactivated. Now they're just dead men again. They were left in the alley behind the Algonquin, like you ordered.'

'Good. Once that security guard from the museum recovers, he'll be able to ID them. That'll put Capone well and truly in the frame.'

'It was a good plan, Johnny,' said Rusty, her voice growing slightly deeper.

Sanguine did not notice that, either.

'You bet your sweet ass it was, baby,' he replied, still gazing with fascination into the eyes of the Martian Falcon.

'Yes,' said Rusty, as the tone of her flawless skin began to change, moving from alabaster to pink to crimson, 'a very good plan. Nothing can stop you now.'

She raised a hand and pointed her index finger at Sanguine's back; as she did so, the perfectly manicured nail grew until the nail varnish cracked and split and floated to the floor in red flakes.

The nail continued to grow until it was ten inches long. It had become as black as the Martian Falcon.

'Nothing except me.'

She plunged the nail into Sanguine's back, slightly to the left of his spine.

He gasped, pulled himself erect, turned to face her, his handsome features contorted in a spasm of fear, shock and agony. He would have screamed a curse at her, were it not for the fact that his throat was already turning to dust.

What happened next took a handful of seconds. Rusty Links closed her eyes and concentrated on the form she wished to assume. Her white blouse and dark jacket split apart beneath a surge of powerful muscles and unfolding wings; her skirt and stockings ripped open and fell to the floor as her pelvis expanded and her legs grew in length, bending with sudden new joints. Her dainty shoes burst like overfilled balloons as cruelly-taloned, three-toed feet spread upon the soft, deep carpet.

Johnny Sanguine fell to his knees and, in the final moment before his eyes turned to steam, looked into the hideous, drooling face of the foul red thing Rusty had become.

'Sorry, Johnny,' it said in a voice like an earthquake. 'Someone else needs this… someone much more important than you.'

As the Vampire King of Brooklyn collapsed into a contorted heap of dust, the thing grabbed the Martian Falcon with a clawed hand, strode to the open window and squeezed itself onto the ledge outside. Then, spreading its vast bat-like wings, it took to the air and flapped away across the city.

CHAPTER 6
Crystalman

The thing that had been Rusty Links – that was *still* her – soared into the hot June sky, the muscles on its crimson back flexing and bulging with each flap of its black, membranous wings as it left the noisy streets of Brooklyn far below. It glanced once at the glinting spires of the city to the east, and then turned its course northeast across Long Island.

Flying high enough so that to anyone on the ground it would have appeared as nothing more sinister than a slightly odd-looking bird, it made its way past the towns and villages that dotted the island, past Garden City and Uniondale, Brentwood and Holbrook, out past Manorville and the Hamptons, only losing altitude at a point midway between East Hampton and Montauk.

It descended quickly towards a large estate surrounded by a high stone wall that was topped with wrought iron spikes. At the centre of the estate stood a gigantic Neo-Renaissance mansion with a three-storey tower at each corner and an elaborately turreted roofline. Modelled on Mentmore Towers in Buckinghamshire, England, which had been designed by Sir Joseph Paxton in 1852 for Baron Mayer de Rothschild, and constructed of pale ochre ashlar, this mansion was by far the largest and most impressive of all the great houses of Long Island.

Little was known about the man who owned the house, although rumours abounded concerning the source of his wealth. Some said it had come from oil, others suggested precious metals or commodities; still others opined that he was a European breakfast cereal magnate who preferred the Mediterranean to New York – hence the infrequency of his visits to his Long Island Shangri La. No one could agree on where his money had come from, but all agreed that there was plenty of it.

The one thing they did know was his name: Felix Carlton.

And about that, they were wrong.

The red, winged creature flew low over the immaculately-tended grounds surrounding the house and alighted on the flagstones of an elaborate stone portico, within which a heavy, iron-studded door stood closed and locked.

The glistening batwings folded upon the creature's back and diminished in size, merging with the muscles, which were themselves already shrinking, returning to their former size and configuration. The skin of the beast likewise turned from hell-red to soft, smooth alabaster. When the transformation was complete, a woman, beautiful, naked and entirely human, stood before the door.

In her left hand she held the Martian Falcon. With her right, she tugged on the large wrought iron bell-pull. From the other side of the door, a tinkle sounded, faint as the bell of a ghost ship.

There was an electrical click, and the door unlocked. Rusty Links turned and smiled in the direction of the concealed camera. She knew this house well – the house and its defensive installations. She turned the handle, opened the door and stepped into a vast, empty entrance hall.

Her bare feet made no sound on the marble floor as she crossed the hall, heading for another door set in the flank of the colossal staircase that curved up and around to the minstrel's gallery spanning the entire length of the room.

There was a heavy, lifeless silence which Rusty's instincts told her extended throughout the house. No one was here, and the stark emptiness of the place, combined with the chill of the air made her shiver slightly.

She went quickly through the door at the base of the staircase and along a short corridor which terminated in a set of double doors, made of grey steel and shut tight. She pressed a brass button set into the wall, and the doors hissed open to reveal a featureless cubicle about ten feet square.

As she stepped across the threshold and the doors slid shut behind her, a male voice, soft and gentle, issued from a hidden loudspeaker. 'Welcome, Rusty,' said the voice. 'I see you've brought me a gift... how very kind of you.' The voice chuckled, and Rusty Links shivered again.

*

With a slight judder, the elevator began to descend into the bedrock beneath the house. Rusty forced herself to breathe deeply and evenly, growing more and more uncomfortable in her nakedness. For ten cents, she would have changed back into her previous form and met her host on slightly more equal terms. Reluctantly, she shrugged off the temptation, since those terms would indeed have been only *slightly* more equal; and in any event, he had told her more than once that he far preferred her human form to any other.

She should have been flattered, she supposed.

For several minutes (which to Rusty felt like several hours) the elevator continued its descent. The only sound was the faint hiss of the lowering piston on which the elevator car was mounted. She held the Martian Falcon between her breasts, gripping it tightly, as if it might offer her some protection.

You don't need protection, she thought. *You can handle yourself... even against him.*

And then she thought: *Yeah, you just keep telling yourself that.*

Presently, the elevator came to a halt and the doors slid open.

Although she had been here several times before, Rusty still hadn't got used to the scene which greeted her. She doubted that she ever would. She doubted that she would ever want to.

The cavern was immense. Its ceiling, dripping with stalactites, was at least two hundred feet high, its glistening, roughly-mottled walls perhaps half a mile away, almost lost in the subterranean gloom. At the centre, upon a vast circular rug whose embroidered designs made her slightly dizzy to look at, were the furnishings of an elegant drawing room: leather sofa, wing chairs, tables bearing exotic and not-quite-identifiable ornaments, and freestanding bookcases filled with leather-bound volumes. The only things missing were the walls that normally would have enclosed such a scene.

Far off to the right, a vehicle constructed of strangely-curved metal components sat upon a single rail, which wound off across the floor of the cavern before vanishing into the semicircular mouth of a tunnel in the far wall.

'A little mood lighting,' said the same voice that had spoken to her when she'd entered the elevator. It echoed strangely in the vast space of the cavern, so that she couldn't decide from which direction it came. 'Romantic, wouldn't you say? I thought it appropriate, given your current state of undress.' The voice gave a soft, ironic laugh.

'Don't flatter yourself, Crystalman,' Rusty said in a loud voice, forcing herself to smile. She stepped away from the elevator car, which had descended on its piston through a hole in the ceiling far above.

The voice laughed again. 'Your confidence is well-placed, of course, since I care not for physical contact with either women or men. But you might have maintained the conceit a little longer.'

'Romance is the last thing on my mind,' Rusty replied. 'Especially in *this* place.'

She caught movement in one of the wing chairs, which had its back to her. A figure stood up and turned to face her. It was tall, a little over six feet, and was dressed in black trousers and a black Nehru jacket. She could not see – had never seen – its face, for it always wore a featureless mask which appeared to have been fashioned from a single piece of smoky quartz.

'I fail to understand your aversion to my home, Rusty,' the figure said. 'I have told you before that these Dero caves have been abandoned for centuries… and even if the Dero tried to reclaim them, they would fail.'

'That makes me feel a whole lot safer,' Rusty said sarcastically.

Chuckling, Crystalman held out a black-gloved hand. 'Come, join me. I wish to see it up close.'

'I don't suppose you have anything for me to wear,' she said as she joined him on the strangely-embroidered rug.

Crystalman wordlessly gestured to the sofa, on which lay a white silk dressing gown.

'How thoughtful,' she said as she handed him the Martian Falcon and went to put on the gown.

'My pleasure,' he replied, without looking at her, his attention fixed totally upon the statue. 'It was very kind of Mr. Sanguine to steal it for us. It saved a lot of trouble. And to think his only motive was to eliminate Mr. Capone from his tawdry little plans for Chicago. I would have expected more from a vampire.'

'Capone's going to be mad, that's for sure,' said Rusty. 'This might even start a war…'

'I doubt it. Capone would rather settle this quickly and quietly, which makes a change for him. He doesn't want this affair to escalate; that's why he's hired some outside help.'

'What do you mean outside help?' asked Rusty.

'He's engaged the services of a private detective, a gentleman by the name of Charles Fort, to get him out of the frame for the theft.'

'Fort… I've heard of him. Got a bit of a reputation, good at his job.'

Crystalman shrugged. 'He knows a little Magick, but nothing serious. A dabbler, rather than a player.'

'How do you know he's involved?'

Crystalman chuckled. 'Because it's my business to know these things.' He produced a small magnifying glass from an inside pocket of his jacket and began to examine the Falcon more closely. 'Magnificent!' he whispered.

'Do you really think it will work?' asked Rusty as she crossed her legs and tapped at the air with her foot.

'Don't you think it's worth a try?' he responded.

'That statue is made of obsidian – nothing more. That's what the report said when the NCPE analysed it.'

'And if it isn't… if there *is* something more to it, if the implications contained within the hieroglyphs found in the temple are even half correct, this may be the most powerful object on the face of the Earth.'

Rusty shook her head. 'The NCPE doesn't think so, otherwise they wouldn't have released it to the Metropolitan Museum.'

'They're fools.'

'Really? They've got some pretty smart guys and gals working for them.'

'And yet *some* of them are unnerved by what the hieroglyphs say, aren't they?' said Crystalman, who was still passing the magnifying glass slowly over the Falcon. 'You said as much, when you returned from your infiltration of Cabo Cañaveral.'

'Yeah, *some* of them, and their colleagues never pass up a chance to rib them about it. If the NCPE were really concerned, they'd have taken the Falcon back from the Museum.'

'Not much chance of that now, is there?' Crystalman chuckled.

'I guess not. Which reminds me: I believe my payment is due.'

'Of course. I'd almost forgotten. Over there.' He indicated an attaché case standing next to one of the chairs.

Rusty stood up, went to the case and picked it up. Had she been dealing with anyone else, she would have opened the case and checked that the money was all there, but she was not prepared even to risk offending Crystalman.

'Ten thousand, as we agreed,' he said. 'I would offer to have one of my men drive you to wherever you wish to go, but I don't suppose that's necessary, is it?'

'No, but I'll take the dressing gown with me. I think it suits me, don't you?'

Crystalman said nothing, merely returned his attention to the Falcon.

'You really don't feel anything, do you?' said Rusty.

'I feel many things, my dear Miss Links… but not *that*. It was something I was simply born without, like a conscience.'

Rusty grinned. 'There speaks the world's greatest super-criminal.'

'You flatter me. I merely follow in the footsteps of greater men: Moriarty, Fantômas, Fu Manchu… they are the real masters. I am merely their acolyte.'

Rusty looked at the elegant furniture standing so incongruously in this strange, dank, frightening place. She wanted to get out as quickly as she could, as always… and yet, as always, something made her want to linger. In spite of the fear even she felt in the presence of Crystalman, something made it difficult to leave. What was it? Curiosity? Admiration? The desire to see what lay beneath his mask – both literally and figuratively?

'Why do you live like this?' she asked suddenly.

'I beg your pardon?' he said without looking at her.

'Here, in this godawful cave, with the Dero still running around on the lower levels, who knows how close by? This furniture belongs in that house up there. Why don't you live there instead of down here in the rotten bowels of the Earth?'

'You're restless today, Rusty,' replied Crystalman quietly. 'Why is that?'

She said nothing.

Crystalman sighed. 'I could live anywhere in the world, but it suits me to live here. For one thing, this little hideaway of mine is utterly impregnable; for another, it amuses me to place a few of the trappings of wealth and comfort down here, in this harsh and ugly environment. It serves to remind me of how ephemeral such things are, how fragile; and because of that fragility, how worthless.'

'You equate fragility with worthlessness?' said Rusty. 'That statue you're holding is fragile, but it's worth a hell of a lot to you.'

'This statue has survived for at least five million years,' replied Crystalman. 'It survived the downfall and destruction of the entire Martian civilisation. I wouldn't call that fragile. It's as permanent as the cavern in which we are standing; it has known vast spans of time. The entire history of human civilisation is but a heartbeat to it.'

'And you think there's a reason for that: you think it's because of what it might contain.'

'Why do you think the NCPE decided against releasing the key to the decipherment of the Martian hieroglyphs?'

Rusty shrugged. 'Probably because they think that to do so would cause more trouble than it's worth. Who knows how many crazies would come out of the woodwork, bombarding them with questions, coming up with all kinds of whacko theories about Mars and the end of the civilisation there? They don't want that distraction.'

'You're wrong,' said Crystalman. 'They've kept the information to themselves because they're afraid.'

Rusty sighed and shook her head. 'Then why give the Falcon to the Metropolitan Museum? Why not lock it up in a vault somewhere?'

'Perhaps they don't trust their own people to leave it alone; perhaps they thought that the museum would be the safest place for it.'

Rusty smiled. 'How wrong they were.'

'Indeed. Now, regarding the hieroglyphs, there's something else I want you to do, something for which your peculiar talents are well suited.'

'Let me guess: you want me to go back to Cabo Cañaveral and steal the ninth rock book.'

'Quite so. I need it, and I must have it.'

'It'll cost you.'

'I'm aware of that. Your fee for this service will be one hundred thousand dollars.'

Rusty's breath caught in her throat, but she maintained her composure. 'That's a good fee.'

'I'm aware of that also. I would like you to begin immediately.'

'It'll take a much deeper infiltration than last time – you do realise that, don't you? I'll need to access areas of the complex I didn't need to before.'

'I do realise that. Open the case.'

Rusty glanced down at the attaché case, then placed it on the sofa and opened it. Inside, lying on top of the neatly-packed wads of banknotes was an unmarked manila envelope.

'That contains all the information you will need,' said Crystalman. 'You will know what to do with it.'

Rusty closed the case, picked it up and began to walk towards the waiting elevator. She hesitated, and turned back to Crystalman. 'If you're right about the Falcon and I get the ninth rock book for you... what are you going to do?'

Crystalman looked at her, and she could sense him grinning behind his quartz mask. 'That's not the right question, Miss Links. The right question is: what am I *not* going to do?'

CHAPTER 7
Carter and Wiseman

Fort was asleep in bed when the street-doorbell rang. He opened his eyes and looked at the clock on the nightstand. It said 12.30 am. He waited in the darkness.

The bell rang again.

He sighed, got out of bed and went to the telephone-box by the corridor door and lifted the receiver. 'Yeah?'

'Charlie,' said a tinny voice. 'It's John Carter.'

'It's twelve thirty, Lieutenant,' said Fort.

'I know. Mind if we come up and talk to you for a few minutes?'

'Who's "we"?'

'Dave is with me.'

'Wiseman?'

'Yeah, Wiseman,' said another voice. 'Come on, Fort, open up.'

Fort was about to say something, decided not to, and instead pressed the button that released the lock. He went into the bedroom and put on his dressing gown.

A couple of minutes later, there was a knock at the corridor door. Fort opened it and said, with exaggerated innocence, 'What's this all about, officers?'

'You know damn well what it's about,' said Wiseman as he and Carter stepped into the hall.

Fort smiled as he led them through to the living room. 'Have a seat, boys,' he said. 'You want some coffee?'

'No, thanks, Charlie,' said Carter.

'I think I'll make some anyway,' said Fort, and went to the tiny adjoining kitchen.

'Damn it, Fort!' said Wiseman loudly.

Fort heard Carter remonstrating with Wiseman in hushed tones while he made coffee. When he returned to the living room with the coffeepot and a mug, he saw that Carter had taken a seat on the sofa, but Wiseman was still standing.

The two policemen made an odd pair. Lieutenant John Carter was tall and lean in the manner of a welterweight boxer, with good strong features and piercing eyes, while Detective-sergeant David Wiseman would have had to lose fifty pounds to qualify as a heavyweight. His heavy-lidded eyes and flabby jowls, however, belied the fact that he was every bit as quick and astute as his superior.

'Sure you boys won't have some?' asked Fort, pouring coffee and sitting at the small table beside the slightly-open window, through which a light breeze entered the room tentatively, as if eavesdropping on them.

'No thanks, Charlie,' said Carter.

'You ready to talk now, Fort?'

'About what?' asked Fort, taking a sip of coffee.

'About Al Capone,' said Carter quietly.

Fort shrugged and said nothing.

'We know you went to see him yesterday,' Carter continued. 'We always keep an eye on the Algonquin while he's in town.'

'That's how we know you were there,' rumbled Wiseman. 'You arrived with three deadwalkers, waltzed right on in like you owned the place. What did you and Capone talk about, Fort?'

'We talked about the Martian Falcon,' Fort replied matter-of-factly.

Carter gave a small smile. 'Thanks for being straight with us. So… what was said?'

'That's none of your business.'

Carter sighed. 'Come on, Charlie! Do you really want to continue this conversation down at the station?'

'No, *you* come on, John. What cause do you have to pull me in?'

'How about accessory to theft?' said Wiseman, with a smug look on his fat face.

'You think I helped Capone steal the Falcon?'

'Tell us we're wrong, Fort,' said Wiseman, leaning forward. 'Tell us *why* we're wrong.'

Fort sighed, took his tobacco pouch from the table and rolled himself a cigarette. He lit it and tapped ash into the ashtray at his elbow. 'Capone didn't steal the Falcon.'

'How do you know?' Carter asked.

'Johnny Sanguine did – at least, that's what Capone believes.'

'Sanguine?' said Carter.

'Yeah. Capone wants me to help him prove it – that's why he had his goons pick me up. He thinks Sanguine's planning to muscle in on his Chicago territory, and used zombies to steal the Falcon so that suspicion would immediately fall on Capone. With the Diesel-Powered Gangster fingered for the heist, the Vampire King of Brooklyn will have a clear run at Chicago.'

'That fits,' said Carter.

'My ass,' said Wiseman.

Carter gave him a warning look.

Fort glanced at each of them in turn. 'What do you mean it fits?'

'Three deadwalkers were found in the alley behind the Algonquin a short time ago,' Carter said. 'Deactivated, just your run-of-the-mill corpses. We took mugshots and showed them to the security guard who survived the heist at the Metropolitan Museum. He ID'd them. They're the ones who stole the Falcon.'

Fort smiled. 'Yeah, but you don't think so, do you Dave?'

Wiseman shook his head. 'Doesn't ring true to me. Maybe Capone had the bird stolen, then cooked up this cockamamie story to point the finger at Sanguine to get him off his back.'

Fort sighed. 'It's a tough one, all right. Got you going round in circles, huh boys? Did Sanguine steal the bird to finger Capone, or the other way round? Yep, it's a tough one all right. But think about this: Capone wouldn't dispose of his goons like that – it's way too messy. They were obviously planted in that alley…'

'By whoever was really controlling them,' added Carter.

Fort nodded, blowing smoke across the room. 'If this was Sanguine's doing, it would make sense for him to plant the deadwalkers outside Capone's hotel; but if it was Capone, trying to make it *look* like Sanguine was framing him, he wouldn't do it that way. It's too complicated, too clumsy. Occam's razor, boys.'

'Whose razor?' said Wiseman.

'It's a scientific principle, genius,' said Fort. 'It means that the more complicated an explanation is, the less likely it is to be correct. Capone steals the Falcon and tries to make it look like Sanguine stole it and is attempting to frame Capone? Come on! *That's* what doesn't ring true.'

'And you'd know about that, wouldn't you, Fort?' said Wiseman.

Fort stubbed out his cigarette. He immediately began to roll another.

'Pretty nervous, aren't you?' said Wiseman.

'I'm tired and I want to get back to bed, so why don't you two gentlemen take a hike? I've told you nothing you didn't already know, so either tell me the real reason you're here at twelve-forty in the goddamned morning or get lost.'

'Watch your mouth, Charlie boy,' said Wiseman with sudden heat in his voice.

Fort dropped his newly-rolled cigarette and stood up. 'Or what, pussy cat?'

'That's enough,' said Carter, 'both of you. Charlie, sit down.'

'It's bad manners to sit when your guests are about to leave,' Fort replied, his eyes still fixed on Wiseman.

'Johnny Sanguine is dead,' said Carter.

'He's a vampire – they're all dead,' said Fort.

'I mean he's *really* dead. He was staked in his apartment yesterday afternoon. Now… will you please sit down?'

Fort sat down. 'Someone murdered him?'

'That's what it looks like,' replied Carter. 'Can't say too many people will be sorry. In any event, word is out already.'

'Do you have any idea who did it?'

'We were kind of hoping you'd know something about it,' said Wiseman.

'I don't.'

Wiseman turned to Carter. 'I'm tired of this, John. Let's take him in. Fort, get dressed.'

Carter held up a hand, and his partner fell silent. 'You have to help us out here, Charlie. Was Capone responsible?'

'I don't know.'

'Bullshit,' said Wiseman.

Fort picked up his cigarette. 'I'm telling you the truth, boys. You can take me in if you like, stick me in a cell and bring me breakfast in the morning – I like my eggs over easy – but you'll get the same answer, today, tomorrow and the day after that. But tell me something: if Sanguine was staked in his apartment, how could Capone be your guy? I mean, that's what you're implying, right? An inside job?'

Neither of the policemen said anything.

'Maybe one of Sanguine's men was working for Capone…'

Carter and Wiseman maintained their silence.

'Pretty unlikely, huh? Given the loyalty vampires show toward each other – especially mob vampires. So… who did it?'

'Maybe you,' said Wiseman.

'Do I look like I could go up against someone like Johnny Sanguine and win? And even if I did manage to get into his apartment, how could I have got out again without being flayed alive?'

Wiseman shrugged. 'Way I see it, you contacted Sanguine and asked for a meet. Maybe you told him that Capone was onto him, and you had some information that might be useful to him. The details don't matter at this stage. What matters is that you managed to get into his apartment, staked him, and managed to get out again.'

Fort chuckled. 'Details don't matter? That could be your motto, Dave. Putting aside the fact that what you've just said undermines your own theory, you're painting with a pretty big brush, aren't you? Come on! You know that bird won't fly – although I understand why you'd want it to. It would make your job an awful lot easier, wouldn't it? The way I see it, you've got a big headache. Not only do you have to find out who really killed Johnny Sanguine, but you have to do it before a war starts between Sanguine's vampires and Capone's bunch.'

'If that happens,' said Carter, 'the entire city's going to go up in flames. Nobody wants that.'

Fort blew another stream of smoke. 'I'll say. So why don't you boys run along and stop it from happening?'

Carter gave him a miserable look. 'Are you sure there's nothing else you can tell us, Charlie?'

'Nothing, John. But I promise I'll keep my eyes and ears open.'

'Let's go, Dave,' said Carter.

Wiseman smiled at Fort in a humourless way. 'Thanks for your help Fort, what little there was of it.'

Fort raised his half-empty coffee mug in an ironic toast.

'What are you going to do now, Charlie?' asked Carter. 'And if you say "go to bed", so help me God I'll run you in.'

Fort chuckled and stubbed out his cigarette. 'As far as I'm concerned, the case is closed. Sanguine's out of the picture – whoever did it. There's no more reason for me to have any involvement with Capone. I won't lie to you – I'm glad about that. But that's it, for me.'

Carter smiled. 'I envy you.'

'Like I said, I'll still keep my eyes and ears open.'

Carter and Wiseman left without saying another word. Fort closed and locked the door behind them, then went back to the living room and poured himself more coffee. He sat at the table, smoking and drinking, for a long time.

CHAPTER 8
Zombie Autopsy

Fort had offered to pick up Lovecraft at his apartment on Clinton Street, but Lovecraft had declined, saying he preferred to meet the private detective at the Manhattan Municipal Building. Something in Lovecraft's tone told Fort that his new employee didn't want him to see the depressed circumstances in which he was forced to live, and Fort had agreed without further comment.

It was 8.45 in the morning when the bullet-nosed upway train carrying Fort glided on its single rail into the station in the tower of the Municipal Building on Center Street. The cobweb-like network of upway lines that covered New York City had been built following the Interborough Rapid Transit Company's discovery of several Dero caverns during its excavation of the first subway tunnels in the 1890s. The entire subway project had been abandoned a few weeks later in favour of the upway system, since although the caverns had apparently not been used for years or even centuries by the Dero, the IRT's planners did not relish the prospect of the creatures returning to wreak havoc with paying passengers.

Fort stepped onto the platform, which was decorated in the same grand Beaux-Arts style as the rest of the building, to find Lovecraft already there, waiting for him.

'What time did you get here?' asked Fort.

'About an hour ago. I thought I would take some time to admire the architecture of the station.'

'You've been wandering around the place for an hour?' Fort shook his head and smiled. 'Okay, let's go.'

'My favoured mode of existence is nocturnal,' said Lovecraft as they joined the lines of office workers filing towards the elevators. 'I much prefer the peace and darkness of the night when writing; but when circumstance requires that I be abroad during the day, I am a habitual early riser.'

'That's good to know,' said Fort as they stopped in front of the bank of elevators and watched, along with the other commuters, the arrows above the doors slowly rising.

'May I enquire,' continued Lovecraft, 'as to our reason for being here?'

'I want to talk to the City Medical Examiner,' Fort replied.

'For what purpose?'

Fort lowered his voice as he replied: 'The three zombies who stole the Martian Falcon were found, deactivated, in an alley out back of the Algonquin yesterday. I need to get a look at the autopsy report. Maybe it'll tell us who created them.'

'Will you be allowed to do so?' Lovecraft asked in surprise.

'The Medical Examiner owes me a favour. A big one. A while back, I got rid of an imp which his ex-wife had sent to bug him. Nasty little bastard it was. Made his life a misery.'

'How did she…?'

'Hired a wizard in the Bronx. I took care of the imp without having it bounce back on him. Now he owes me a favour, too.'

'Are *you* a wizard, Mr Fort?'

'Charlie.'

'Sorry… Charlie?'

'Not as such, but I do know a little Magick. I can take care of myself on that score.'

The elevator arrived, and Lovecraft and Fort squeezed themselves in amongst the commuters. Lovecraft opened his mouth to say something else, but Fort gave him a warning look, and he closed it again.

They left the elevator on the fifth floor, and Fort led the way along several crowded corridors. In spite of his greater height,

Lovecraft struggled to keep up with his rapidly-striding employer. The sounds of voices and footsteps bounced from the Art Deco walls and marble floor, and Fort weaved in and out of the throng with the grace of a ballet dancer.

When they finally arrived at the outer door to the Office of the Chief Medical Examiner, Lovecraft was quite out of breath.

Fort looked him up and down. 'Not one for exercise, are you Howard?'

'I've never really experienced the necessity to take any,' Lovecraft replied in a contrite tone.

Fort grinned unsympathetically. 'That may change, pal, that may change.'

He opened the door and strode into a large room, one wall of which was dominated by the seal of the Chief Medical Examiner's Office, a winged caduceus combined with the scales of justice on a blue background.

The receptionist, a bespectacled woman in her middle years with an immaculate hairdo and a no-nonsense attitude, looked up at him. 'May I help you?' she asked curtly.

'Good morning, ma'am,' said Fort. 'I'd like to see Mr Dunsby.'

She raised a carefully-plucked eyebrow. 'Do you have an appointment?'

'No.'

'In that case, I'm afraid Mr Dunsby is very busy.'

'I've no doubt,' Fort smiled, 'with three deadwalkers in his lap. Just tell him Charles Fort would like a word.'

The receptionist sniffed at him. 'That won't be possible. If you'd just like to…'

'Mr Fort?' said a voice from the open door to an inner office.

Fort and Lovecraft turned to see a small, balding man in his late fifties, whose neatly-pressed suit couldn't hide the fact that its occupant had seen better, less stressful days.

'Good morning, Mr Dunsby,' said Fort. 'Any chance of a quick word?'

'About what?'

Fort's smile grew broader. 'I need a favour.' He nodded at the door in which Dunsby was standing. 'Do you mind if my associate and I step inside for a few minutes?'

The Chief Medical Examiner hesitated, then said to the receptionist: 'Miss Davenport, hold all calls.'

'Yes, Mr Dunsby,' she replied, before giving Fort an extremely dirty look.

'A pleasure, ma'am,' he said, then beckoned to Lovecraft to follow him into the office.

'How are things, Mr Dunsby?' asked Fort when Dunsby had closed his office door and motioned him and Lovecraft to a pair of chairs facing his cluttered desk. 'No more problems with supernaturals, I take it.'

'None whatsoever,' Dunsby replied. 'Whatever you did, it worked.'

'By the way, this is my associate, Howard Lovecraft.'

Lovecraft leaned across the desk, offering his hand, which Dunsby shook reluctantly.

'You wanted a quick word, you said.'

'That's right.'

Dunsby smiled humourlessly. 'Now I understand why you refused payment when you got rid of that imp.'

Fort shrugged. 'Now you understand.'

'I thought money was the only thing that mattered to you guys.'

'Far from it, Mr Dunsby.'

Dunsby sighed. 'Well… what can I do for you?'

'You can give me a peek at the autopsy report on those three zombies that were found outside the Algonquin yesterday.'

Dunsby frowned. 'What's your interest in them?'

'I had a run-in with some of their pals yesterday morning in Brooklyn.'

'What… *kind* of a run-in?' Dunsby asked slowly.

'That's not important.'

Dunsby sat forward in his chair. 'Listen, Mr Fort. I accept that you're calling in a pretty big favour, but you have to square with me. Why do you want to see the autopsy report?'

Fort sat forward in his own chair. 'All right, I'll square with you. Johnny Sanguine has been murdered, and the police are looking at me pretty hard.'

'They think you might have had something to do with it?'

'They do, and as if that weren't enough, they also think I might have had something to do with the theft of the Martian Falcon. Seems like those boys have got me lined up to take the rap for half the crimes in New York.'

'John Carter is heading up that investigation,' said Dunsby.

'Yeah, him and his boyfriend Dave Wiseman. I need them off my back, especially since the vampire mob will also be looking for someone to blame for their boss's death, and if word gets out that I'm a suspect, I'll be in more trouble than even I can handle.'

'We must also confront the likelihood,' Lovecraft added, 'that the police will be trying very hard for a speedy resolution to their murder investigation, before a war erupts between the Capone gang and Sanguine's vampires. If they can pin Sanguine's murder on Mr Fort, it's all the more likely that a war will be averted.'

Dunsby glanced sharply at Lovecraft. 'Are you implying that Lieutenant Carter would pursue Mr Fort under false pretences?'

'Er...' said Lovecraft.

'No, he's not saying that,' said Fort with a quick, narrow-eyed glance at Lovecraft. 'Mr Lovecraft chose his words poorly.'

'I'm afraid I did,' said Lovecraft.

'Look, Dunsby, here's the thing: I need to know exactly who created those zombies, whether it was Sanguine or Capone, and I need to know real fast. Are you going to help me out?'

Dunsby sighed and began to search the clutter of papers on his desk. 'The autopsy was conducted yesterday evening. We always put supernatural cases to the top of the list: we don't like to keep such things in the building any longer than we have to.'

'Very wise, sir,' said Lovecraft.

Fort gave him a look that said 'zip it'.

Dunsby found what he was looking for and handed a sheet of paper across the desk to Fort. 'Preliminary report,' he said, 'but I think you'll find everything you need there.'

Fort scanned the page, then passed it to Lovecraft as he returned his attention to Dunsby. 'So, no residue of Enochian Magick,' he said.

Dunsby shook his head. 'They had no symbols about their person, and nothing showed up on the æther scanner when we put them through it. No, it looks like they were created through other, more subtle means…'

'Subtle enough for a vampire?' asked Fort.

'That would be my conclusion. Does that answer your question?' Dunsby's tone of voice suggested that he fervently hoped so.

'I guess it does,' said Fort as Lovecraft handed back the sheet of paper. 'Capone didn't create those zombies. Looks like he was on the level with me.'

'I'm glad to hear it,' said Dunsby, in a tone which suggested he really didn't give a damn either way.

'Well,' said Fort, rising from his chair, 'thanks for your help Mr Dunsby.'

'Are we even now?' asked Dunsby as he shook Fort's hand.

'Yeah, I guess we are.'

*

'Come on,' said Fort when they had left the office. 'Let's go grab some coffee. I need to think.'

They went to a small coffee shop on the far side of the building and sat at a table. Fort watched, frowning, as Lovecraft put four spoonfuls of sugar into his coffee.

'Bit of a sweet tooth, huh?'

Lovecraft nodded, stirring his coffee with agitated little flicks of his spoon. He took a sip, grimaced and added another spoonful. 'Did the autopsy report confirm your assumptions?' he asked.

'Pretty much,' Fort nodded. 'Æther scanners don't lie. If those zombies had been created with Enochian Magick, which Capone favours, the psychic residue would have shown up in the readings.'

'So the likeliest explanation remains that Sanguine was responsible for the theft of the Martian Falcon.'

'Yeah, but that doesn't explain why Sanguine was offed.'

'Some internal problem in his gang?' suggested Lovecraft.

Fort shook his head. 'Pretty unlikely. Sanguine was by far the most powerful amongst his bunch. None of them would have had the moxie to go up against him, even if they'd wanted to.'

'Then surely Capone must be behind it.'

'That doesn't make sense, either,' said Fort. 'Or rather, it *would* have made sense if he hadn't brought me in. I mean, why do so if he intended to off Sanguine all along?'

'Perhaps he changed his mind after speaking with you.'

'No,' said Fort. 'He wouldn't have changed his plan so quickly. Something else is going on, Howard. There's a big piece of the picture which we're not seeing.'

'You think someone else is involved in this affair? Someone whose identity is unknown to us?'

'Yeah,' said Fort miserably. 'That's what I think.'

CHAPTER 9
Father O'Blivion

The Visitation Rectory stood on Richards Street, in the Red Hook district of Brooklyn, an oasis of light in a desert of iniquity – at least that was how Father Cormack O'Malley saw it. He thought of all the Catholic churches in New York that way, and to him it was far more than a metaphor. His ancestors had lived in the wild countryside of County Cork, in the far south of Ireland, and the echoes of that hard and simple life rang through him with every beat of his heart.

As he descended the stone steps from the Rectory's front door to the street, O'Malley glanced up at the huge bulk of a skycrawler that had just heaved itself into the air from the docks in Gowanus Bay to the south. Like a fat, misshapen insect, the giant aircraft lumbered through the sky, its Cavorite-coated outer skin glowing an unpleasant and unnatural shade of green even in the bright sunlight of midday. O'Malley shook his head and cursed it silently.

He mistrusted the strange science that had spawned machines like the skycrawler and raised cities like New York upon the face of God's Earth; that mistrust was vindicated in the misery, greed and vice he saw in the faces of its inhabitants every day. To probe the mysteries of the universe was to bang unceremoniously on the gates to God's Kingdom, and the towers of concrete, steel and glass which rose around him were as Towers of Babel striving insolently to reach a Heaven in which they had no place.

The price of this temporal impertinence was the spiritual squalor that afflicted the city, weighing down the human soul and sullying it with the dark stain of so-called 'progress'.

It was a squalor he had watched infect the heart of more than one young priest, whose mind and soul had yet to be tempered in this unholy forge, which was why he made a point of visiting each new arrival in the city. These visits gave him an opportunity to see how they were settling in, to listen to their hopes and fears, and to gauge their strengths and weaknesses. It was important work – at least as important as ministering to the spiritual needs of his flock – and Father O'Malley was nothing if not mindful of his responsibilities.

He had grave concerns about the young priest, Father Desmond Maguire, whom he had just left. The lad was barely out of the seminary, and here he was already in the panting maw of New York, with a head full of dreams about offering salvation to the heaving, self-obsessed masses. Optimism and high ideals were fine – essential, in fact – but the greatest test for a man of God was how he handled the situations in which those ideals seemed doomed to failure and irrelevance.

When that happened (and he believed it was *when*, not if) he would see the real Desmond Maguire.

As he walked along Richards Street toward the Columbia Street upway station, O'Malley became aware that he was being followed. A glance in the wing mirror of a parked car told him that there were two of them: rough-looking types, unshaven and shabbily-dressed, a pair of street hoodlums, the dregs of humanity drifting along the street the way excrement drifts along a sewer pipe.

Forgive me, Father, O'Malley thought. *I know I should not consider them that way. They are your errant children, as are we all...*

'Hey, Father!' called one of the men.

O'Malley stopped and turned to face them. 'Yes, my son?'

'Me and my buddy, we got a question for you.'

'And what is your question?' O'Malley asked.

The other man grinned at him. 'How much you got in your wallet?'

Suddenly, they lunged at him, sweeping him off the street and into a narrow alley filled with stinking garbage. They thrust him against a wall, and while one held O'Malley's throat in an iron-fast grip, the other started to search his pockets. He could smell their whisky-tainted breath, the stink from their unwashed bodies, and he pitied them.

'Where's your fuckin' wallet, Father, huh?' said one.

'Hurry it up!' said the one who was holding O'Malley by the throat.

'I have little money,' said O'Malley, struggling to get the words out past the hoodlum's grip.

One of the men found what he was looking for in the back pocket of O'Malley's pants. He held up the wallet for his friend to see, and then grinned at the priest. 'See, Father?' he said. 'That wasn't so hard, was it?'

The one who was holding O'Malley drew back his arm, made a fist and said: 'Lights out, Father.'

O'Malley smiled at him and brought his knee up sharply, directly into the man's crotch. The man gasped and dropped instantly to his knees, while O'Malley whipped his elbow around and struck the other hoodlum square in the face, flattening his nose with a crunch like that of walnut shells crushed underfoot. O'Malley then launched himself from the wall against which he had been pinned and aimed a powerful uppercut to the man's solar plexus which lifted him clean off his feet. He dropped like a sack of potatoes and writhed on the filthy ground.

'Do you still think that wasn't so hard?' said the priest.

'Son of a *bitch!*' gasped the other man, who was still holding his genitals, his eyes tightly shut. 'You fuckin' *bastard!*'

'Your profanity is an insult to God!' shouted O'Malley as he leaned forward, grabbed a handful of the man's hair and yanked up his head. 'As is your very life!'

He punched the man three times, shattering his jaw and knocking out several of his teeth.

'What the fuck you doin'?' gasped the other hoodlum, who had managed to get some of his breath back.

O'Malley glanced at him. He was still holding his ruined nose with one hand, blood flowing from between his fingers. 'You're a fuckin' *priest!*'

O'Malley released his grip, and the man fell face forward and lay still. He approached the other hoodlum, who crawled towards the wall.

'And because I'm a priest, you thought me easy game. How many others have you thought that about, you and your buddy? How many others have you dragged into alleys like this, and robbed and beaten?' O'Malley picked up his wallet, returned it to his pocket and crouched down beside the cowering man. 'How many?'

'None, Father, none, honest!'

'You're a lying little bastard.'

'It ain't no lie, I swear to you.'

'You don't know who I am, do you?'

'No… why should I?'

O'Malley stood up and thrust out his foot, pinning the hoodlum's head to the wall. The man moaned in pain and terror.

'I am Father Cormack O'Malley.'

'Oh Christ!' said the man through gritted teeth. 'Father O'Blivion!'

'That's me.' O'Malley gave a mirthless grin. 'And don't take your Saviour's name in vain, nor call on Him for protection, for he has already sent me to save you. You and your buddy are going to change your ways. From this moment on, you will turn away from the path of evil.'

'Yes,' whispered the hoodlum.

'From this moment on, you will forsake your wickedness and turn toward the light that God in His infinite wisdom and mercy has shown you.'

'Yes, we will, honest!'

'Through your actions from this moment forward, you will bare your souls to God, and through those actions, and the repentance they represent, will your souls be cleansed of the filth which sullies them.'

With difficulty, for O'Malley's shoe was still planted firmly against the side of his head, the man nodded.

'Do you think that your soul is yours to do with as you see fit?'

'I… I dunno,' said the hoodlum.

O'Malley pressed harder against his head.

'Aahh! No! No! I don't think so! I don't think so!'

'And well you should not, for your soul belongs to God, and every wicked act you perform is an insult to Him who endowed you with it. Do you understand?'

'Yes, Father,' the man whimpered. 'I understand.'

'I'll be watching you,' said O'Malley. 'Don't think I won't. And if you stray once from this new path, so help me, I will cut you down myself and send your souls to Him for judgment! Do you understand?'

The hoodlum began to weep. 'Yes, Father.'

Father Cormack O'Malley gazed down at the man, and smiled. 'If you're smart, my son, those are the last tears you will ever cry.'

He was about to turn away and leave the alley, when a movement in its shadowed depths caught his attention.

He stepped away from the hoodlum. 'Who's there?' he called out. 'Come on now, show yourself!'

From out of the shadows, a tall figure approached, making no sound as it glided along the garbage-strewn ground. It was dressed in a suit of alabaster-white, and was surrounded by a pale, subtle radiance.

O'Malley recognised the figure long before it finally drew up to him. He turned to the hoodlums and said: 'Get going, you lads.'

The hoodlums didn't need to be told twice. They dragged themselves to their feet and fled the alley.

O'Malley returned his attention to the figure dressed in white. 'I thought you were dead,' he said.

'You sound disappointed,' said the figure.

'I am. I thought the world had finally been rid of your vileness.'

'That hurts, Father.'

'I doubt it,' O'Malley said. 'What do you want?'

'I need your help.'

'Don't make me laugh!'

'It's true,' said the figure. 'And you're quite right: I *am* dead. I have passed through the final death. But I still need your help.'

O'Malley smiled a smile that was more a grimace. 'All right then, I'll play along. What can a humble priest do to help the ghost of Johnny Sanguine?'

CHAPTER 10
No Rest for the Wicked

'I'm not a vampire anymore, Father,' said Johnny Sanguine.

'What are you, then?' asked O'Malley, putting his hand in his pocket.

'Just your average ghost,' Sanguine replied, glancing down at O'Malley's pocket with a half-smile.

'What do you want?'

'Like I said, I need your help.'

By way of response, O'Malley suddenly withdrew a silver crucifix and thrust it toward Sanguine.

The ghost's smile grew broader. 'That never bothered me before… why should it now?'

O'Malley glanced at the crucifix and put it away. 'I thought you might have become transformed into something worse than a vampire.'

'Transformed…' said Sanguine, a slight frown clouding his pale features. 'An interesting choice of words.'

O'Malley sighed. 'I'm busy, Sanguine.'

'Yes, I noticed. Busy cleaning up the streets, sweeping up stray souls and pointing them in the right direction, which is up rather than down, right?'

'That's my mission, my calling.'

'Your mission! Your calling!' Sanguine snorted. 'Sisyphus! One day the boulder's going to come crashing down on you, crushing you like a stray dog under the wheels of a car.'

'I'm ready for whatever fate God has planned for me,' said O'Malley in a level voice. 'And since you claim to need my help, I wouldn't go running off at the mouth like that.'

Sanguine nodded. 'You're right – although it's not just me you'll be helping.'

'You're talking in riddles. Get on with it or be on your way!'

'All right, Father,' said Sanguine, raising his hands in a placatory gesture. 'I was killed yesterday afternoon… staked.'

'Who was responsible? Capone?'

Sanguine laughed. 'No, not Capone.'

'Surprising. I'd have thought he'd be the only one with enough balls to go up against you.'

'You'd have thought so, wouldn't you? But it wasn't him.'

'Who, then?'

'Rusty Links.'

O'Malley's eyes widened. 'Your girl?'

'My girl.'

'Why did she do it?'

'She was acting on someone else's behalf.'

'How do you know?'

'She told me… as I was dying.'

'Whoever he is, I'd like to shake his hand.'

'Believe me, Father, you wouldn't.'

'Why not? Who is it?'

'Crystalman,' replied Sanguine.

'She told you that?'

'No, but I'm dead, and the dead know a great many things that the living don't.'

O'Malley said nothing. His face became set in a grim mask.

'And that's not all,' continued Sanguine. 'Rusty Links is not human. She's a shapeshifter…'

'The devil you say!'

'Another interesting choice of words, considering the form she took when she staked me.'

'Why did she do it? Or maybe I should ask why Crystalman told her to do it?'

'I was responsible for stealing the Martian Falcon…'

'You?'

'Yes. I used zombies for the heist, so suspicion would fall on Capone. But Rusty stole it from me. The last thing she said to me was that someone else needs it – someone much more important than me.'

'And you know for a fact that that someone is Crystalman.'

Sanguine nodded.

'Why does he want the Falcon?'

'Because of what it contains.'

'And what does it contain?'

The smile that had been playing upon Sanguine's lips faded. 'The Falcon must be retrieved from Crystalman and returned to Mars,' he said.

'*What?*' cried O'Malley. 'What the hell are you talking about, Sanguine?'

'It's true, Father.'

'I'll tell you what's true, lad: you always were a gobshite, and you always will be!'

'It's true,' Sanguine repeated.

'And how, precisely, is that to be achieved? Assuming Crystalman is kind enough to give it back, are we to sprout wings and fly to Mars?'

'The NCPE is building the X-M 2 right now. They'll soon be ready to launch the next expedition. When that ship blasts off, the Martian Falcon *must* be aboard.'

'Why?' said O'Malley, taking a step forward. 'You didn't answer my question just then. What does the Martian Falcon contain that's so important to Crystalman?'

'Something terrible,' said Sanguine.

'Ah, bullshit! Feckin' bullshit, lad! It's just a statue – priceless, yes, but just a statue.'

'You're wrong.'

'How do you know?'

'Because the Primal Mind told me.'

'The what?'

'The Primal Mind of the Universe: the intelligence which you call God.'

'Oh!' said O'Malley, folding his arms and regarding the ghost of Johnny Sanguine with undisguised contempt. 'So *God* told you to come here and waste my time, did He?'

'That's right, Father. You must understand that what I was before, I am not now. When Rusty Links staked me, when my body collapsed into ash, my soul was freed… but my soul is still tainted with all the evil I have committed throughout my un-life. And when the Primal Mind appeared to me, I cowered before it, fully expecting to be punished. But that didn't happen, for the Primal Mind is wise and compassionate beyond the comprehension of humanity. It offered me the chance to redeem myself, to rescue my own soul from the punishment that awaits it.'

'And that chance involves returning the Falcon to Mars,' said O'Malley.

'It's my only opportunity for redemption, Father, the only way I'll be able to find peace. I don't want to think about the alternative.'

'And you want my help.'

Sanguine nodded.

'Why should I, after all the evil you've done?'

'You know the answer to that question,' said Sanguine. 'It's your duty as a man of God to help souls to find redemption.'

'You always were a liar, Johnny,' said O'Malley with a shake of his head. 'How do I know you're not lying now?'

'What reason would I have to lie to you, Father? I'm already dead and finished. My time on Earth is at an end; all I have left now is the chance to perform a service which will allow me to pass fully from this world into the realm of the Primal Mind.'

'You mean Heaven?'

'If you want to call it that…'

'Heaven… *you*… the Vampire King of Brooklyn, who has caused more mischief and suffering than anyone else in this city, save Capone himself!'

'Your duty stands, Father,' said Sanguine quietly. 'Regardless of your own attitude to me and what I've done. I have asked you to help me redeem my soul. You have no choice but to do so, even if you think I'm lying to you.'

'I *do* think you're lying to me, Sanguine.'

'You're free to do so... but your duty stands.'

O'Malley stood in silence for several moments. Presently, he said: 'What happens if the Falcon isn't returned to Mars?'

'A vast and ancient evil will be released... a scourge from the black seas of infinity which will visit itself upon the Earth.'

'And what is the *nature* of that evil?'

'Will you help me, Father?'

O'Malley thought some more and then sighed. 'How am I supposed to get the Falcon from Crystalman? How am I to put it on the next rocketship to Mars?'

Sanguine smiled at him. 'You'll find a way. I'll help you, however and whenever I can. What do you say?'

CHAPTER 11
A Warning

A MESSAGE FROM MARS?

FAMOUS INVENTOR RECEIVES
TRANSMISSION FROM THE RED PLANET

ANCIENT CIVILIZATION MORE
ADVANCED THAN PREVIOUSLY
THOUGHT

TELEVISION PICTURES SHOW
PLANETWIDE CATASTROPHE

Dr. Nikola Tesla, inventor of polyphase electric current and the AC motor, pioneer in high-frequency transmission, predecessor of Marconi with the wireless and inventor of the Tesla Force Beam, claimed yesterday to have detected an electrical transmission originating on Mars.

Using the 'Teslascope', a device he designed and constructed at his laboratory in Colorado Springs, Dr. Tesla was engaged upon an experiment in long-distance wireless transmission and reception, when his equipment detected the signal.

Initially, he thought that the signal might have been a natural non-terrestrial radio source such as that produced by the magnetosphere of the giant planet Jupiter; however, acting on the kind of hunch which is emblematic of his genius, Dr. Tesla ran the signal through his televisualizing equipment and was astonished to see moving images of scenes on a planet other than the Earth...

'Hey, Howard, look at this,' said Fort, pushing that day's edition of the *Herald Tribune* across the counter.

They had gone for lunch at the drugstore on Atlantic Avenue. Lovecraft had decided to try Hans's meatloaf, having been advanced a week's pay by Fort, and reluctantly he put down his knife and fork to take the paper. He read the front-page report quickly, his nostrils twitching at the insistently delicious aroma drifting up from the two slabs of meatloaf, the mashed potatoes, greens and thick brown gravy, all of which lay as yet untouched on his plate.

As he read, he gradually forgot about his food.

'A transmission from Mars?' he said. 'That's astonishing! How can it be?'

'Read on,' said Fort, digging in to his cheeseburger.

Lovecraft read aloud: "'According to Dr. Tesla, the moving images recorded on his equipment show scenes of devastation covering the entire planet: cities in ruin, strange-looking people running in panic or lying dead upon the ground, and something vast, hazy and indistinct hovering in the sky. The scientist believes that the images show events on the planet Mars – events which occurred at least five million years ago. He added that there are more images, but they are too indistinct to reveal much information. He is working hard to process them through his highly-specialised equipment, hoping to increase their resolution.

"'When asked how such images could have been transmitted to Earth, in view of the fact that nothing lives on the Red Planet now, Dr. Tesla replied that somewhere on Mars there must be some kind of mechanical apparatus which is still functioning.'"

Lovecraft put down the newspaper and glanced at Fort. The sight of his employer munching on the cheeseburger reminded him of his own lunch. He picked up his knife and fork and began to eat. 'The headline is quite right,' he said between mouthfuls. 'The ancient Martian civilisation must have been far more advanced than hitherto assumed.'

Fort nodded.

'It's astonishing,' Lovecraft continued, 'that the transmitting apparatus is still working after such an incredible span of time. It's been sending out its strange message for millions of years!'

'What makes you think that?' asked Fort.

'I beg your pardon?'

Fort crunched loudly on a dill pickle. 'Why do you think it's been transmitting constantly for the last five million years?'

'How's da meatloaf, Mr Lovecraft? Pretty good, huh?' shouted Hans from the kitchen.

'Excellent, thank you,' Lovecraft replied.

'Damn right it's excellent,' said Hans, cracking an egg onto the hotplate.

Lovecraft indicated the newspaper. 'I'm not sure I understand your question. Isn't it obvious that it's been transmitting for all that time? I mean… Dr. Tesla has intercepted it.'

Fort smiled. 'If it's been transmitting ever since the heyday of the Martian civilisation, how come it wasn't picked up by the X-M's receivers during the expedition? You'd think they'd have mentioned it.'

Lovecraft chewed thoughtfully on a piece of meatloaf. 'I see what you mean.'

Fort chuckled. 'Glad the penny's finally dropped, Howard. Now, what does that imply to you?'

It only took Lovecraft a moment to make the connection. 'Good Lord!' he cried. 'The implication's obvious, isn't it? The transmitting apparatus must have been activated following the departure of the X-M on its return flight to Earth…'

'Coincidence?' prompted Fort.

'Unlikely, I'd have to say. It must have been the presence of the rocketship which activated the apparatus.'

'Could well be,' replied Fort. 'On the other hand, it could be that the removal of the Falcon was what caused the activation. Either way, we're left with the same question.'

'Which is?'

'Why? Why did the arrival of travellers from another planet – and/or the taking of the artefact we know as the Martian Falcon – trigger the transmission of that message?'

Lovecraft scooped up a forkful of mashed potatoes. He was about to pop it into his mouth when he stopped suddenly. 'A warning,' he said. 'Given the contents of the transmission – the devastation, the people fleeing and dying – there can be no other reason. But the question remains: what *caused* the catastrophe, a catastrophe that seems to have wiped out an entire civilisation?'

'Maybe it had something to do with the thing in the sky. "Something vast, hazy and indistinct",' Fort quoted. 'Sounds weird enough for one of your stories, Howard!'

'Indeed,' said Lovecraft, who, it was true, had begun to consider the fictional possibilities for such an intriguing event. 'But if it *is* a warning…'

'Then we could be in a whole heap of trouble,' said Fort. 'And by "we", I mean the entire human race.'

Lovecraft put down his fork. Suddenly, he had lost his appetite.

'You're not going to finish that?' said Fort.

Lovecraft shook his head, so Fort grabbed the plate and slid it in front of him. 'Great meatloaf, Hans!' he called.

'Damn straight,' replied Hans over his shoulder.

'What are we going to do?' asked Lovecraft.

'I think we should take a trip out to Colorado and see Dr. Tesla. I want to get a good look at that transmission, see exactly what it contains, and what he thinks about it. I mean, what he *really* thinks – not what he's told the press. I also want to see if he's managed to increase the resolution on the images.'

'I've never been to Colorado before,' said Lovecraft.

'Well, grab your spurs, Howard, 'cause we're heading out west.'

'*Scheisse!*' yelled Hans suddenly from the serving hatch leading to the kitchen.

Everyone at the counter jumped and looked at him.

'What's up, Hans?' asked Fort.

The kobold pointed at the street door.

Two zombies had just walked in.

'God damn it, not again,' muttered Fort.

'You know, Charlie,' said Hans, shaking his large blue head, 'I'm startin' to worry about the company you keep.'

'What makes you think they've come for me?' asked Fort in a weary, sardonic tone.

'Fort,' said one of the zombies. 'Come with us.'

Hans shrugged. 'That.'

'Back to the Algonquin, boys?' said Fort.

'Not this time,' the zombie replied.

'I don't suppose there's any point in asking where?'

'Not much.'

Lovecraft leaned towards Fort. 'Shall I come too?'

'Hell yeah.'

*

The limo which was parked at the kerb outside was a lot bigger than the one Fort had ridden in the previous day; in fact, this one was more like a bus than a car. Although it still looked like a Studebaker, an average-sized automobile could have fit under its hood with room to spare.

'Good grief!' whispered Lovecraft into Fort's ear as they approached. 'Look at the size of that thing!'

'It's Capone's personal limo,' Fort replied. 'He had it built specially. It's the only car he'll fit into.'

One of the zombies opened the rear passenger door, which was twice the size of a normal car door, and motioned them inside.

Fort and Lovecraft climbed in and sat side by side on the rear-facing bench seat. Capone sat opposite. They regarded him in silence, Fort with weary resignation, Lovecraft with undisguised terror. The two zombies sat on either side of their boss.

'Who's your pal?' asked the Diesel-powered Gangster, gesturing with a huge metallic paw.

'This is Howard Lovecraft,' Fort replied. 'A new associate.'

Lovecraft nodded vigorously without saying anything.

'Looks like he belongs in a library,' said Capone.

I do, Lovecraft thought miserably.

Capone turned his attention to the zombie in the driving seat. 'Tony, drive – and don't stop for nothin' or nobody.'

As the car's twenty-litre engine gave a thunderous growl and the enormous vehicle pulled swiftly away from the kerb, Capone said: 'Got to keep movin' now. Too dangerous at the Algonquin. The smart move would be to get out of New York altogether – head back to Chicago… but I ain't never run from nothin' in my life, and I ain't gonna start now.'

'You're talking about Sanguine's boys,' said Fort.

'You catch on quick, Charlie. Yeah, Sanguine's boys. Someone staked him, and now the shit's flying hot. We're goin' to the mattresses on this one. Things are gonna get ugly.'

Fort was about to ask Capone if he was responsible, thought better of it, and instead said: 'Do you have any idea who might have done it?'

'You think it was me, Charlie?' asked Capone, leaning forward in his seat. The pistons powering his artificial body hissed ominously.

'That wouldn't make sense, Mr Capone,' Fort replied quickly. 'I mean, why bring me in if you intended to take care of the Sanguine problem yourself?'

Lovecraft nodded again. Capone glanced at him, and he stopped.

'Yeah, well, you're right. I didn't order the hit.'

'Do you know who did?' Fort repeated.

Capone shook his head. 'But word on the street is that the Brooklyn vampires are lookin' for Rusty Links. Seems she's gone missing.'

'Sanguine's squeeze?' said Fort. 'You think she might have had something to do with it?'

'How the fuck do I know?' Capone growled. 'You know she's a shifter, right?'

'I'd heard rumours.'

'Yeah, well, they're true, and word is Sanguine's boys think she's working for me…'

'But she isn't.'

'Hell no! I don't like shifters: can't trust 'em. But you're right, Links might have had something to do with it. In any case, she's gone, and there could be two reasons for that: either she's running scared 'cause she knows who did it, or she's skipped 'cause *she's* the one who did it – and neither option looks too good for me.'

'I understand,' said Fort. 'And believe me, I sympathise. Looks like you've exchanged one problem for another.'

'That's what I wanna talk to you about.'

Oh Christ, here it comes, thought Fort.

'The terms of our agreement have just changed, Charlie,' said Capone. 'You've got to get the vampires off my back – prove to them that I had nothing to do with offing their boss.'

'How the hell am I supposed to do that?' said Fort, his voice rising in incredulity.

Capone leaned forward again. 'I'm sorry, Charlie, I don't think I heard you.'

This time, Fort leaned forward as well. 'I *said*, how the hell am I supposed to do that?' The order was so outrageous, so impossible, so downright suicidal, that he no longer cared about offending the mob boss.

Capone gave him a long look, and then his fat, cruel face twisted into a smirk. 'You got balls, Charlie,' he chuckled. 'You'll think of a way. No one wants a war: it's bad for business. But a war is what's comin' unless this mess gets sorted out. And the fact is there's no way out for you. Word is already out that you're workin' for me. The cops know you went to the Algonquin with my boys yesterday. And if the cops know, you can bet your ass the vampires do too. You're in the shit as deep as I am, Charlie boy; now it's up to you to get us both out.'

'Hey, boss,' said the zombie who was driving.

Capone glanced at him. 'What?'

'We got company.' The zombie jerked a glistening thumb (minus nail) over his shoulder.

Capone twisted in his seat to look through the limo's rear window. Fort and Lovecraft stood up to get a better view.

The car immediately behind was large and sleek, its windows tinted almost completely black. With a screech of tyres it swerved suddenly, revealing an identical car behind. The second car swerved in the opposite direction, and both accelerated until they were flanking Capone's limo.

'Oh, crap,' said Fort. 'Vampires.'

CHAPTER 12
Death Has No Speed Limit

Without waiting to be told, Tony the driver gunned the car's massive engine, and Lovecraft and Fort simultaneously grabbed the leather handgrips on each side of the cabin as the vehicle surged forward.

'Oh good grief!' cried Lovecraft.

'Hang on to your hat, librarian,' said Capone, his face contorted in a mirthless grin. 'Tony'll get us out of this.'

'Right, boss,' Tony gurgled, spinning the steering wheel suddenly.

There was an ugly crunch of metal against metal as the limousine shunted the car in front out of its way. Lovecraft and Fort looked through the side window in time to see the car spinning off the road and into a storefront, where it disappeared in a messy, multicoloured cloud of exploding fruit and vegetables.

'Mr Capone,' said Lovecraft. 'I wonder if you might drop us off and forge ahead without us. I assure you we'll be wishing you the very best of luck.'

'Hey Charlie,' said Capone. 'I like this guy: he's got a sense of humour like yours!'

Fort glanced at Lovecraft and saw in his eyes that he wasn't joking; and that, he realised, was funny. He started laughing and held onto the handgrip with all his might as Tony barged another car off the road. The zombies sitting on either side of Capone looked straight ahead, their dead faces completely expressionless, like two bored passengers on a bus.

The sleek, black vampire cars drew level with the limousine once again. Their rear passenger windows rolled down and the muzzles of a distressing number of Tommy guns poked out.

'God damn it!' said Fort. 'Is this car armoured?'

'Of course it is, Charlie,' Capone replied nonchalantly, as the deafening stutter of machine gun fire erupted from the vampires' cars, accompanied by the metallic clatter of shells striking the polished flanks of the limousine. 'But they're gonna get tired of that pretty soon, I'd say… and then they'll try something else.'

'And what might that be?' asked Lovecraft, hanging onto his own handgrip as the car swerved this way and that, braking and accelerating in quick succession as Tony tried to shake their pursuers.

'Probably try to run us off the road and use their strength to rip open the doors…'

Lovecraft ratcheted up the look of horror on his face by several notches. 'And then?'

'They'll probably rip your heads off and beat me to death with them.'

'Charles,' said Lovecraft.

'Yes, Howard?'

'I resign.'

Tony swerved once again, this time taking the car onto the onramp leading to the Brooklyn Queens Expressway. As they reached the elevated section, Lovecraft caught a glimpse of New York Harbor, with Governors Island sprawling in the near distance and the Statue of Liberty beyond. He realised that he would have given pretty much anything to be at either of those places at that moment.

Tony gunned the engine again, and the limousine surged forward. Fort guessed their speed to be around eighty miles an hour. He glanced over his shoulder at the road ahead and prayed that Tony wouldn't need to shunt anymore cars out of the way. If he did, the weight of the limousine would easily push them through the crash barriers and onto the road below. Fortunately, the traffic was fairly light, and Tony settled for swerving around the cars ahead instead of ploughing straight through them. Fort guessed that their driver did this in order to maintain their speed, rather than through any concern for the other road users.

Capone was right in his assumption about the vampires' next move. While the rain of bullets continued from one car, the other dropped back a few feet and began to swerve into the limousine's rear end. The car jerked and shuddered with each metallic clank, and Tony fought the steering wheel in an effort to keep on a straight course. Fort had been worried about other cars being shunted off the elevated section of the Expressway; but now he realised that the vampires were trying to do precisely that to the limousine. He guessed that they were about fifty feet up. If the limo went over the side, he didn't give much for their chances of surviving the fall.

'Okay,' said Capone suddenly. 'I've had just about enough of this shit.'

With a hiss of pistons he leaned forward, reached under his seat and brought out what looked like a Thompson submachine gun – although the distinctive drum magazine was twice the normal size.

'I don't think that's going to be much good against a bunch of vampires, Mr Capone,' observed Fort, as another shunt from the car behind nearly threw him to the floor.

'Correction, Charlie boy,' replied Capone as he cocked the weapon with a loud click. 'Your normal Chicago typewriter carries .45 ACP cartridges, which have about as much effect on a nightwalker as bad language; but *this* baby has rock crystal shells full of holy water – and *that's* a different story!'

'Chicago typewriter?' said Lovecraft.

'It's a nickname for a Tommy gun, Howard,' Fort replied.

'Oh… I rather like that.'

'Glad you approve, librarian,' said Capone as he reached up and pressed a button set flush with the ceiling of the passenger cabin. A large panel in the ceiling slid forward, and Capone stood up so that his head and upper torso were poking through the opening.

The pistons mounted where a human's hips would be hissed and flexed as the Diesel-powered Gangster pivoted around and brought the modified Tommy gun to bear on the vampire car which was still in its flanking position at the limousine's side.

'Hey, dumb fucks!' he shouted at the top of his artificial lungs. 'Get a load of this!'

He began firing through the open windows of the vampires' car. Fort and Lovecraft could hear the resulting screams even above the roar of the limousine's engine and the stutter of competing gunfire. The car behind ceased its attempts to shunt the limo off the road. Fort guessed that the drive had been taken by surprise at this new turn of events.

The arms holding the machine guns, black-sleeved and gloved, began to jerk violently, so that the bullets flew in all directions. One uncontrolled volley struck the rear end of a large delivery truck in front of the limo. Several bullets hit the tyres, which exploded with loud rubbery bangs.

The truck began to swerve back and forth across the road as the driver fought to control the wheel. It took just a few moments for him to lose the battle with his vehicle's high centre of gravity. The truck threw itself over like a child having a tantrum, spilling its contents across the road and sliding along the asphalt in a shower of sparks.

'Oh shit,' said Tony as he tried to avoid the wreck, but the driver of the second vampire car had seen his opportunity and accelerated sharply, ploughing into the rear of the limo and shunting it forward just as the zombie driver spun his steering wheel to the left. The huge vehicle slewed across the road, its oversized tyres screeching in protest.

'Hold onto your hats, boys,' said Capone as he ducked down and dropped onto the rear seat, crushing one of his zombies to a stinking pulp as he did so. 'Oh... sorry, Pauly.'

'Dat's okay, boss,' the zombie gurgled, just before his head fell off and rolled messily onto the floor.

With a sickening crunch, the limousine hit the upended delivery truck side-on. Fort, Lovecraft and the other zombie were thrown violently to one side of the cabin by the impact, and then to the floor. Fort's head collided with that of the crushed zombie.

'Oh shit,' he said. 'Sorry, Pauly.'

'Dat's okay.'

Still brandishing his modified Thompson, Capone flexed one piston-driven leg and kicked the rear passenger door clean off its hinges. It skittered across the scarred asphalt towards the two vampire cars, which had come to a halt behind the limo.

The cars were Duesenbergs, their styling aggressive and elegant, and entirely in keeping with the nature of their occupants. Their black paintwork glinted in the sunlight, as did the highly-polished chrome of their radiator grilles and headlamps. Their heavily-tinted windshields were like the black sunglasses of implacable assassins.

Capone climbed from the limousine and stood before them with his steel legs planted firmly apart upon the road, ignoring the honks and squealing tyres of the oncoming traffic that swerved to avoid the wreck. 'All right, you nightwalkin' cocksuckers!' he shouted. 'You wanna dance? Then let's dance!'

The doors of the Duesenbergs opened, and eight vampires emerged. They were dressed entirely in black, right down to their shirts and ties, and each wore a black leather mask which completely covered his head. Their eyes were hidden behind goggles as heavily tinted as the windows of their cars. From inside the limo, Fort could see that a couple of them were standing awkwardly, half bent over. They must have been the ones who were hit by Capone's shells: the holy water must have seeped through the fabric of their suits, eating into their skin like acid.

'Buncha deadbeats!' shouted Capone. 'Think you can take me, huh? Then let's go!'

'What do you think our chances are of emerging from this altercation alive?' asked Lovecraft.

Fort glanced at him. 'Not great, Howard. Not great.' He hesitated, then added: 'I'm sorry.'

'It's my aunts I feel sorry for,' Lovecraft replied. 'My death will hit them very hard.' There was sadness and resignation in his voice, but no fear. Fort gave him a longer look but said nothing.

They returned their attention to the scene outside the limo. Capone had trained his weapon on the vampires, who had in turn brought their Thompsons to bear on him. Fort noted that they were aiming high: when the shooting started, they would go for headshots, since it would be futile to fire at Capone's massive, armoured body.

As far as Fort knew, Capone's head was as vulnerable to injury as his body once had been. He didn't give much for the Diesel-Powered Gangster's chances against the vampires: bullets filled with holy water was a good idea on paper, but in practice all it seemed to have done was piss them off even more.

And when they were done with Capone…

Fort glanced again at Lovecraft. 'It's been nice knowing you, Howard,' he said.

CHAPTER 13
The Telaug Machine

Rusty Links had been mistaken when she assumed that Crystalman was in danger from the Deros. It was understandable enough, of course, since he had not been strictly accurate when he told her that he was simply occupying caverns that they had long ago abandoned.

The fact was that he had taken these upper chambers from them, and they had capitulated without a fight. They were well aware of his reputation, not to mention his true identity: the penetray machines which they kept in the deeper caverns and through which they observed events in the upper world told them that it would not do to make an enemy of Crystalman.

His reputation had preceded him, even into the nighted realms of the Inner Earth.

The Deros had left behind much that was useful to Crystalman when they had departed these upper chambers, including several of the fantastic machines which were their inheritance from the long-vanished civilisation that had spawned them. One of the machines contained the thought-records of the Atlans, the spacefaring race that had come from the uncharted interstellar gulfs to colonise Earth in the far-off night of prehistory.

For countless millennia, the Atlans had lived in peace and utopian splendour upon the Earth, which they called Lemuria, making the world their own and raising beautiful and mighty cities on its surface.

Then, five million years ago, something had happened to the Sun. The nature of the catastrophe was not explained fully in the thought-records of Lemuria, and Crystalman guessed that so utterly appalling was the event that the Atlans could not bring themselves to set it down in the great chronicle of their civilisation. As far as he understood it, the chemistry of the Sun had undergone a radical change, as if the star had succumbed to some terrible disease, and had begun to radiate a form of energy that was exceedingly harmful to the Atlans, and which they called *disintegrant energy*, or *de*.

Their civilisation under threat, the Atlans excavated gargantuan caverns and tunnels far below Lemuria's surface, in which they built enormous cities which would have dwarfed any human city of the present. These subterranean realms shielded the entire Atlan population, some three billion individuals; however, the underground cities did not prove a permanent solution, and 20,000 years ago Lemuria/Earth was abandoned in favour of younger, cleaner star systems.

Many Lemurians had already fallen victim to the debilitating effects of the Sun's harmful radiation and were forced to remain in the cavern cities of the Inner Earth, where they degenerated into the race of disfigured, idiotic and malicious beings known as the Dero. This name was a contraction of the Atlan word *abandondero*, a compound word meaning negative and subservient. Hence the Deros were, literally, controlled by negative forces.

These fiendish, sadistic and perverted beings abducted thousands of surface-dwellers every year and took them into their cavern cities, where they were tortured, used as slave labour or eaten. Although fundamentally stupid and brutal, the Dero nevertheless knew how to use the fabulous machinery left behind by the Lemurians, and were able to spread evil and destruction throughout the world by means of their *dis* rays.

Many governments, including that of the United States, had sent military expeditions into the cavern systems to try to solve the Dero problem. None had returned, and the League of Nations had decided unanimously that, while an all-out confrontation with the cave-dwellers was both necessary and inevitable, it would have to wait until humanity had reached a level of technological sophistication which would allow it to destroy the enemy completely once and for all.

When that day would finally arrive, no one knew, save that the future of humanity depended upon it.

Crystalman walked across the stone floor of his singular drawing room and climbed into the strangely-curved vehicle which sat upon its single rail. He pulled a lever, and the vehicle moved smoothly and silently off across the cavern, gradually picking up speed as it approached the tunnel mouth in the far wall. The vehicle was one of the many relics of the once-mighty Atlan civilisation; the rail upon which it travelled was part of a planet-wide network, much of which was now in hopeless disrepair, but which had once linked every continent on Earth through tunnels winding endlessly through the living rock of the world.

The vehicle followed the track as it curved through the tunnel, the darkness relieved by the single headlamp which cleaved the eternal night of this subterranean realm. Presently, the vehicle emerged in another, smaller chamber, an excavated cube perhaps eighty feet on a side, which contained nothing from the human world of light and sanity.

Like many chambers of the Inner Earth, the walls were decorated from floor to ceiling with bas reliefs depicting scenes from the life of the Atlan civilisation. The bas reliefs were sweeping in scope and exquisite in execution – although the ones in this chamber had been largely defaced by the malicious and idiotic Dero, who saw no sense in beauty, and for whom the illustrious history of their ancestors was but a cruel and mocking reminder of all that they had lost.

Crystalman brought the vehicle to a halt, climbed down and regarded his hoard of ancient and outrageous machines. Some had long ago fallen into complete disrepair, so that even their functions were now a mystery... but others were still in working order, and it was towards one of these that Crystalman carried the Martian Falcon.

The Atlans had called it a telepathic augmenter, or telaug, and it was a miracle of their arcane and long-forgotten science. In appearance it was as bizarre as any of their other devices: it gave the impression of having been melted, drawn away by intense heat from its original form, so that it was now warped and etiolated, a painterly smear in three dimensions, a confusion of sweeping curves and iridescent bulges that stood upon the floor of the chamber like an idol devoted to some incomprehensible alien god.

Its purpose was to transmit thought. Once an individual's brain patterns had been recorded, the telaug machine acted as a powerful transceiver which would allow instantaneous telepathic communication. Crystalman had found the device extremely useful on more than one occasion. Over the last few years, several high-ranking figures in politics, industry and law enforcement, in America and other countries, had been Crystalman's guests here in the upper caverns of the Dero. Of course, they had been sedated at the time, and had no memory of their temporary abduction, or of the recording of their brains' electrochemical impulses, as distinctive and unique as fingerprints, which allowed Crystalman to step inside their heads whenever he chose, and to read their minds at his leisure. Their every thought and plan, their every intention and secret (dirty or otherwise), were his to peruse as easily as one might scan the pages of a newspaper. Through the subtle manipulation of the person's will, he guided some plans and intentions towards fruition when he decided that they would be beneficial to him; others, those he considered contrary to his interests, he caused to be abandoned.

The telaug was indeed a wonderful device, by far the most useful of Crystalman's many useful possessions, but today he hoped it would surpass itself.

Today, he hoped it would allow him to divine the true nature of the Martian Falcon.

The telaug sensed his approach and slowly opened its maw, the misshapen metal of its flank splitting apart to reveal the twitching, cilia-like sensors within. Crystalman placed the statuette inside, stepped back and began to manipulate the machine's controls, bringing the sensors to full awareness. A low hum slowly spread through the cavern, like tendrils of ink exploring a piece of blotting paper. A myriad of glowing, crisscrossing lines appeared in the bulbous, asymmetrical monitor screen above the controls.

Crystalman frowned and leaned forward to examine the strange pattern more closely. It was no surprise, of course, that the pattern was so unusual, so utterly unlike anything he had ever seen before. The important thing was that there was a pattern at all. He gave a shallow sigh of satisfaction. There *was* something inside the Falcon, some form of energy, an invisible matrix of information coherent enough for the telaug to detect and record.

The lines on the screen twisted and writhed, glowing an ugly shade of green – the green of disease and decay, the green of rotten meat, of the sky before a thunderstorm.

An indicator light told Crystalman that the process was complete, that the energy signature of whatever was inside the Martian Falcon had now been recorded. He manipulated more controls, calling up his own brain pattern from the depths of the machine's memory. His gaze fell upon the lever that would connect the two patterns, placing him in direct contact with the pattern inside the Falcon.

He hesitated, glancing again at the green tendrils that writhed across the monitor screen.

He pulled the lever.

He gasped, his mouth open wide behind his quartz mask. He reached up with hands that had become desperate claws and tore the mask from his head. It skittered away across the stone floor of the chamber as he fell to his knees, panting, his eyes tightly shut.

He groaned, and somewhere in the depths of his mind the realisation came to him that the voice was not his.

A series of sense impressions flooded his awareness.

Confinement... aeon-long and terrible beyond enduring.

The stillness of stone, the silence of ages, trapped within an implacable polymerized lattice of volcanic glass, coughed out of Mars when the planet was still young.

And *rage*… rage as powerful as the great volcano that had birthed his prison, powerful enough to smite worlds and scrape the screaming life from them.

Crystalman gasped again, dragged himself to his knees and reached with a violently-trembling hand towards the lever that would shut down the telaug machine. He pulled the lever and fell onto his back, once again feeling air surrounding him instead of stone, once again feeling limbs, skin, bone and senses instead of the unendurable stillness and darkness that had enclosed him.

Panting, he turned his head to look at the Martian Falcon, standing still and serene within the telaug.

Still, serene and silent.

And containing something that wanted out, something that wanted out very badly indeed.

Crystalman took the Falcon, walked unsteadily back to the railed vehicle and returned to his 'drawing room' in the immense cavern beneath the house. Still breathing raggedly, still unsteady on his feet, he crossed the floor and sat in an armchair.

There was something powerful inside the Falcon – no doubt about it. A raging mind, a soul in torment, anger and terror fused into a terrible new alloy… but behind it, beyond it… yes, there was something else, some*where* else, something far worse… and it was that which had thrown Crystalman to his knees. He had touched it for the briefest span, and the touch had nearly annihilated him. He closed his eyes and forced himself to breathe more evenly.

'The power of it,' he whispered. 'Yes… the power. When the time comes, I will need to forsake this body, this fragile flesh; I will need to return to that of which I am the merest fragment. And then…' He smiled and looked up at the ceiling of the cavern far above. 'I know what you are… and I humbly send you greetings.'

CHAPTER 14
Reprieve

The vampires approached slowly and steadily, their weapons still trained on Capone's head.

'Buncha numb-nuts,' said Capone. 'Whataya waitin' for? Let's go!'

'You're going to pay for what you did to Johnny Sanguine, garbage can,' said one of the vampires.

'Oh yeah? And who's gonna make me pay? You?'

'Wait a minute,' said Fort, stepping forward suddenly. Four of the vampires immediately trained their weapons on him. 'Capone had nothing to do with your boss's murder.'

'Shut it, Fort,' said the vampire. 'We'll get to you next.'

'It's true,' Fort persisted.

'I said shut it!' The vampire returned his attention to Capone. 'Was the bird really worth that much to you? Was it really worth your life, you metal maggot?'

'What the hell are you talkin' about, nightwalker?' said Capone.

'Rusty Links, that shapeshifting bitch! We know she's working for you. We know you paid her to stake Johnny and take the Falcon. Why? What's it worth to you? Tell us, and we'll make it quick and easy for you.'

Capone laughed. 'The sunlight must be gettin' to you. Like I said to my friend Charlie here, I don't deal with shifters – they can't be trusted. Guess old Johnny found that out for himself, didn't he?'

Fort glanced back along the road. The traffic had come to a halt behind the wreckage of the truck and Capone's limousine. The people in the cars were wisely staying put; no one was getting out. Fort saw ashen faces through windshields. Further back along the road, drivers who couldn't see what had caused the wreck were honking their horns in frustration. The traffic was quickly backing up. In a few minutes, the cops would show up. Fort hoped that he and Lovecraft would still be alive when they did.

One of the vampires had the same thought. He stepped forward. 'Carmine,' he said to the lead vampire. 'Let's just do them and get out of here. Cops'll be here soon.'

'Shut it, Vinnie,' said Carmine.

'You should ask yourself why Sanguine stole the Falcon in the first place,' said Fort, resisting the temptation to check his wristwatch. *God damn it*, he thought. *Cops'll show up on your doorstep in the middle of the night, but when you actually* need *them...*

'I told you to shut up, Fort,' said Carmine.

'Or what? You'll shoot me? You're going to do that anyway. What did Sanguine know about the Falcon?'

'Nothing.' Carmine turned his machine gun on Fort. 'What do *you* know about it?'

'We know it's dangerous,' Lovecraft piped up.

Carmine's gun twitched in his direction, and Lovecraft took an instinctive step back. 'Dangerous how?'

'It's entirely possible that it destroyed the Martian civilisation,' Lovecraft replied.

Fort thought about telling him to shut up, but they still needed to play for time, and the way Carmine's gun wavered a little told him that Lovecraft was doing a pretty good job.

'What are you talking about?' said the vampire.

'Sanguine stole it thinkin' he could put me in the frame for the heist, didn't he?' said Capone. 'Only he didn't figure on Rusty Links double crossing him. I thought Johnny was smarter than that...'

'Shut up about that!' said Carmine. 'I don't wanna hear about that. I'm talkin' to slim over there. What do you mean it destroyed the Martians?'

'I take it you didn't read this morning's newspapers,' said Lovecraft.

'I had other things on my mind,' said Carmine.

The distant wail of police sirens drifted along the road.

'Damn it, Carmine, come *on*!' said Vinnie.

'Vinnie, so help me...'

Another vampire stepped forward. 'Vinnie's right,' he said. 'We gotta get going. Let's just do Capone and take these two with us. Then we can make them talk.'

'Sir,' said Lovecraft, 'you don't need to *make* us talk. We will quite happily tell you whatever you want to know, so please... put your typewriters down.'

Vinnie glanced at the other vampires. 'Typewriters? Is this guy for real?'

'Okay, we'll do it your way,' said Carmine, taking aim once again at Capone's head. 'Kiss your diesel-powered ass goodbye, Capone...'

Lovecraft and Fort winced in anticipation of the coming hail of bullets, but instead of firing, Carmine hesitated and glanced up at the sky. The other vampires did the same and then looked at each other in apparent confusion.

'What's happening?' whispered Lovecraft.

'I'm not sure,' Fort whispered back.

The vampires lowered their weapons and stood still, with their heads raised, as if they were listening to something.

'What the fuck are you doing?' said Capone. 'You got cold feet?' He slammed his fists into his metal chest. 'Come on!'

'Shut up, shit bucket,' said Carmine. He beckoned to the other vampires, and they huddled together, speaking quietly to each other.

Then, with a final glance at Capone, they returned to their cars and took off, skidding across the central divide with a grind of metal on concrete and hurtling back along the Expressway.

'What the fuck?' said Capone. 'Why'd they take off like that?'

'I have no idea,' Fort replied. 'But I think it may be worth our while to find out.'

'Another time, maybe,' said Capone, jerking his head at the oncoming traffic on the other side of the central divide, and the two police squad cars that were rapidly approaching. 'See ya later, boys.'

With that, he ran to the edge of the elevated highway and leaped over. A couple of seconds later, Lovecraft and Fort heard the crunch of metal on asphalt and a sudden cacophony of honking horns and screeching tyres. They ran to the edge and looked over to see Capone racing off amongst the swerving traffic.

Fort sighed and shook his head, as the squad cars skidded to a halt and four cops piled out, guns drawn. 'Son of a bitch,' he said.

*

Twenty minutes later, Lovecraft and Fort were sitting on uncomfortable chairs in a small, drab room in the 7th Precinct stationhouse on the Lower East Side. Lovecraft had expected to make a statement and be politely thanked and allowed to leave, but Fort knew better.

Lovecraft glanced at Fort, who was leaning forward, face cradled in palms, his elbows planted on the cheap table in front of them. The table had once been white, but years of cigarette smoke had persuaded it to give up the pretence.

'Not even coffee, eh?' said Lovecraft.

'Not even coffee,' Fort replied, taking a hip flask from an inside pocket of his suit. He unscrewed it, took a lengthy sip and then offered it to Lovecraft.

'No, thank you, Charles. I never indulge.'

Fort sighed. 'Of course you don't, Howard.'

'We've given our statements. For how long do you think we're going to be detained?'

At that moment, the door opened and John Carter and Dave Wiseman entered.

'Well well,' said Fort. 'If it isn't Tweedledum and Tweedle-dumber. How you doing, boys?'

Wiseman gave him a humourless grin. 'From the look of things, a hell of a lot better than you, Fort.'

Carter and Wiseman took the two empty chairs across the table from Lovecraft and Fort.

'So,' said Fort. 'You got me on the detain-on-sight list, huh?'

'Not quite, Charlie,' Carter replied. 'Cops took statements from the witnesses on the Expressway. They saw what happened with you and Capone and the vampires; they also saw Capone leaving the scene.'

'When they called it in,' added Wiseman, 'we decided to bring you in for further questioning.'

Fort smiled. 'Thanks. Saved us having to walk back.'

Carter smiled too, and then glanced at Lovecraft. 'So… what's your story, Mr. Lovecraft?'

'Er… my story?'

'How did you come to be mixed up in all this?'

'He's my new research assistant,' Fort began, but Carter held up a hand.

'I think the gentleman can speak for himself, don't you, Charlie?'

Fort shrugged, folded his arms and sat back on his chair.

'I am a writer, sir,' said Lovecraft. 'One who has, regrettably, been forced by parlous financial circumstances to seek regular employment. Mr. Fort was kind enough to offer me such employment…'

Wiseman grunted. 'That *was* kind of him. Where do you live?'

Lovecraft told him.

'And where are you from, originally? Boston?'

'Providence, Rhode Island.'

'What are you doing in New York?'

'I was married, briefly. I moved here with my then-wife.'

'Where is she now?'

'Cleveland.'

Wiseman leaned forward. 'And what were you and Mr. Fort here doing in Al Capone's limousine?'

Lovecraft hesitated, shrugged and said: 'Being chased by vampires.'

'Don't get smart, Mr. Lovecraft,' Wiseman rumbled. 'You're in a heap of trouble.'

Lovecraft swallowed audibly.

'Don't listen to him, Howard,' said Fort. 'He doesn't know what the hell he's talking about.'

Wiseman cackled like a witch and shot a glance at Carter. 'Get this guy, John! I don't know what I'm talking about. Well, Mr. Fort, why don't you set me straight? Let's start with what you said last night. The case is closed, you said. No more reason to have anything to do with Capone, you said. And yet, here you are the next day, running around with him in his limo. What's the deal, Charlie boy?'

'You still think I was involved in the Falcon heist,' said Fort. 'Me and Capone.'

Wiseman gave an elaborate shrug. 'Like I said last night: tell me why I'm wrong.'

Fort shook his head sadly. 'Such two-dimensional thinking.'

Wiseman frowned. 'What the hell's that supposed to mean?'

'Mr. Lovecraft and I swung by the Medical Examiner's office this morning and took a peek at the autopsy report on the three deadwalkers who were found in back of the Algonquin. They didn't belong to Capone...' Fort glanced from Wiseman to Carter. 'But of course, you already knew that, didn't you? No traces of Enochian Magick, which is the method Capone uses for reanimation.'

'So Sanguine stole the Falcon after all?' said Carter.

Fort snapped his fingers. 'Bingo! Yeah, Sanguine stole the Falcon, and got staked for his trouble.'

'Do you know who by?'

'According to Sanguine's boys, it was Rusty Links...'

'What?' said Wiseman with an incredulous snort. 'You're telling us a girl took out the most powerful vampire in New York?'

Fort smiled, his gaze remaining on Carter.

'She's a... shapeshifter?' Carter said.

'The penny drops,' said Fort. 'Hallelujah.'

Carter nodded contemplatively. 'She could have taken the form of something so dangerous and powerful not even Sanguine would have stood a chance.'

'You're actually buying this bullshit?' said Wiseman.

'Hold on, Dave,' said Carter, leaning forward. 'All right, Charlie, let's just say that you're right…'

'Not me,' said Fort. 'Sanguine's boys – and they were there.'

'Okay, fine,' said Carter. 'But why?'

'Because she wanted the Falcon, and she took it. Sanguine's boys think she stole it on Capone's orders, but I don't think so. I think she stole it for someone else.'

'Who?'

'I have no idea, but I need to find out. We *all* need to find out, and quickly.'

Carter hesitated. 'Because of Tesla…'

'*Tesla?*' said Wiseman. 'What the hell has *he* got to do with this?'

'You know, Dave, you should try reading the front pages once in a while instead of just the funnies,' said Fort.

Wiseman ground his jaw but said nothing.

His gaze still fixed on Carter, Fort continued: 'There's something more going on here than two wiseguys knocking the shit out of each other – something much more. You know it, Howard and I know it, and given time, even Einstein here'll figure it out. The Martian Falcon is more than just a statue, a relic from a dead civilisation. The question is: what is it?'

'And why does… *someone* want it?' added Carter.

'Yeah, that too.'

'You don't think it's Links?'

Fort shook his head. 'I'd be surprised if she were acting alone. This seems too ambitious. I think there's someone pulling her strings, someone who knows – or suspects – what the Falcon really is. That's the person you should be looking for.'

Carter nodded. 'We'll issue an arrest warrant for Links…'

Fort chuckled. 'Good luck with that.'

Carter shook his head miserably. 'Yeah, I know. How do you bring in a shapeshifter? She could look like anyone or anything.'

'That's your problem, boys,' said Fort, trying not to look too smug.

'It's your problem too, Fort,' said Wiseman. 'You and your pal here aren't off the hook yet.'

Carter ignored him and said: 'What's next for you, Charlie? From what you've been saying, you're not going to walk away from this.'

'Damn right I'm not. As soon as you cut us loose, Mr. Lovecraft and I are heading out to Colorado to have a talk with Dr. Tesla about the transmission he intercepted from Mars…'

'The hell you are!' said Wiseman. 'You're not skipping town until this investigation is put to bed.'

Fort slammed his fist onto the table. 'Damn it, Wiseman, why can't you get it through your thick skull that this isn't about gangsters? It never was! It's about all of us – the entire human race. Tesla has detected a transmission coming from Mars, a transmission that only began *after* the departure of the X-M expedition from the planet – a transmission that shows the destruction of the Martian civilisation.'

'And you think the Falcon has something to do with it?' said Wiseman.

'That's what we need to find out,' said Fort. 'Because if the transmission *was* triggered by the removal of the Falcon from that temple on Mars – and I'd put money on that being the case – then it stands a chance that the Falcon is somehow connected with the catastrophe that wiped out the Martians five million years ago.'

Carter and Wiseman glanced at each other. Wiseman shook his head slowly.

'Gentlemen,' said Lovecraft, 'let's not forget that the crew of Rocketship X-M have not been the same since they returned to Earth, and that the Martian Falcon was displayed at the museum in a lead-lined case. There is something very strange about that object – and not just that it's from Mars.'

Carter considered this and then sighed. 'All right, Charlie. Get out of here. Go to Colorado, but do me a favour and don't stay there too long, huh? Capone and the vampires are getting ready to go head to head – an all-out war on the streets of New York. There's going to be a bloodbath unless we can crack this case, understood?'

Fort stood up. 'Understood.'

CHAPTER 15
Cabo Cañaveral

Rusty Links hated Florida.

She hated the flatness of the landscape, the incessant, cloying heat that fastened itself on the skin like an unwanted lover, the humidity that hung upon the air, as if the air itself were sweating. She hated the Spanish moss that clung like rotting hair to the branches of the Southern Live Oaks and Gulf-cypress, and the tough, broad-bladed St. Augustine grass that covered the ground like a carpet of tiny green knives. She reserved a special loathing for the Atlantic coast in particular, due to its proximity to the Devil's Triangle, the area of ocean bounded by the three points of Miami, Bermuda and Puerto Rico, and the horrors it contained.

Florida, she thought as she flew on her vast, membranous wings high above the East Coast Highway, casting nervous glances at the ocean on her left. *A dangling haemorrhoid on the ass of America.*

As she flew over Titusville, she noted the position of the sun in the sky and calculated that the time was around a quarter past seven. Down there in that steaming little town, at an address mentioned in the dossier Crystalman had given her along with her ten thousand, her target would be finishing breakfast with his family and preparing to leave for the day. He would then drive south along the East Coast Highway to his office at Cabo Cañaveral, where he worked as Chief Archivist for the X-M Program. His name was Aldous Bradlee.

Rusty peered down at the buildings lining Main Street. They seemed exhausted by the heat that, even at this early hour, was gathering its strength for another of its daily onslaughts. The buildings held no interest for her. Titusville was just another pointless smudge on a useless landscape. With a contemptuous flap of her wings, she accelerated away from the town.

She flew for a few more miles before descending and alighting on the side of the road. There was one advantage to this place, at least: out here, people were few and far between. There wasn't a car in sight, nor were there any houses. There was just the road, the sea to the left and the flat, sweating land to the right.

She reassumed her human form and walked behind one of the low dunes lining the road. She waited, feeling the steadily-rising heat of the morning sun on her naked back, and listening to the whispering sea…

A few minutes later, a glint of chrome appeared in the distance. Another half minute, and the glint became an automobile drifting at a leisurely pace along the highway.

'Red Packard Sport Roadster,' Rusty said, and smiled.

She clambered up and over the dune, waving her arms frantically and screaming: 'Help me! Oh God, please help me!'

The car braked immediately, and a man got out. He was tall and athletic, with a swimmer's supple yet powerful body. He had left his hat in the car, and his blond hair fluttered in the humid breeze. His face was wide-eyed and open-mouthed as he watched the naked woman half running, half staggering towards him.

'Please help me!' Rusty repeated, her face twisted in terror.

'What the hell?' said Aldous Bradlee. 'Oh God, what the *hell?*'

'Please,' cried Rusty. 'They're after me.'

'Ma'am, what happened?'

Rusty flung herself into Bradlee's arms. 'Please, get me away from here!'

Bradlee cast a fearful glance at the dunes from which Rusty had come. He took off his suit jacket and flung it around her shoulders. 'Come on,' he said hurriedly. 'Let's get you out of here and to the police.'

In an instant, Rusty's expression of terror vanished. She smiled at him and said: 'That won't be necessary.'

Bradlee frowned at her in confusion. The frown became a grimace of agony as her knee came up savagely into his groin. He gasped and collapsed on the sandy ground. Rusty reached down, took his head in both hands and twisted sharply, feeling the crunch of bone and cartilage as Bradlee's neck snapped. His body went limp. Rusty placed a finger on the side of his neck, under the jaw-line. There was no pulse.

She stood up and looked at his body. A shadow of remorse flitted across her mind, but it was gone almost before she noticed it. She bent and reached under Bradlee's armpits and dragged his body behind the dunes, briefly adding mass to her muscles to aid in the dragging.

Ten minutes later, Rusty Links, wearing Aldous Bradlee's form and dressed in his clothes, walked from behind the dunes to his car. She climbed in, started the car and continued along the highway towards Cabo Cañaveral, leaving his naked body buried beneath the sand.

*

Rusty brought the car to a halt at the entrance to the approach road leading from the East Coast Highway to Cabo Cañaveral. She had never been one to dwell upon romantic notions; for her, they were mere distractions that only served to divert her from the more important business of survival. It took a lot to impress her, to give her pause and make her consider anything but her own agenda.

Cabo Cañaveral was one such thing.

The rocket complex was dominated by two objects rising from the flat land like metal cathedrals and pointing at the blue sky and the depths of interplanetary space beyond. One was the gargantuan Vehicle Assembly Building, the largest building on Earth, looking like an aircraft hangar with a parabolic cross-section, but many, many times larger. It was in this behemoth, whose white flanks reflected the sunlight as if it were its own source of illumination, that Rocketship X-M had been built, and it was here that construction of the X-M 2 was nearing completion.

The other object was the launch gantry standing three miles from the Vehicle Assembly Building. Like the VAB, it was five hundred feet high, but looked much more delicate – unfinished, almost, as if some grand architectural project had been abandoned upon completion of its underlying structure: a glinting metal lattice speckled with machinery so complex that its details were lost in the haze of distance – a Kandinsky painting in three dimensions.

The rocket complex struck Rusty as both magnificent and ludicrous: magnificent for its expression of human ingenuity and the desire to know the universe and its secrets; ludicrous for its assumption that there was any place for humanity in the vast darkness beyond the tiny sphere of Earth.

In her opinion, humanity was a child running towards a busy freeway…

The thought conjured an image of Crystalman, chuckling behind his quartz mask while he examined his prize. No, she corrected herself, the prize wasn't the Martian Falcon, but whatever was inside it.

A child running towards a freeway, she thought. *But was Crystalman the child… or the freeway?*

She gunned the car's engine and glided swiftly along the approach road to the complex's main gate. She stopped at the security checkpoint as a uniformed guard approached. The guard bent to look inside the car as Rusty took Aldous Bradlee's security pass from an inside pocket of his jacket.

'Good morning, Mr. Bradlee,' said the guard.

Rusty smiled. 'Good morning.'

The guard frowned as he checked the pass. 'Everything all right, sir?'

'Of course. Why do you ask?'

'Nothing. Your voice just sounds a little odd.'

'Oh! Just a sore throat. Nothing, really.'

The guard nodded, smiled and handed back the pass.

'I'm sorry to hear that, sir. Hope you feel better soon.'

'Thanks. I'm sure I will.'

The guard signalled for the barrier to be lifted, and Rusty took the car into the complex, annoyed that apparently she had not got Bradlee's vocal chords quite right. She began to reconfigure them, but then stopped. According to the dossier Crystalman had given her, Bradlee worked until six. She doubted she would stay at Cabo Cañaveral until then, and a sore throat would be a good excuse to leave early, so she left her vocal chords as they were.

The road led her into a miniature town composed of machine shops, design offices, a conference centre and other support buildings, all one or two storeys and all constructed from pristine white concrete.

Rusty knew exactly where to go. She parked the car in Bradlee's parking space outside one of the larger buildings, got out and, carrying Bradlee's briefcase, walked confidently through the main entrance.

A couple of corridors took her to a door with a burnished steel plaque which read:

ALDOUS BRADLEE
CHIEF ARCHIVIST, X-M PROGRAM

She opened the door and entered an outer office occupied by Bradlee's secretary, whom the dossier had named as Bridget Sullivan.

'Good morning, Bridget,' she said.

Bridget looked up from her typewriter and returned Rusty's smile. 'Good morning, Mr. Bradlee. How are you?'

'Not great, as it happens. Bit of a sore throat. I wouldn't get too close if I were you. In fact, I may have to skip out early.'

'Oh dear,' said Bridget. 'I hope it's nothing serious.'

Rusty smiled and shook her head. 'I doubt it. But better safe than sorry, huh?'

'I suppose so. Does this mean you'll be missing the conference this morning?'

'Conference?'

'With Director Olson and the other department heads.' Bridget offered a smile. 'Surely you haven't forgotten, sir. It was only scheduled yesterday.'

Rusty gave a rueful grin. 'Oh, of course! Sorry. Head's a bit fuzzy. You know, I think it might be an allergy of some kind. No, I, er, I'll be here for the conference. What time was it?'

Bridget's smile grew broader. 'Ten o'clock in the main conference room. The details are in your desk planner. Would you like some coffee?'

'I'd love some, thank you,' Rusty replied as she crossed the room to the door of Bradlee's office.

She closed the door, sat at his desk and thought for a moment. This was inconvenient. The last thing she needed was to spend a protracted length of time in the company of other NCPE personnel. The longer she did so, the more likely it was that someone would notice something odd about 'Aldous Bradlee'. The dossier which Crystalman had given here was pretty detailed, but it didn't contain enough information to allow her to impersonate the archivist indefinitely. Her intention had been to get in, grab what she needed, and get out again as quickly as possible. Now, it looked like she would be spending the entire morning here, in the company of people who knew Bradlee well.

I guess I'll just have to play up the illness angle, she thought.

She consulted the desk planner. The entry under that day read: EMERGENCY CONFERENCE, 10AM, OPEN-ENDED. LOCATION: MAIN CONFERENCE ROOM, BUILDING A. SUBJECT: MARTIAN TRANSMISSION, NATURE AND IMPLICATIONS FOR X-M 2 EXPEDITION.

Rusty sat back and thought about this while Bridget brought in a cup of coffee. Rusty thanked her and sipped the coffee as Bridget left the room. She grimaced. Shit. Cream and sugar. Rusty preferred her coffee straight up, like her bourbon. Never mind.

She glanced again at the entry in the desk planner.

Emergency conference on the Martian transmission, she thought. *That might be worth sticking around for.* She glanced at the bank of file cabinets beside the desk and then looked at Bradlee's watch. *An hour and a half until the conference. I'd better get some reading done – and quick.*

She opened the file cabinet, yanked out Bradlee's files and began to read them, cramming the information into her head as fast as she could, her eyes dancing across the typewritten pages.

By a quarter to ten, Rusty was sitting back in Bradlee's chair, staring blankly into space and thinking: *Oh shit...*

CHAPTER 16
Never Trust a Vampire

Fort had just finished packing his travelling valise when the street-door-bell rang. He went to the telephone-box and lifted the receiver.

'Yeah?'

'Good morning, Charles,' said the voice of Lovecraft.

'Morning, Howard,' said Fort, checking his wristwatch. Nine o'clock on the dot. He was gratified but not surprised that Lovecraft was on time. He pressed the button to open the street-door. 'Come on up.'

When he opened the corridor-door, Fort noted that Lovecraft was visibly excited. 'You're chirpy this morning,' he said as he led him through to the living room.

'I've never flown before,' Lovecraft replied, putting down his own valise by the sofa. 'The furthest from Providence I've ever been is Key West, and I've certainly never been anywhere near an airliner.'

'Well, you're in for a treat, I guess. Coffee?'

'Yes, please.'

Lovecraft followed Fort through to the kitchen.

'Do you think we'll encounter them?'

'Encounter what?'

'Why, the sky beasts, of course!'

'Oh. Well, I guess. Longer flights usually do. That's why big airliners are fitted with heavy weapons.'

Fort poured a cup of coffee, handed it to Lovecraft and pointed to the sugar bowl on the countertop.

'Thank you,' said Lovecraft. 'I've always wanted to see them, in the flesh, as it were. I've seen photographs of them, of course, in the *National Geographic*, which carried a fascinating piece on them by Sir Arthur Conan Doyle a few years ago, but they must be a truly magnificent sight up close.'

'Be careful what you wish for, Howard. They're pretty impressive, no doubt, as long as they don't get too close. Most of them are harmless enough, but some are pretty nasty – especially if they're hungry.'

Lovecraft hesitated before sipping his coffee. 'Indeed,' he said.

At that moment, the street-door-bell rang again.

'Damn it,' said Fort. 'If that's Carter and Wiseman, I'm going to shit bullets.'

He went back to the telephone-box and lifted the receiver. 'Yeah. What is it?'

A voice he recognised immediately replied: 'Now is that any way to greet an old friend?'

'Cormack!' said Fort, pushing the button. 'Come on up.' He opened the corridor-door and waited while O'Malley climbed the stairs. Lovecraft stood in the middle of the living room with an expression of curiosity on his long face.

'Charlie, my lad,' said O'Malley, stepping into the apartment. 'How have you been?'

'Just dandy, Cormack,' Fort replied, shaking the priest's hand and beckoning him through to the living room. 'How about some coffee?'

'I won't, thank you.'

'This is Mr. Howard Lovecraft,' said Fort. 'A new associate.'

'A pleasure to meet you, Mr. Lovecraft,' said O'Malley, offering his hand.

Lovecraft shook it, replying: 'How do you do, Father.'

'I'm sorry to say this,' said Fort, 'but I'm afraid we don't have much time to talk. We have a plane to catch.'

'Working on a case?'

'Yeah.'

O'Malley nodded. 'Then I'll be brief. Charlie... I need your help.'

Fort motioned him to the sofa. 'Sure. What's up?'

'I need you to help me find the Martian Falcon,' said O'Malley.

Fort and Lovecraft glanced at each other. 'Well now,' said Fort with a grim chuckle. 'Sounds like half of New York wants to find that damned thing, and they're all coming to me for help. I wish I'd never heard of it!'

'So do I, Charlie, believe me,' said O'Malley.

Fort sighed. 'Howard and I are working on the same case, and it looks like it's about much more than a turf war between two gangsters. All right, Cormack, suppose you tell us how *you're* involved with this caper.'

The priest echoed the private detective's sigh. 'You don't know who has the Falcon right now, do you?'

'Not a clue.'

O'Malley hesitated, and then said: 'There's no easy way to say this, Charlie, so I'll just come out with it. Crystalman has it.'

Lovecraft gasped, reached for his coffee cup and drained it in a single gulp.

Fort looked at his old friend for a long moment, fists on his hips, his face set in a grim expression. 'How do you know that, Cormack?'

'Johnny Sanguine told me.'

'Sanguine's dead,' said Fort. 'Really dead – the kind of dead you don't come back from.'

'I wish that were true,' said O'Malley in a quiet voice. He went on to describe his encounter with the ghost of Johnny Sanguine.

When he had finished, Fort said: 'Now let me get this straight. Sanguine wants you to help him get the Falcon back from Crystalman and return it to Mars so he can redeem his soul in the sight of the Almighty.'

'That's about the size of it,' said O'Malley.

'Does anything about that story strike you as... oh, I don't know... bullshit?'

'Of course it does!' cried O'Malley. He stood up and began to pace back and forth. 'The only part of his story I believe is that he wants to get his hands on the Falcon – although God knows why. And speaking of God, all that stuff about the "Primal Mind" and cleansing his soul of all the evil he's done… well, we all know Sanguine. I've spent my life guiding God's children towards redemption, but that little bastard is beyond it. But I *do* believe he wants the Falcon.'

'Because of what it contains,' said Lovecraft.

'Exactly. There is something inside that thing, something of immense power. I don't know what it is, but I *do* know I don't want it in Sanguine's hands.'

'Or Crystalman's,' added Fort.

'But how on earth can we go up against Crystalman?' asked Lovecraft, glancing desperately from the private detective to the priest. 'No one knows who he is or *where* he is, and those who have tried to find out…'

'Have all wound up dead,' said Fort, 'in a variety of unpleasant and imaginative ways. I should have told Capone to go screw himself. At least a bullet in the head's quick and simple.'

'Really, Charles,' said Lovecraft, 'that's no way to talk.'

'Mr. Lovecraft's right,' said O'Malley. 'A defeatist attitude breeds its own defeat.'

'Wise words, Cormack,' said Fort in a tone which suggested he thought they were anything but.

'Just a moment,' said Lovecraft. 'How could Sanguine know all this? The nature of the Martian Falcon, the fact that Crystalman has it. As far as we know, he was killed almost immediately upon taking possession of it.'

'He didn't tell me,' replied O'Malley. 'But the answer seems plain enough.'

'He must have followed Rusty Links,' said Fort. 'When she died the final death, his spirit was released, and he followed her to Crystalman. So he knows where Crystalman's hideout is. He didn't tell you, Cormack?'

The priest shook his head.

'I have another question,' said Lovecraft.

Fort sighed. 'Ask away, Howard.'

'Why would Sanguine tell you that the Falcon must be returned to Mars?'

'What are you getting at?' asked O'Malley.

'Well, it seems a very specific necessity, don't you think?' Lovecraft replied. 'Why would Sanguine say it if it weren't true, or if he didn't *believe* it to be true? Why not simply tell you that the Falcon must be disposed of on Earth?'

O'Malley glanced at Fort. 'Good question.'

'Funny thing is,' said Fort, 'returning it to Mars may be the best thing to do with it.'

'How so?' asked O'Malley.

'You've read about Tesla's discovery in the papers?'

'The transmission from Mars?' O'Malley hesitated, and then whispered: 'O good Lord!'

'Yeah,' said Fort. 'Right now, my guess is that the transmission was triggered by the X-M mission two years ago, and I'd put money on it having something to do with the Falcon. Howard and I are heading out to Colorado to get the rest of the story from Tesla.'

O'Malley lowered his head. 'A vast and ancient evil, he said; a scourge from the depths of space. But what in God's name could Sanguine want with such a thing?'

'More to the point,' said Fort, 'what does Crystalman want with it?'

'On the subject of Crystalman,' said Lovecraft, 'since we know that he has the Falcon, shouldn't we just go to the police and tell them? They're doubtless better equipped to go up against him than we are.'

'That shower of bastards?' said O'Malley. He shook his head. 'This is too important to leave in the hands of New York's finest! No, we need to handle this ourselves, but to do that we need more information.' He paused. 'Yes, we need more information. And I think I know where I may be able to get it. Of course, I'll need to call in a big favour...'

'What are you talking about, Cormack?' asked Fort.

'I'm talking about making a trip to the Vatican to see an old friend,' O'Malley replied.

Fort raised his eyebrows. 'You mean the Pope?'

'The very same.'

'Are you saying you're friends with Pope Pius XI?' asked Lovecraft incredulously.

'I am indeed. Ambrogio and I go way back... back to our days together as combat exorcists. He'll grant my request, I'm sure of it.'

'What request?' asked Fort.

'I'm going to ask him to give me access to the Vatican Archives. I'm going to ask him to allow me to consult the *Kitab Al Azif*.' O'Malley paused and smiled grimly at Fort's and Lovecraft's open-mouthed stares. 'That's right, lads, I'm going to read the book that should never be read, the book that contains the secret history of the Earth and the Solar System – the very universe! The book of the Mad Arab, the *Necronomicon*... and may God protect me and forgive me!'

CHAPTER 17
The Bel Geddes

LaGuardia International Aerodrome sprawled across a thousand acres of northern Queens on the waterfront between the East River and Bowery Bay. After O'Malley left, Lovecraft and Fort took a cab from Fort's apartment to Terminal 2, which operated domestic flights.

As they got out of the cab, both looked up as the air was shaken by the thunderous drone of an airliner taking off. The vast silver chevron of a Bel Geddes Number 4 swept majestically overhead, its twenty propeller engines clawing at the air and hauling it up into the cloud-mottled sky. Lovecraft wondered how something so huge could get off the ground, let alone climb to an altitude of fifteen thousand feet and fly for hours.

In spite of his trepidation, in spite of all the doubts he had begun to entertain about the wisdom of accepting Fort's job offer and the perils to which it had exposed him, Lovecraft was looking forward to this journey.

They made their way into the terminal building, where Fort bought two two-way tickets to Denver at the sales desk. Then they checked in their travelling valises with an immaculately uniformed young woman who smiled an immaculate smile at them and wished them a pleasant journey.

Twenty minutes later, their plane was ready for boarding. Lovecraft looked through the panoramic windows of the departure lounge and was gratified to see that it was another

Bel Geddes Number 4. The boarding tube, all polished oak and thick carpeting, connected the departure lounge with the main embarkation hatch in the starboard pontoon.

The airliner was a thing to behold, a steel behemoth with nine decks and a wingspan of just over five hundred feet. Beneath the shallow V of the colossal wing which formed the main fuselage, and which contained suites and staterooms for overnight flights, each pontoon contained five decks marked by circular portholes peppering its flanks. A small lookout tower stood at the port and starboard wingtips, while the engine section with its twenty propellers – ten facing forward and ten aft – was a smaller echo of the main fuselage, and was mounted towards the leading edge on two sturdy pylons directly above the flight deck.

Looking at the aircraft, Lovecraft briefly recalled his dislike of the skycrawlers drifting through the air above New York, which seemed so emblematic of the city's profound otherness, and realised that there could be no comparison with the magnificent object standing before him now. The skycrawlers represented the ugliness of commerce, unfettered and unheeding, a base pursuit of the bottom line that was its own reason for existing.

But the Bel Geddes... this was *romance*, a great sweep of silver whose natural habitat was the blue void of the sky and the countless unknown destinations beyond. Lovecraft could hardly wait to get on board.

He and Fort joined the line of passengers making their way through the boarding tube, which took them into the main embarkation foyer on deck three of the starboard pontoon. From there they climbed to deck five on a wide Art Deco staircase that would not have been out of place in the finest Long Island mansion.

As they made their way forward to the vast observation lounge at the front of the aircraft, with its armchairs and settees all upholstered in rich burgundy leather, Lovecraft glanced to his left and caught a glimpse of the main dining room and the lozenge-shaped stage at the rear, where the orchestra were busily setting up their music stands and unpacking their instruments.

The dining tables were all bare, save for their immaculately pressed white linen tablecloths: the dining staff would wait until the airliner had levelled off at its cruising altitude before setting them and serving lunch.

Mindful that this was Lovecraft's first flight, Fort moved quickly towards the front, choosing two armchairs close to one of the fourteen huge square windows set into the gigantic fuselage's leading edge. Fort took out his tobacco pouch, rolling papers and matches and tossed them onto the ornate smoking table between the two chairs, while Lovecraft looked through the window, eyes wide with anticipation.

When embarkation had been completed, the air trembled slightly with a sound like distant thunder coming from above as the propeller engines roared into life and the airliner began its leisurely movement away from the terminal building and onto the taxiway. The engines settled into a steady, mildly soporific drone which could not be completely silenced even by the soundproofing between the decks.

A gentle yet authoritative voice issued from hidden loudspeakers throughout the airliner's interior. 'Good morning, ladies and gentlemen,' it said. 'I am Captain Everett C. Parker, and on behalf of my crew, I would like to welcome you aboard Transcontinental Flight 19 to Denver, Colorado. We will be cruising at an altitude of fifteen thousand feet, and our flight time to Denver will be six hours and thirty minutes. I hope and trust that you will have a pleasant flight. Thank you.'

Fort rolled and lit a cigarette and glanced at Lovecraft, who was leaning forward in his chair and watching rapt as they approached the main runway. *Queer bird*, he thought. Capone was right: he *did* belong in a library, but he had proved that he could keep his head in a crisis, and that counted for a lot in Fort's line of work.

All the same, Fort wondered if he had done this mild-mannered fellow a disservice in offering him the job. They had already come within a hair's breadth of death at the hands of Sanguine's crew, and Fort doubted that the sailing would be any smoother from here on in. Lovecraft appeared to scare easily, but he kept his nerve in spite of it, and that, Fort reflected, was the true mark of courage.

The airliner reached the main runway, turned and paused, as if gathering its strength for the long climb ahead. Then the drone of the engines rose in pitch and Lovecraft and Fort were pushed gently back into their armchairs as the Bel Geddes accelerated along the runway. The deck pitched up at a shallow angle as the airliner left the ground, and Lovecraft caught his breath as the distant skyline of New York sank beneath the lower edges of the forward windows. There was a faint mechanical whine as the eighty wheels comprising the craft's massive undercarriage withdrew into the pontoons.

'And we're off,' said Fort.

'Miraculous!' whispered Lovecraft.

*

The first lunch sitting was an hour after takeoff. Lovecraft and Fort went aft through a wide, arched doorway into the dining room and took a table near the port bulkhead as the band began to play a Bix Beiderbecke number.

'How do you like your first flight so far, Howard?' asked Fort as they both looked over their menus.

'Astonishing,' Lovecraft replied. 'More so than I expected, in fact. Normally, I'm not one to sing the praises of modern technology, but this… well, this is entirely different.'

'How so?'

'I suppose because it embodies mankind's yearning for discovery, for travel to distant and unknown places, to seek and to find that which is unknown, to divine the true nature of existence, and man's place therein.'

Fort glanced at Lovecraft over the top of his menu. He smiled and shook his head. 'Man's place in the true nature of existence, huh? I don't think you'll find that in Denver.'

'Perhaps not,' Lovecraft replied with a smile of his own. 'But I'm willing to bet we *will* find it in Colorado Springs – or at least a clue to it.'

Fort glanced at him again, this time more thoughtfully. 'Yeah… I guess you could be right, Howard.'

A waiter drifted over and asked them if they were ready to order. Fort chose the prime rib, while Lovecraft decided on the East Indian lamb curry with rice.

Fort raised an eyebrow. 'You like that stuff?'

'Indeed!' enthused Lovecraft. 'I was introduced to it not long ago by a friend and correspondent, Mr. E. Hoffmann Price. I like spicy food exceedingly, and I'm hoping that this dish will be particularly vigorous…' He glanced around at the other diners. 'Although I suspect my hope will be a forlorn one.'

'How so?'

'The galley may well be hamstrung by the dull trepidation of the pedestrian American palate,' Lovecraft replied, with apparently genuine sadness. 'I have little doubt they would prefer the kind of curry that's safe for women and children – a pallid, gutless, quite innocuous sauce; not the blighting, blasting, searing curry of the true Indian fashion, one drop of which has been known to draw blisters from a Cordovan boot. *That* is the kind I crave.'

'Well,' said Fort after a brief hesitation. 'Good luck.'

'I take it you don't particularly care for exotic cuisine, Charles?' said Lovecraft.

'I don't mind it, but my stomach does. Plays hell with me afterwards.'

'I'm sorry to hear that.'

Fort shrugged. 'I can live with it.'

'Your friend, Father O'Malley…' Lovecraft began.

'What about him?'

'A rather strange chap – but evidently well-connected.'

'Right on both counts,' Fort smiled.

'How long have you known him?'

'Longer than either of us care to remember. Before he joined the priesthood, he was a boxer. Could have gone all the way, but he found a higher calling. That's how he got his nickname: Father O'Blivion. Got a left hook like you wouldn't believe, which he still uses on occasion.'

Lovecraft raised his eyebrows. 'Really?'

'One of his specialties is guiding street punks onto the path to righteousness. Well… I say "guide", but it's more accurate to say he *punches* them onto the right path. And very few of them stray afterwards. One conversation with Father O'Blivion is enough for most.'

'I don't doubt it,' said Lovecraft quietly.

'Anyway,' said Fort, 'why don't you tell me a little bit more about yourself, Howard?'

Lovecraft gave him a quizzical look. 'Why? What do you wish to know?'

'Well, if we're going to work together, we should get to know each other, don't you think? We've hardly had the chance, so far, and we've got more than six hours to fill.'

Lovecraft considered this. 'Very well. Let me see… I was born on August the twentieth, 1890 in Providence, Rhode Island. When I was three years old, my father, Winfield Scott Lovecraft, was confined to Butler Hospital following a complete collapse while on a business trip to Chicago.'

'I'm sorry to hear that,' said Fort. 'What was the diagnosis?'

'The doctors told my mother that he had suffered a general paralysis – nervous exhaustion brought on by overwork. I regret to say that he never recovered. He died five years later. I was raised by my mother, Sarah, my aunts Lillian and Annie Phillips, and my maternal grandfather, Whipple Van Buren Phillips.'

'Must have been a pretty bad shock for you all,' said Fort.

'Of course,' Lovecraft nodded absently. His eyes had suddenly become unfocused, looking over Fort's left shoulder. 'My mother also died in Butler Hospital.'

Fort raised his eyebrows. 'Was she there for… the same reason as your father?'

'Similar,' Lovecraft replied. 'My mother was of a peculiarly depressive cast, and suffered from frequent bouts of hysteria. She was committed to the hospital six years ago, where she died two years later.'

Fort was beginning to regret asking Lovecraft to talk about himself. The poor guy's family history seemed to be one of unmitigated tragedy.

Lovecraft caught his expression, and gave a small smile. 'That said,' he continued, 'I must add that my childhood was one of utter contentment. Following my father's death, the position of family patriarch was assumed by Grandfather Whipple, who was a highly successful businessman, and it was in his library that my love of literature was kindled.' The small smile grew broader. 'Yes, it was there that I encountered the *Iliad* and the *Odyssey* for the first time, where I first read *The Arabian Nights*, and so many others. It was there also that I developed my interest in science – chemistry and astronomy in particular – and where I first conceived my intention to become a professional astronomer.'

'Why didn't you?' asked Fort.

The smile vanished and was replaced by an expression that, to Fort's eyes, seemed to combine both anger and shame. 'Mathematics,' Lovecraft said, as if the word were the name of an old enemy.

'Mathematics?'

'It was the subject with which I had most trouble at school, in spite of my great fascination with it. In fact, I confess that I completely failed to master it, which as you know is a requisite for entry into the field of professional astronomy. I suppose that one could say this resulted in a breakdown of sorts; in any event, I came to feel at an inappropriately young age that life no longer held any meaning or promise, that the death of this one dream signalled the death of all dreams.'

'What turned you around?' asked Fort.

'The UAPA,' Lovecraft replied.

'The United Amateur Press Association.'

'I suppose one could say that that splendid institution saved my life, for I had been contemplating suicide for some time. But in the UAPA, I found companionship and likemindedness, and I have made many splendid friends as a result of my association with it.'

Fort nodded. 'Why did you move to New York?'

Lovecraft told him about the failed marriage to Sonia and her departure for Cleveland after only a few months.

Fort sat back in his chair as the waiter brought their lunch. 'Jesus, Howard, doesn't look like you've been served a whole heap of luck so far.'

'Oh, I don't know,' Lovecraft replied as he leaned forward to take in the aroma of the lamb curry. 'I have my health and my writing. I need little else beyond that.' He took up his fork and tasted a piece of lamb.

'How is it?' asked Fort.

'Something of a curate's egg, I'm afraid. The meat is tender and flavourful, but as to the sauce, it's as I feared: a pale approximation of what it could have been.'

Fort suppressed a smile. 'I'm sorry to hear that.'

'That's not to say that the dish is a failure,' Lovecraft added hurriedly, anxious that his disappointment not be taken for impoliteness. 'It's still thoughtfully prepared, and the necessary spices are all present and correct.'

Fort chuckled as he cut into his steak.

'Anyway, that's quite enough of my uneventful life,' Lovecraft continued. 'What about you, Charles? What's your story?'

'Oh, there's not much to tell. I was born in Albany in 1874. Did a lot of travelling in my youth, out west, and also in Europe…'

'Ah!' said Lovecraft. 'Now that is an experience I envy you. I would so love to see those parts of the world which I only read about in books and periodicals. But do go on.'

Fort was about to, but at that moment the airliner gave a sudden shudder, and the port wing dipped sharply. Throughout the dining room, a hundred plates slopped their contents onto pristine tablecloths while glasses were upended and a loud collective murmur of alarm rose from the diners.

Almost immediately, the voice of Captain Parker issued from the loudspeakers. 'Ladies and gentlemen, this is Captain Parker. I apologise for the slight turbulence. Seems we've caught the attention of a sky beast, which has just given us a small nudge. This is a little unexpected, as the electro-scanners at LaGuardia didn't detect any in our vicinity. I assure you, however, that we are in no danger: looks like it's just curious. For those of you who may be on your first flight, I should explain that it's common for these animals to give aircraft a little exploratory tap now and then. The sky beasts are, by and large, gentle creatures; however, the Purser tells me that there have been some spillages in the dining room, for which I apologise. If you would kindly–'

He was interrupted by another jolt, this one much harder than the first. The alarmed murmur of the passengers became a collective cry of fear. When Captain Parker resumed, there was an edge of tension in his voice. 'Ladies and gentlemen, please stand by.'

Lovecraft looked over Fort's shoulder through the arched doorway separating the dining room from the observation lounge. Through the huge forward windows, he caught a glimpse of something flitting past from left to right. It wasn't a bird – didn't even seem to be an object as such: more a narrow ripple in the air, like a heat haze, which briefly distorted the deep blue void of the sky.

A moment later, he saw another one. This one moved more slowly, so that he could take in its detail. It was a slender, translucent strand, bounded on each side by a slightly darker line. Like the first, it was long; Lovecraft couldn't see the ends. Another appeared, hanging parallel with the other one, and then another, which unfurled from above like the proboscis of a colossal insect.

Several of the other passengers caught sight of the swaying, translucent tendrils. A woman screamed, a child began to cry loudly, chairs were overturned as people jumped to their feet.

Fort turned and looked through the forward windows as something descended into view from above. It looked like a parachute, a vast pale blue circle in the sky, mottled with darker patches and strung with a myriad of branc ing purple lines, like veins. The edges of the thing undulated slowly, like a jellyfish drifting in a gentle ocean current.

The tendrils that had descended around the airliner were attached to the object – those and many more besides. The craft lurched again, even harder this time. The thickly-carpeted floor heaved upwards, throwing people from their feet and upending tables and chairs. The screams of the women grew louder, the wails of the terrified children more desperate.

Lovecraft and Fort got unsteadily to their feet as the deck pitched to the left. The dining room was filled with the sound of breaking plates and glasses, which momentarily drowned out the cries of the passengers.

'Charles,' said Lovecraft, 'what's happening?'

'This isn't an exploratory nudge, Howard,' Fort replied, struggling to remain upright on the shifting deck. 'We're under attack!'

CHAPTER 18
The Death of a Distant World

Still thinking about what she had read in Aldous Bradlee's files, Rusty Links made her way to the Main Conference Room in Building A, which was at the far end of a sunlit walkway lined with palm trees. She could have been on any college campus in Florida, she reflected; the Cabo Cañaveral rocket complex had that kind of look and feel to it – apart from the gargantuan Vehicle Assembly Building and launch gantry, of course, which kind of undermined the impression.

She entered the windowless, brightly-lit conference room to find several people already there, sitting around a horseshoe-shaped table of polished teak. One wall of the room was dominated by a large projection screen, and Rusty noted that a movie projector was mounted on the opposite wall. Off to one side stood a table bearing coffeepots, cups and a large platter of donuts and pastries. With a muted 'Good morning,' she poured herself a cup of coffee, remembering to add cream and sugar, and took a seat at the table. She looked at the faces around her, matching them to the photographs in the dossier which Crystalman had given to her.

'Okay,' said the Chief Administrator, whose name was Troy Martell. 'Let's get started. We've all seen the images from the Martian transmission, but I think they bear another viewing before we discuss what to do about them. David, would you get the lights, please?'

'Sure thing,' said David Kaplan, the Flight Director, who stood up and flipped the switch by the door.

Martell stood up and went to the projector. He switched it on and the brief darkness was broken by the bright white beam, which threw a legend onto the projection screen.

NATIONAL COMMITTEE ON
PLANETARY EXPLORATION
HIGHLY CONFIDENTIAL MATERIAL
DO NOT DISSEMINATE

'This is the enhanced footage from Tesla's lab?' asked Kaplan.

'Yeah,' said Martell.

'And you've discussed it with him?'

'I called him yesterday evening,' Martell nodded. 'It wasn't the friendliest of conversations, but in the end I managed to persuade him to hold off on any further revelations to the press until we've had a chance to evaluate this material properly.'

Kaplan nodded and returned his attention to the screen, as did all the others. Rusty glanced around the table, putting names to faces: Brian Canning, Deputy Administrator; Monica Quinlan, Chief Scientist; Larry Donahue, Director of Exobiology; Pete Medina, Flight Systems Analyst; Deborah Pellin, Director of Space Medicine...

And Aldous Bradlee, Chief Archivist.

Rusty felt an uncomfortable and irritating twinge of nerves as she realised that Bradlee would be expected to contribute in no small measure to the conversation that would follow the screening of the material. She doubted that feigning a sore throat would be of any help whatsoever. She took a deep breath, sipped her coffee and watched as the video reel began.

From the outset, it was clear that whatever refinements Tesla had made to his receiving equipment had yielded stunning results: these images were orders of magnitude clearer than the ones he had initially received with his Teslascope. As the reel progressed, Rusty found herself wishing they weren't. She glanced periodically at the other faces around the table, at the expressions of wonder and awe that were gradually transformed into horror and disbelief. They had seen this footage before, but clearly the horror was still fresh, as if they were seeing it for the first time.

Although sympathy was not a trait she possessed in any great measure, Rusty sympathised with them now.

The images seemed to have been spliced together in the manner of a newsreel, telling a story concisely and in apparent sequence. They showed a planet that didn't look like Mars: it was green, forested, with oceans and lakes of bright, crystalline blue that glittered beneath fronds of milk-white cloud.

Taken from high orbit, thought Rusty. *So the ancient Martians were capable of space travel.*

The next image was of a vast city of white stone, or perhaps metal – it was difficult to tell. The buildings, huge and eerily beautiful, were highly geometrical in design: there were cubes and tall cylinders, slender pyramids and perfect spheres supported by graceful pylons, star-shaped towers and shallow cones... all punctuated with thousands of circular windows and connected to each other by thin, tube-like structures. Clearly, this was an advanced civilisation, at least on a par with modern humanity.

The next image was of people – the Martians themselves – and Rusty was struck by how human they looked. There were differences, of course: they were incredibly tall and slender, doubtless an evolutionary response to their world's low gravity; and their faces were alabaster-pale, with no need of melanin to protect them from the weakened rays of a distant sun.

They were standing in a wide plaza beneath a bright blue sky, looking up at a balcony protruding from the lower section of a colossal pyramid. Another Martian, dressed in robes of iridescent prismatic colours, was standing on the balcony and was apparently addressing the throng. His long, slender arms were raised, as if he were delivering a speech of unparalleled importance.

A leader of some kind, thought Rusty. *Maybe this was their capital city. No sound… wonder why. Maybe there was no need, or maybe the sound was lost from the transmission…*

The point of view switched suddenly. Now they were seeing the pyramid from a great distance – ten miles at least – and from a height of perhaps a thousand feet. The apex of the pyramid had begun to glow – if 'glow' was the right word. In fact, it was more like a stain on the air, a dull patch of purple, like meat that had been left hanging for too long.

The camera panned upwards as the purple stain seeped into the sky in a long, thin tendril – a beam of something that was trying to be light.

What the hell is that? thought Rusty with a quick glance around the table. *Serious technology… or perhaps something else…* She felt something clutch at her stomach with ghostly fingers – something profane… obscene.

The tendril of un-light reached slowly into the blue Martian sky, higher and higher, and then began to open into an inverted cone. It reminded Rusty of a fan vault flowering across the distant ceiling of some vast cathedral. It was made of the same dark purple substance as the tendril that had birthed it. The tendril began to sway and bulge intermittently with a disgusting peristaltic movement, as if something was inside it… something that was making its way with relentless pulsating spasms towards the unseen mouth of the cone.

Rusty glanced at Deborah Pellin, the Director of Space Medicine. She had covered her mouth with a trembling hand. Next to her, Pete Medina, the Flight Systems Analyst, had shut his eyes and was shaking his head. He didn't want to see what was about to happen next. None of them did.

Rusty returned her attention to the screen in time to see something emerging from the mouth of the cone. A thing blacker than the depths of space… a thing made of darkness that writhed and whipped and spilled into the air like liquid or a dense, heavy gas.

And then Rusty Links realised what had been attempted on Mars five million years ago. 'You stupid bastards,' she whispered.

Troy Martell glanced at her. 'What was that, Aldous?'

She gave a small start. 'Nothing,' she replied quietly. 'I... this is difficult to watch.'

'Damn straight,' said Pete Medina.

Martell gave a small nod. 'There's not much more.'

The writhing mass of darkness grew and spread with a rapidity that was stunning, terrifying. It erupted from the mouth of the cone and fell upon the city, flooding streets, smashing buildings to fragments, seizing and absorbing the screaming inhabitants. The thing's hunger was vast – as vast as Mars itself. Within a few minutes, it had leached the planet of its atmosphere, turning the sky from blue to pale, lifeless pink.

The point of view switched again to Mars as seen from high orbit. A ruddy stain was spreading rapidly out from the region which had been named Cydonia by the humans who had ventured there five million years later. The stain was like fire consuming tissue paper, annihilating everything with which it came into contact: forests, pastures, lakes, oceans... and cities. But it was not fire that smothered Mars and turned it from a living world to a dead husk of oxidised rock. It was something much, much worse.

Rusty knew exactly what it was, and the knowledge made her want to go back to Long Island and tell Crystalman what he could do with his hundred thousand.

Again the point of view shifted. This time the movements of the camera were jerky, as if whoever had been holding it was running or staggering. There was a room in which several Martians were holding the one who wore the iridescent robes. He was on his knees, and appeared to have been badly beaten. It was difficult to see exactly what was happening due to the sudden, erratic movements of the camera; clearly, the catastrophe that had destroyed Mars and its inhabitants was still occurring outside the room.

Another sudden jerk, and the screen was filled with some kind of machine. There was something about the lines of the machine that made the skin crawl; its very shape suggested somehow that it should never have been built, that its design should not have been given form in three dimensions. Its glinting, bulbous flanks split open like misshapen mouths, revealing two chambers within. One chamber was empty save for a complex tracery of dangling, silvery filaments.

The other chamber contained the Martian Falcon.

Kicking, struggling, screaming in eerie silence, the Martian in the iridescent robes was dragged towards the machine and thrust into the empty chamber. The doors closed. The camera jerked again as pieces of masonry began to fall from the ceiling. Another Martian began to manipulate the machine's controls, which consisted of numerous dials, switches and levers.

Moments later, the doors of the machine opened again. The robed Martian fell to the floor, clearly dead. The others left his body where it lay and took the Martian Falcon from the neighbouring chamber.

Again the point of view changed. Now the Martians were half running, half staggering along a corridor lit intermittently by flickering electric lights. One of them clutched the Falcon to his breast. The building's power supply was being interrupted, would doubtless soon give out altogether. The effect was like a strobe light, giving rapid, disjointed glimpses of what was happening.

The corridor opened into a large chamber which Rusty immediately recognised from the newsreels she had seen of the X-M expedition. It was the room in which Captain Thorne Smith and his crew had discovered the Martian Falcon two years ago.

A final jerk of the camera, and the screen went dark.

Martell stood up and switched off the projector. Taking his seat again, he said: 'That's all she wrote. Thoughts?'

'The one in the robes,' said Monica Quinlan. 'He was clearly a leader, perhaps *the* leader. And it looks like he was responsible for the destruction of their world.'

'But how?' asked Pete Medina. 'That pyramid was more than a building. But what was it? A machine of some kind? And what did it do? It looks like it projected something into the sky, but what?'

'It was clearly a technological device,' said David Kaplan. 'As to what it was *for*... a new type of power source? A weapon?' He shrugged and shook his head.

'Whatever it was,' said Larry Donahue, the Director of Exobiology, 'it produced something that was utterly inimical to all life – and not just life. Did you see how the sky changed colour? It sucked the entire atmosphere off of Mars! It consumed *everything* – the life of the planet, the very air itself.'

Troy Martell leaned forward. 'Do you think it could have been some kind of life form, Larry? An alien being of some kind?'

'It looked that way to me,' Donahue nodded. 'It acted almost like... like a single-celled organism, reaching out and absorbing everything it touched, but on a colossal scale, a scale large enough to suck an entire planet dry.'

'Those poor people,' said Deborah Pellin. 'Destroyed... *consumed*...' She shook her head.

'It seems to me we have two questions to answer,' said David Kaplan. 'One: did that thing leave once it had consumed everything on Mars, or is it still there, perhaps lying dormant, waiting? And two: what did the Martians do to the guy in the fancy robes?'

'I'd say they were punishing him,' said Brian Canning, the Deputy Administrator. 'Whatever they did, he wound up dead as a result. But where does the Martian Falcon fit into all this?'

'It was somehow part of the punishment,' said Monica Quinlan. 'It *had* to be. Perhaps the power source for the machine that killed the leader... a battery of some kind?'

Brian Canning shook his head. 'That can't be true. We examined the Falcon before we shipped it off to New York. It's obsidian, nothing more. No internal structure. It's a piece of art, not a technological device.'

Monica Quinlan gave a snort. 'Is that why we insisted it be kept in a lead-lined container?'

'That was just a precaution, Monica,' Martell replied. 'And the theory that it adversely affects mental states is just that – a theory. There's no known mechanism by which it could do that, but, as you know, we decided to err on the side of caution.'

'But what about the X-M crew?' Quinlan persisted.

'Same thing,' Martell said with an edge of irritation. 'The psych boys are still working on them. Their state could be put down to the effects of space travel; it could be completely unrelated to Mars or anything they found there. We still don't know for sure, but there's no concrete reason to tie it to the Falcon.'

'Until now,' said Larry Donahue.

Martell was about to answer, but David Kaplan interrupted him. 'Perhaps it had some ritual meaning,' he said.

'That doesn't ring true to me,' said Quinlan. 'It was definitely a machine that they put him into, and it looks like he sure as hell didn't want to go. It's as if he knew what was about to happen to him.'

'Why was the event filmed?' asked Pete Medina suddenly. All eyes turned to him. 'If that transmission was sent as a warning...' He paused, considering the implications of his own question. 'I can understand why the initial event was filmed: it was clearly the culmination of some great enterprise. And the catastrophe that followed – it stands to reason that the camera would have captured that as well. But the punishment of the guy in robes... why did they film that? Why did they think they needed to?'

They all thought about this. Martell glanced at Rusty. 'Aldous,' he said, 'you've been pretty quiet so far. Any thoughts?'

Damn it! Well, it had to happen sooner or later, and at least she was being asked to speculate rather than show any prior knowledge. 'Aldous Bradlee' folded his arms and sat back in his chair, frowning pensively. 'An opposing faction,' he said. 'A group who knew that what the guy in robes was planning was a bad idea. It looks like they couldn't stop him – maybe he was too powerful, maybe Monica is right and he was the Martians' supreme ruler. In any event, when the catastrophe occurred, they were prepared, and they jumped on him immediately. Maybe they thought that by killing him they could put a stop to what was happening...'

'They were sure as hell wrong about that,' said Deborah Pellin.

'And then,' Rusty continued, now talking more to herself than to anyone else, 'while the catastrophe was occurring... knowing that they too would be dead soon… they set up the transmission equipment. But they didn't set it to transmit immediately… no, they didn't do that. Instead, they set it to transmit only in the event that Mars was visited in the future. Now… why did they do that…?'

The others looked at each other in silence. Then Medina said: 'Maybe they didn't want to advertise the fact that something terrible had happened. Warnings can sometimes be lures, you know? For God's sake don't come here! Oh, really? Why not? Let's go there and find out!'

Larry Donahue nodded. 'That's possible, I guess. But that leaves us with another question, doesn't it? What triggered the transmission? Was it the arrival of Rocketship X-M? Or was it the taking of the Falcon? Whatever they did to their leader, the Falcon had something to do with it.'

Rusty looked at Donahue. *Yeah*, she thought, *the Falcon had something to do with it.*

'If that's really the case,' said Quinlan, 'then we have another question and another problem: we don't know where the Falcon is. It's been stolen…'

'The New York police think it was stolen by the mob,' said Martell. 'Most likely, Al Capone.'

'Yeah,' said Quinlan, 'but is that true? Or was it stolen by someone else?'

'What are you getting at, Monica?' asked Martell.

Quinlan sighed. 'I don't know. It's just that, well, the timing… it strikes me as too close to be coincidence. What if it wasn't Capone or any other gangster? What if someone else knows something about the Martian Falcon… something we don't?'

Martell sighed. 'Unfortunately, that's out of our hands. Let's just hope that the New York police are half as good as they think they are…' He paused. 'And let's hope that you're wrong about whoever stole the Falcon.'

Brian Canning nodded. 'I guess it's time we turned to the main reason for this meeting: the X-M 2 expedition. Where does the transmission leave us? If it's a warning, do we go ahead, or do we abort?'

'I see no reason to abort,' said Martell.

'Why not?' asked Canning.

'Whatever happened on Mars happened five million years ago. It's over. Finished. Whatever destroyed them is long gone: the fact that the X-M crew made it back alive is proof of that. There's a hell of a lot of money tied up in the X-M program – a *hell* of a lot – and I can't imagine that Washington will be too pleased if we tell them we've decided to scrap the whole thing because of a message that was recorded five million years ago. They're just not going to go for it.'

'You say that whatever destroyed Mars is finished,' said Monica Quinlan. 'But Troy… are you *sure*?'

Martell sighed. 'Of course I'm not, but space travel is a dangerous business, we all know that. We have to weigh risk against investment…'

'We?' said Quinlan.

Martell paused. 'They. The bean-counters in Washington who are holding our purse strings. They're the ones we answer to, ultimately, and they have the final say. When you get right down to it, all we can do is make recommendations.'

'I suppose you're right,' said Quinlan glumly. 'But I still don't like it.'

'I'm not too thrilled about it myself, Monica,' muttered Martell. 'I'd like some more time – time to properly evaluate what we're dealing with here. But the optimum launch window to Mars won't stay open for much longer, and I can tell you for a fact that Washington won't stand for what they'll see as an unnecessary delay.' He turned to Rusty. 'All right. Aldous, I think it's time for an update on the ninth rock book. Why don't you bring us up to speed on what you've learned so far?'

Rusty gave a slight start, and felt her heart sink. *An update?* she thought. *Oh shit…*

CHAPTER 19
The Sky Beast

The Bel Geddes lurched and heaved again, the deck jumping like a tossed pancake as the sky beast's tendrils wrapped themselves around the aircraft's wings. The distant squeal and groan of crushed metal echoed through the craft in counterpoint to the tuneless opera of the passengers' screams. Crockery, furniture and the band's instruments flew through the air, smashing against bulkheads and deck as the pilot throttled up the aircraft's engines to maximum, their desperate drone competing with the cacophony inside. From unseen points above and below, a metallic, staccato chittering began: the machine gun batteries mounted on the Bel Geddes's dorsal and ventral surfaces. The great airliner wasn't going to go down without a fight.

'It's trying to pull us in!' yelled Fort, pointing through the archway leading to the observation lounge and the panoramic windows. 'If we can't break free, it'll make a meal of us!'

'I don't think so!' Lovecraft shouted back. 'Look at it, Charles! Look at its colour!'

At first, Fort wondered what the hell Lovecraft was talking about. Then he peered more closely at the blue and pink striations that had begun to ripple across the creature's vast circular canopy. 'My God, Howard, you're right!'

'You'll note the species, as well,' Lovecraft continued. '*Peregrinans placidus…*'

He was right about that, too, Fort realised. *Peregrinans placidus*... gentle walker. The sky beast shouldn't have been a threat: this particular species was perhaps the most docile of all the atmospheric Medusozoa; there were no known instances of a *Peregrinans placidus* ever having attacked an aircraft.

'I read about these in the *National Geographic*,' said Lovecraft as he ducked to avoid a flying double bass. 'Those colours, that pattern...'

'I know,' said Fort. 'They're a mating display. The damned thing doesn't want to eat us... it wants to screw us!'

'Well,' said Lovecraft, 'I wouldn't have put it quite *that* way, but...'

The rate of fire from the defensive batteries increased. Lovecraft and Fort watched as a score of streamers of hot metal hurtled towards the sky beast. They didn't seem to be doing much good. The aircraft lurched again as yet more tendrils flew from the creature's underside and wrapped themselves around its wings.

Fort looked up at the ceiling. 'Damn it, Howard, even if it doesn't want to eat us, if those tendrils damage the engines or the control surfaces...'

'We're still done for,' agreed Lovecraft. 'The question is, what are we going to do?'

At that moment, the air was shredded by the sound of breaking glass – but this was no falling wineglass or decanter. The sound was distant, but it filled the dining room and made the passengers scream even louder and cover their ears. It was as if every piece of glass in the world were shattering at once.

Fort cringed beneath the sound. 'Jesus Christ!'

'It must be the solarium windows,' said Lovecraft.

'Right again, Howard. Come on!'

Half running, half staggering, they ran from the dining room into the port pontoon and aft along the central corridor, past doors leading to the shop, the bar and the infirmary (Fort quickly looked into the infirmary, but saw that it was empty).

The corridor opened into a large vestibule at the rear of the pontoon. The solarium lay beyond at the very rear of the giant airliner's centre section. The vast room was three decks high; its gently sloping ceiling, which met the deck at a shallow angle at the rear of the fuselage, was composed of enormous, rectangular panes of glass – at least, it *had* been until a minute ago. Now the glass lay in a million shards on the deck and the solarium was open to the atmosphere. People who had been sunning themselves or playing deck games were now fleeing madly into the vestibules in the port and starboard pontoons in a desperate attempt to get away from the semi-translucent tendrils that were whipping back and forth, seeking a firm grip on the airliner's hind.

Near the rear of the solarium, a small girl, perhaps nine years old, crouched next to one of the glassless window panels. Her eyes were shut tight and she was covering her ears with her hands, paralyzed with terror.

Somewhere to their left, Lovecraft and Fort heard a woman shouting: 'Madeleine! Madeleine!' They watched as the woman emerged from the tide of fleeing passengers, saw the girl and screamed: '*Madeleine!*'

'Oh good grief!' cried Lovecraft. 'The child… she's…'

The deck lurched again, bouncing the girl up and out of the window. The woman screamed again and fell to her knees.

Fort sprinted towards the windows, glancing up at the tendrils which had now fastened themselves firmly around the steel frames. Lovecraft followed, not wanting to, for he fully expected to see the poor child falling away from the aircraft, cartwheeling through the sky towards a terrible end.

Instead, he saw her lying flat upon the ten feet of fuselage that separated the lower edge of the solarium window from the trailing edge. She was clinging to a small sensor mast which sprouted from the metal skin of the aircraft. It was about the size of a handheld flashlight, one of many such instruments that relayed information on atmospheric conditions, temperature and wind speed. Lovecraft looked at the terror-stricken expression on her face as her tiny fingers tried to maintain their grip on the sensor mast. The aircraft lurched again, bouncing the child up and down.

'*Mommeeeee!*' she screamed.

'My God, Charles,' said Lovecraft. 'What are we to *do*?'

'I'll tell you what *you're* going to do, Howard,' Fort replied, shrugging off his jacket and letting it fall to the deck. 'You're going to grab my ankles.'

'What?'

Fort staggered to the very edge of the deck, grabbing the window frame for support. He took off his spectacles and shoved them into his trouser pocket as the screaming air outside tried to rip his hair from his head.

'Ready Howard?' he shouted.

'One moment,' said Lovecraft, who had realised what Fort was about to do. He took off his own necktie, tied one end to the window frame and the other around his left ankle; then he crouched down and took Fort's ankles in the strongest grip his shattered nerves would allow. 'I'm ready, Charles.'

Fort crouched also, placed his hands on the outer skin of the aircraft and gradually lowered himself until he was lying flat. He reached out in front of him, with the air screaming in his ears and the staccato *clack* of the machine guns hammering in the background. He stretched as far as he could, reaching with outstretched arms towards the girl… but she was still a couple of feet beyond his reach.

'Damn it!' he cried. 'Howard, I'm going to edge forward.'

'All right, Charles, I've still got you!' Lovecraft shouted, his reply all but lost in the howl of wind and rattle of machine gun fire. He hoped that the aircraft's weapons were having some effect on the amorous sky beast, otherwise he and Fort were wasting their time.

Fort raised himself onto his elbows and edged forward. 'It's all right, kid!' he shouted. 'I'm coming for you… nearly there!'

'*I want my mommeeeee!*' the girl cried.

As he continued to inch forward, Fort felt something damp seeping through his shirtsleeves: the outer skin of the aircraft was slick with something. Water? Condensation? No… more like an oily residue of some kind. He wasn't sure, and he gave it no more thought – he had other things on his mind right now…

Feeling his back and shoulder muscles burning with the exertion, he reached out and grabbed the girl's wrist, just as her fingers gave out and released their grip on the sensor mast.

'Got you!' he cried. 'Howard!'

Lovecraft gripped Fort's ankles ever tighter and began to pull him back. Two male passengers rushed forward and lent a hand. In another few seconds, Fort and the girl were back inside.

Her mother staggered across the deck and gathered her up in her arms. 'Thank you!' she cried. 'Oh thank you, thank you!'

'Well done, sir!' said one of the passengers who had helped haul Fort back in, clapping him on the back as he slowly got to his feet.

Fort rubbed his right shoulder with his left hand. 'I'm going to feel this tomorrow, mark my words.'

At that moment, the deck ceased its heaving and the stutter of machine gun fire became sporadic and then stopped altogether. The only sounds were the drone of the engines and the whistle of the wind outside. 'I think they've done it,' said Fort. 'They've fought off the beast!'

A ragged cheer went up from the passengers.

'Thank God,' said the woman, who was still clutching her child to her breast. 'Oh, thank God.'

'Good job, Howard,' said Fort.

Lovecraft looked down at Fort's arms. 'Charles,' he said, 'what's that on your shirt? And what on earth is that *smell?*'

*

Captain Parker was standing at the forward windows of the flight deck, scanning the sky with binoculars when the purser entered, followed by Fort and Lovecraft.

'Captain,' said the purser, 'I'm sorry about this – I know it's highly irregular – but you may want to hear what these gentlemen have to say.'

Parker turned from the windows and cast an unsympathetic glance at all three of them. 'You're right,' he snapped. 'It *is* irregular. We're a little busy up here, Wentworth.'

Lovecraft gazed around the flight deck with undisguised wonder, taking in the huge banks of instruments lining the bulkheads and gawping at the countless gauges, switches and levers, and the members of the flight crew who were moving hurriedly between them, checking the aircraft's systems and making numerous adjustments.

Fort stepped forward. 'A *Peregrinans placidus* tried to mate with us, Captain,' he said. 'That's never happened before, as far as I know. Want me to tell you why?'

Captain Parker hesitated. 'You mean you know?'

'I sure do. Sniff my arms.'

'I beg your pardon?'

'You heard me,' Fort replied, raising a forearm and waving it back and forth beneath Parker's nose.

The captain grimaced. 'My God, what a stink!'

'You know what this is, don't you?'

'Of course I do! It's a secretion, a mating pheromone produced by a female *Peregrinans placidus*. But how come it's all over your shirt?'

Fort told him about rescuing the girl, and concluded: 'This stuff was on the liner's outer skin. It must be all over the fuselage. It's what put that male in the mood for a little hanky panky.'

'But that's impossible,' protested Parker. 'How the hell could it get onto the fuselage?'

'I was hoping you might have some ideas,' said Fort.

With obvious reluctance, Parker leaned forward and sniffed again. 'It seems to be somewhat diluted. Still stinks to high heaven, mind you, but…'

'Diluted?' said Fort.

Parker nodded. 'When secreted from a live *Peregrinans placidus*, this pheromone is much more pungent. Undiluted, it would have cleared the flight deck, believe me – none of us could have stood it for more than a few seconds.'

'So it's diluted… what with?'

'How should I know? Water, presumably.'

'Water,' echoed Fort. He glanced around the flight deck. 'How much damage have we taken, Captain?'

'A fair bit, but nothing catastrophic, since we're still in the air.' Parker indicated the main scanner, a large circular display at the centre of the main instrument panel just below the forward windows. 'The beast has returned to the upper atmosphere – I guess he figured we weren't worth the trouble thanks to our gun batteries. As for us, we can make it to Denver, although the ship won't be making the return flight to New York as scheduled. She'll need to go to the workshop for repairs to some of the control surfaces, and she'll need to be checked for interior and exterior structural integrity…'

'She'll need a good bath as well,' Lovecraft added. 'They'll need to wash that unholy stench off her skin. Any trace of it could attract another sky beast.'

Fort glanced at him. 'What did you say?'

Lovecraft gave him an uncertain look. 'I… said she'll need a good bath…'

Fort clicked his fingers. 'A bath – that must be it! That must be how the pheromone got onto the outer skin.'

'What the hell are you talking about?' demanded Captain Parker.

'The pheromone must have been added to the cleaning solution when the ship was washed during pre-flight maintenance…'

Parker looked at him incredulously. 'Are you saying that someone did this deliberately? That the ship was… *sabotaged?*'

'That's exactly what I'm saying, Captain,' Fort replied.

'*Why*, for God's sake?'

Fort hesitated, and then replied: 'I have no idea, but it's the most plausible explanation, don't you think? How else could the pheromone have been diluted and deposited on the skin of the ship?' He paused and added: 'Anyway, I think we've taken up more than enough of your time. We'll head back down to the passenger decks. There's a lot of clearing up to do, and I noticed that some of the passengers are lending a hand. I think we will, too. Thank you, Captain Parker. Come along, Howard.'

Fort seized Lovecraft by the elbow and half-dragged him from the flight deck.

*

Fort said nothing until they had descended the staircase leading down from the flight deck. When he was sure they were out of earshot of any of the crew or passengers, he said: 'Damn it! Me and my big mouth!'

'What do you mean, Charles?' said Lovecraft.

'I shouldn't have mentioned sabotage.'

'Why not?'

'Listen, Howard. I think I know why the pheromone was sprayed onto this aircraft. It's because someone wants us dead – you and me. They knew we'd be on this flight. They wanted to make it look like an accident – a sky beast attack on our plane – and they weren't too concerned about taking out four hundred other people in the process.'

'Someone in Crystalman's employ?'

'I'd put money on it.'

'So why didn't you tell Captain Parker? And why shouldn't you have mentioned sabotage?'

'Because if Parker thinks we know anything about what happened, he'll radio through to Denver and have us picked up by aerodrome security as soon as we land. There's going to be a big investigation into this incident, and we don't have the time to get dragged into it.'

Lovecraft nodded. 'Yes, I see. But if Crystalman *is* behind this, how did he know we'd be on this flight? How did he know we'd be going to Denver?'

'That's what bothers me, Howard. We only told three people about our travel plans: Carter, Wiseman and Cormack.'

'You mean…?'

'I think we have to face the possibility that one of them is working for Crystalman. He must have reported to Crystalman, who then sent one or more of his goons to pose as maintenance crew at LaGuardia. They must have put the pheromone into the tanks of detergent before the plane was washed.'

'But why didn't the other maintenance men notice the smell?' asked Lovecraft.

'Because they're all required to wear face masks with air filters when handling the detergent; it's powerful stuff – gives off some pretty noxious fumes. None of the legitimate maintenance guys would have noticed anything unusual, and by the time we got into the air, the water and detergent would have evaporated from the skin of the ship, leaving the pheromone to do its work.'

'That all sounds plausible enough,' said Lovecraft. 'But how on earth did Crystalman get his hands on a reproductive pheromone from a sky beast?'

Fort sighed. 'I'm not sure, Howard, but I do know that Crystalman's a genius; a warped bastard to be sure, but a genius nonetheless. He couldn't have evaded the law for so long, otherwise.' He thought for a moment and added: 'You know, I wouldn't put it past him to chemically synthesise the active compounds in the reproductive pheromone. He's got the knowledge, and chances are he's got the equipment...' He grimaced. 'Which reminds me, I need a shower and a change of clothes.'

CHAPTER 20
As Dead as Mars

Rusty looked around the conference table at the expectant faces looking back at her. *An update*, she thought. *They want an update. Okay... okay.*

'Well,' she said, 'I'm still conducting my analysis and evaluation...'

'And?' said Troy Martell.

'To be honest, there's not too much to report at this stage...'

'Is that all you've got to say?' asked Canning with a glance at the others. 'Come on, Aldous! I mean, you were the one who recommended that we keep the ninth rock book. You said it might contain the key to deciphering the hieroglyphs in the other books. You were pretty adamant about it, in fact.'

'Brian's right,' said Martell. 'You've been pretty cagey about your research so far. I decided to cut you some slack, in view of the difficulty of your work – trying to interpret the words of an alien language with nothing to compare them to. It's a tough job, I'll grant you, but you must have come up with something by now.'

Rusty had an answer for them – or rather, Aldous Bradlee did, but she had no way of knowing if he had already mentioned it in a previous meeting. If she told them what they already knew, she'd be in trouble; they'd know something was up. But, she decided, she had no choice: she had to tell them *something*, so she went for broke and told them what she had read in Bradlee's files.

'Okay... I wasn't going to share this with you just yet; I was going to do some more work, to make sure I wasn't wrong, to make sure I wasn't *crazy*... but you need an answer now, so here it is. We know that the Martian rock books are – or were – their favoured means of literary expression. They're masterpieces of craftsmanship, both in design and execution: thin slivers of basalt, granite, onyx and other minerals bound together with metal rings and containing text and images. We have no idea how they were made; it's as if the different minerals were somehow shaped and manipulated to produce the images on each page.'

'We know all this, Aldous,' said Canning with more than a trace of impatience. 'We know what they look like; we want to know what they *mean*.'

'I'm getting to that, Brian,' said Rusty. 'They're more than just books whose pages are made of rock – much more.'

'What do you mean?' asked Martell.

'I believe they're the product of a highly-advanced technology, which I've called "lithotechnology".' Rusty scanned the faces of the others. Their bemused expressions told her that this was news to them, that she was still on safe ground. She began to relax a little. If they'd never heard that word, it followed that they'd never heard the rest of it.

'Lithotechnology? What the hell does that mean?' said Pete Medina.

'Simply put,' Rusty replied, 'it means that the ninth rock book is an information storage device, but not in the way a normal book is. Oh, it has text and images, but it contains much more than that. Somehow... *somehow*, it's capable of communicating with whoever looks at it.'

The others cast incredulous glances at each other.

'Communicating?' said Martell. 'How?'

'It takes a long time to get going,' Rusty replied, 'which is why no one has noticed it before. It could be because our brain patterns are different from those of the Martians. It takes longer for the book to key into the electrical field generated by the human brain. But I've spent an awful lot of time staring at the pages of the ninth book – enough time for the lithotechnology to align itself with my brain pattern…'

'Excuse me, Aldous,' said Monica Quinlan, 'but are you saying that the rock book *speaks* to you?'

'Not as such,' Rusty replied. 'It's difficult to describe the sensation. When I look at the pages of the rock book, it's as if memories are triggered in my brain – memories I obviously don't possess. It's like I'm *remembering* things I never experienced, things I never knew before.' She paused and shook her head. 'It's a very unsettling experience. The book isn't *telling* me anything as such; it's… *implanting* information without my realising it, and then prompting me to remember what's been implanted.'

'You mean it's communicating with your subconscious mind?' said Deborah Pellin.

'Yes, I think that's a pretty good way of describing it. The information is somehow transferred to my subconscious, and since that's not a normal event, the subconscious doesn't know how to process it, so it rejects it, in effect; it shunts the information up into the waking consciousness, which experiences it as memories. At least, that's my guess.'

'Fascinating,' murmured Pellin.

'Do the other rock books have this ability?' asked Martell.

Rusty shook her head. 'I don't think so. I tried it with them, but they're completely inert. They may have been damaged in some way. The ninth book is the only one that does this.'

'Incredible,' said Pete Medina in a tone which suggested he wasn't entirely convinced. 'What you're describing certainly sounds like tech of some kind… but in *rock?* How the hell does *that* work?'

Rusty shrugged. 'Like I said, it's highly advanced.' She nodded at the projector on the wall. 'We've just seen images of Mars taken from orbit, so we know they were capable of spaceflight. They were on a level with humanity as far as technology goes, and I suspect that they were pretty far in advance of us. Somehow they had a way of embedding their technology – in terms of communications at least – in mineral forms. Don't ask me how.'

'All right,' said Martell. 'Let's leave that aside for now. What did the book tell you?'

Rusty hesitated before replying: 'It told me that what we call the Martian Falcon utilises the same technology. It told me what the Falcon really is.'

'And what's that?' asked Martell.

'A prison,' Rusty replied.

The others glanced at each other again.

'A prison for who, or what?' asked Medina.

'The one in the robes,' said Rusty. 'The one who destroyed Mars and every living thing on it. The bird isn't really a falcon, of course – although it's a pretty close analogy to a terrestrial falcon. It was their symbol for justice, and it was the way they punished their criminals. They didn't have prisons like ours, with criminals locked up in cells. Those who were convicted of serious crimes were placed in the machine we saw, and their minds – their life force, the very essence of what they were – were transferred to a statue like the one we brought back from Mars. They were trapped there for the length of their sentence while their physical bodies were kept in a kind of... I don't know what you'd call it – suspended animation?'

'That sounds awful,' said Deborah Pellin, who gave a visible shudder.

'Yes... yes it does,' said Rusty. 'It was a highly symbolic punishment: the total confinement of the mind and soul within the physical representation of justice. When they did it to the one in the robes – his name was Haq ul'Suun – they allowed his body to die. They knew that they were condemning him to an eternity trapped within the mineral matrix of the Falcon. It was the only fitting punishment for the utter destruction he had wrought upon Vattan.'

'Vattan?' said Medina.

'That was their name for Mars,' said Rusty.

Martell leaned forward, planting his elbows on the conference table. 'So... you're saying that this Martian–'

'Vattanian,' Rusty corrected.

'This Vattanian, Haq ul'Suun... his mind is still inside the Falcon?'

'I believe so.'

'And is it dangerous?' asked Martell.

'He was called the God-King of Vattan,' Rusty replied. 'That was how the Vattanians considered him. I don't know if he was really a god. I doubt it, since they effectively killed him – his body at least. But his intellect was immense, and he had access to information about the universe which would make him very dangerous indeed if he were ever to be released from his prison.'

'What information?' asked Brian Canning.

'What we saw in that vid was a ritual of sorts, but not an occult ritual. It was based on a scientific theory. Don't ask me how he knew this, because the rock book didn't give me that information...' (*At least*, thought Rusty, *it wasn't in the notes I managed to read.*) '...but Haq ul'Suun had figured out how to create a portal between this universe and another – what he called "a place between the spaces we know".'

'Between the spaces we know?' said Medina. 'What the hell's that supposed to mean?'

'I think it means he found a way to access other dimensions of reality,' Rusty replied. 'The pyramid *was* a machine – a machine of immense power and sophistication, capable of opening a way between our reality... and another.'

'And the thing that came through?' said Pellin. 'The thing that destroyed Mars?'

'Something from outside... or I should say something from *between*. An entity from between the four dimensional axes of our universe – length, breadth, height and time.'

'So this guy Haq ul'Suun,' said Martell. 'He was up there with Einstein – way above him, in fact.'

'*Way* above,' said Rusty. 'Haq ul'Suun must have thought he could harness the power of the *between*. I don't know what he was planning to do with that power, or what he *thought* he could do; the rock book didn't tell me that. But whatever his intentions were, they failed...'

'That's an understatement,' said Medina with a snort. 'Makes what happened to the *Titanic* look like a minor inconvenience.'

'Does the rock book say what happened after the thing destroyed Mars?' asked Martell. 'Where did it go? Is it still there?'

Rusty shook her head. 'I'm sorry, Troy. It may contain that information, but if it does, I haven't managed to access it – not yet.'

'All right,' Martell nodded. 'Keep trying. We need to know as much about this as we can.'

'What about the X-M 2?' asked Canning. 'Do we still go back to Mars?'

Martell sighed. 'I'll have to take this to the Senate Committee on Planetary Exploration. It's not a call I can make. They'll have to decide, and I'm pretty sure I know what their decision will be.'

'They'll decide we should go back,' said Canning.

'That's my guess. They'll figure that since the first expedition made it back alive, it'll be okay to send another.'

'But you're not convinced,' said Pellin.

'Who *could* be?' Martell sighed. 'They know full well that Thorne Smith and his crew haven't been the same since they got back, but they're putting it down to the stress of space travel. They think the replacement crew will be better prepared – and I'm not convinced of that, either.'

'We still have the problem of the Falcon, and what's inside it,' said Canning.

'Not to mention whoever really stole it,' added Medina.

Martell shook his head. 'Like I said, that's out of our hands.' He turned to Rusty. 'This is all riding on you now, Aldous.'

'Me?'

'Yeah. You implied that you haven't got everything the rock book has to give – not yet. Well, we need you to get everything, every scrap of information that that thing contains. Understood?'

Rusty saw her chance to skip out. 'Understood, Troy. I'll get to work on it right now.' She stood up. 'If you'll excuse me?'

Martell nodded. 'Go to it, pal.'

Rusty nodded to the others and left the room.

Five minutes later, she was back in Aldous Bradlee's office, looking around for the place where he had put the rock book. She checked the file cabinets and his desk drawers. Nothing. Then her eyes fell upon a wall safe with a combination lock. *Got to be in there*, she thought.

She went back to the outer office where Bridget Sullivan was typing up some correspondence. Modifying her vocal chords so that she sounded even rougher than before, she said: 'Bridget, would you please do me a favour?'

'Of course, Mr. Bradlee.'

'Would you be a dear and pop along to the pharmacy for me? I think I really am coming down with something…'

'Some linctus, that's what you need,' Bridget said, standing up.

Rusty smiled. 'Bless you, you read my mind. I would go myself, but Troy just dumped a load of work in my lap – wants it pronto.'

'No problem, Mr. Bradlee,' Bridget smiled. 'I'll get you some straight away.'

'You're a doll.'

When she heard to door to the outer office open and close, Rusty turned to the wall safe. Of course, she had no idea what the combination was, but with Bridget out on her errand, Rusty no longer needed it.

She took off Bradlee's suit jacket, tie and shirt, which would have been shredded by what her upper body was about to become. She closed her eyes and concentrated, and her torso and arms expanded, changing from lithe and supply-muscled to brutally, supernaturally powerful. A few seconds later, a hybrid thing that possessed Aldous Bradlee's legs and the upper body of a Bavarian forest troll – a thing that was, nevertheless, still Rusty Links – stood before the wall safe.

With a single swipe of its fist, the thing smashed away the dial of the combination lock. Then it thrust a stubby finger into the resulting hole and yanked open the door. The locking mechanism gave with a loud metallic crunch. Rusty reassumed the form of Aldous Bradlee, quickly dressed in his clothes again and looked inside the safe.

Bingo!

She took the Martian rock book and put it on Bradlee's desk, hardly looking at it but marvelling at its lightness. She opened Bradlee's briefcase and put it inside, along with the file containing the notes he had made, then she closed the wall safe and replaced the combination dial. She took a moment to make sure that it looked undamaged, and then went through to the outer office, where she hastily wrote a note for Bridget. The note said that Bradlee was feeling pretty darned sick and had decided to work at home for the rest of the day. The note wasn't in Bradlee's handwriting, of course, but by the time Bridget began to puzzle over it, it wouldn't matter.

Taking the briefcase with her, she left the office and walked quickly out to the car park. She got into Bradlee's car and drove away, thinking about what she had read in his notes – that is, the parts she had not told Troy Martell and the others.

Crystalman's suspicions were on the money, she reflected. The ninth rock book *did* contain the means to access what the Martian Falcon contained – although he was wrong in his assumption that it included the key to translating the other books. They were irrelevant; everything Crystalman needed was in the ninth book, which lay on the seat beside Rusty.

She thought about what the book had told Aldous Bradlee: the images and pseudo memories which it had transmitted to him by means of its strange lithotechnology, and which he had transcribed in his notes. The book had told him that it did not just describe Haq ul'Suun's punishment; it was *part* of it.

She drove north for a few miles and then pulled onto a deserted stretch of beach. She turned off the engine, opened the briefcase and looked through Bradlee's notes. A moment later, she found the page she was looking for. She read it again, more carefully this time, taking in the information slowly instead of skimming over it.

The rock book has provided so much incredible information, but by far the most incredible is the nature of the book itself. The Vattanians punished their worst criminals by confining their minds in the falcons; but since the punishment was never permanent, the mind-transfer was reversible. It seems that the lithotechnological process was encoded within a rock book specially created for the purpose at the time of the transfer.

The book we now have in our possession is the one that was created at the time of Haq ul'Suun's punishment. As far as I can understand, its creation was automatic and unavoidable. The Vattanians who condemned Haq ul'Suun never intended for him ever to be released from his prison; but they didn't have time to reprogram the transfer machine, and so this code book was created as his mind was transferred to the Falcon.

I have little doubt that, given the chance, they would have destroyed the book, but events overtook them. It's for this reason that I am going to request that the book remain with the NCPE here at Cabo Cañaveral, rather than being transferred to the Metropolitan Museum with the others. If it really does contain the key to unlocking Haq ul'Suun's prison, it should never be allowed anywhere near the Martian Falcon. In fact, I am tempted to destroy the thing; perhaps at some point I will, but for now I need to study it further. I know it contains more information – information that may prove vital to the success of the X-M 2 expedition.

I think Troy Martell is correct: the Senate Committee will insist on the X-M 2 mission going ahead, in spite of the dangers – in spite of what Dr. Pellin has reported following her examination of Captain Smith and his crew. Their dreams are horrific. Who could experience such dreams and remain sane? But what is the origin of those dreams? Can the thing that destroyed the Vattanians and their world really still be on Mars – or inside it, bubbling and blaspheming at the planet's core... waiting? And if so, why? Why does it not boil forth to consume the entire Solar System? Could it be that it's somehow linked to Haq ul'Suun, that its fate is *tied to that of the one who summoned it?*

I must talk to Deborah about this. I need to know more about the dreams that Smith and the others are having. I'm convinced that they hold the key to what's happening on Mars and the nature of the thing that may still be there.

Rusty put the notes down on the passenger seat beside her and thought about what she had just read, her fingers tapping the steering wheel contemplatively. So that was the reason why the crew of Rocketship X-M hadn't been seen in public for nearly two years. *Plagued by nightmares*, she thought. *Their minds under siege by something that seeped into our universe five million years ago.... something that's still there, at the centre of Mars. Good Christ! If Bradlee was right, if it's somehow rendered inert by Haq ul'Suun's imprisonment, then what happens if his mind is released from the Falcon?*

She took out the rock book and held it gingerly in her lap. It was beautiful, she had to admit. It was about ten inches by twelve. Each of its mineral pages, twenty-three in number, was as thin as a sheet of heavy-gauge writing paper and was bound with the others by means of an ingenious arrangement of silvery metal hinges. The book appeared to contain a visual chronicle of Haq ul'Suun's crime: the construction of the pyramid-machine, the emergence of the thing that had sucked Mars dry and turned it into a corpse planet, the fleeing and the dying of its inhabitants – all rendered in differently-hued slivers of polished stone, the images merging into one another in ways Rusty could hardly fathom. Beautiful, yes – but horrible also: the silent death scream of an entire world...

What do you want with this, Crystalman? she thought. *What do you really want? Did you know all along what the Falcon contains? You must have, otherwise why go to all that trouble to obtain it? And if I do give you the rock book... if I do give you the key to unlocking Haq ul'Suun's prison, what happens then?*

For the next five minutes, Rusty sat very still, thinking. Then, very slowly, she got out of the car, taking the rock book with her. *If I do this, I'm dead*, she told herself. *As dead as Mars. He'll find me no matter what, no matter where I hide… but if I don't do this, the whole damned planet may wind up dead.*

She walked to the front of the car, holding the rock book in both hands.

Bullshit! He won't find me. No one can find a shifter who doesn't want to be found. No one!

She raised the rock book above her head and brought it down hard on the edge of the radiator grille. The book bounced off, still intact. She tried again, but again the Martian rock book remained undamaged.

'Lithotechnology,' she muttered, and then gave a loud and heartfelt curse.

She dropped the book onto the sand, took off her upper garments and became the troll again. Snatching up the book, she battered it again and again upon the car's radiator – but to no avail. The rock book appeared to be indestructible, unlike the radiator grille, which now sported several sizeable dents.

She resumed Bradlee's form, dressed again and threw herself into the driver's seat, sighing loudly. 'All right,' she said. 'I'll keep it. I'll take it with me to wherever I end up going. I don't know what you think you're doing, Crystalman, but I won't let you do it.'

*

Beneath his house on Long Island, Crystalman stood before the telaug, reading Rusty Links's brain patterns on the machine's misshapen display screen. Not long after they had begun their association, he had sedated her, brought her to this chamber and recorded her patterns, just as he had with so many other useful people. Like the others, she retained no memory of the event. Like the others, her mind was now open and defenceless before his telepathic gaze.

No one can find a shifter who doesn't want to be found.

'Normally, that's true, Rusty,' Crystalman whispered. 'But not in your case, unfortunately.' He smiled behind his quartz mask.

'I'm in your head right now, but you don't know it. My hand is at your throat, but you see me not.'

He switched off the telaug and stepped back from the machine. 'I'm coming for you, Rusty. You have betrayed me, and I'm coming for you.' He inclined his head, gazing up at the ceiling of the chamber. 'And when I have the rock book, when I have released the spirit of Haq ul'Suun, then you too shall be free once again. Do you hear me, father? Though you sleep at the centre of Mars, do you hear me? You will be free again... soon.'

CHAPTER 21
Tesla

Fort and Lovecraft lost no time in getting off the aircraft, collecting their travelling valises and leaving the domestic terminal of Denver International Aerodrome. As they hurried to the car rental office, Fort expected to be apprehended by Aerodrome Security at any moment and taken to a small, quiet room to be questioned about the sabotaging of the Bel Geddes. He only allowed himself a sigh of relief when they were driving south out of Denver, towards Colorado Springs.

They decided to make straight for Dr. Tesla's laboratory in the foothills of Cheyenne Mountain, southwest of the city. The scientist and inventor was famously obsessed with his work, and although he maintained a residence in Colorado Springs, his laboratory contained a small apartment. He was known to spend weeks at a time there, working on a bewildering array of ideas and projects.

The drive was too long for Fort, who was obliged to listen to Lovecraft waxing lyrical about the quaintness and charm of the architecture of the Old West, which, while lacking the elegance of the Colonial style of New England, was nevertheless redolent with the monumental trials and struggles of the frontiersmen and settlers of years gone by.

'I didn't know you were interested in architecture, Howard,' Fort said during one of Lovecraft's infrequent pauses.

'I am indeed, Charles,' Lovecraft enthused, 'for it is only through a study of architecture that one can gain the measure of a place, and its true relationship to the people who live and lived there. Take Rhode Island, for instance. When one travels through it, one senses a subtle magick in the air, originating in the towns through which one passes – the noble domes and steeples, the steep Georgian alleys winding amongst gambrel roofs…'

Oh God, thought Fort.

*

Tesla's laboratory was a rambling, wood-built building at the end of a short, dusty road with a sign that read: PRIVATE PROPERTY. ABSOLUTELY NO TRESPASSING.

'I was afraid of this,' said Lovecraft as they passed the sign.

'Afraid of what?' asked Fort.

'Didn't you see that? We're trespassing, Charles! Intruding upon a man's privacy, which should be considered sacred at all times. We should have phoned through first.'

Fort shook his head. 'Are you for real, Howard?'

'I'm merely saying–'

'I doubt he's going to come out with Smith & Wessons blazing. And if it means that much to you, I'll let you apologise.'

'Splendid,' Lovecraft muttered as Fort brought the car to a halt beside the building and climbed out.

Fort strode up to the door and rapped loudly three times. He waited a few moments and rapped again.

Presently, the door opened to reveal a slender, immaculately dressed man with matinee idol looks and thick dark hair parted in the middle. His neatly-trimmed moustache twitched in irritation.

'Who are you and what do you want?' he demanded.

'Dr. Tesla,' said Lovecraft, hurrying forward, 'I offer our humble apologies –'

'Nicely done, Howard,' said Fort. 'Now, sir, my name's Charles Fort and this is Mr. Howard Lovecraft. We've come from New York to see you on a matter of the gravest urgency – a matter concerning the Martian Falcon.'

Tesla hesitated, looked Fort up and down, did the same with Lovecraft, and finally answered: 'What's your interest in the Falcon?'

'You're aware that the statue has been stolen?' said Fort.

'Of course I am. We do have newspapers out here, Mr. Fort.'

'And do you know who stole it?'

Tesla's frown deepened. 'No. Do you?'

'Yes, we do.' Fort took out his Private Investigator ID and showed it to Tesla.

The inventor sniffed and glanced at Lovecraft. 'Where's yours?'

'I, er, don't have one,' Lovecraft replied. 'Which reminds me, Charles…'

'Not now, Howard. Dr. Tesla, we've been investigating the theft of the Falcon, and our investigations have given us a name: Crystalman.'

Tesla's eyes widened slightly as his frown faded. 'Are you sure?'

'Absolutely certain,' Fort replied. 'The report in the *New York Times* said you were working on cleaning up the transmission from Mars, processing it through your equipment to increase the resolution.'

'That's right.'

'Had any luck?'

'The NCPE have asked me not to comment to the press.'

Fort smiled. 'We're not the press.'

'Why don't the NCPE want you to speak to the press, Dr. Tesla?' asked Lovecraft.

Tesla glanced at Lovecraft and then lowered his eyes. 'Crystalman,' he murmured. 'What does *he* want with the Falcon?'

'That's what we're trying to find out,' Fort replied. 'But you can bet your bottom dollar it's nothing good. May we come in?'

Tesla hesitated and then sighed. 'Very well.'

Fort and Lovecraft stepped through the door into a vast space filled with complex electrical equipment, only some of which they could identify. There were transmitters and receivers, switch and circuit boards, circuit breakers, meters, transformers, batteries, inductors, oscillators and distribution frames, either stacked in metal cabinets or standing upon the numerous workbenches ranged across the floor. The centre of the room was dominated by a conical framework about ten feet high, which supported a large silvery sphere about three feet in diameter.

Lovecraft pointed to the device and asked, fascinated: 'Is that your magnifying transmitter?'

'It is,' Tesla replied. 'I'm trying to perfect a method of wireless power transmission, which I'm hoping will revolutionise the production and distribution of electrical energy, just as telecommunications have been revolutionised by the development of wireless telegraphy.'

'Incredible!' said Lovecraft. 'May I ask how close you are to achieving your goal?'

Before Tesla could answer, Fort said: 'I'm sure this is all very interesting, gentlemen, but can we return to the matter at hand?'

'Of course,' said Tesla. 'Please follow me.'

He led them across the floor of the laboratory to a door in a partition wall, which led to a large office containing a desk, chairs, file cabinets and bookshelves. The desk was strewn with papers on which Fort and Lovecraft glimpsed lines of complex equations which made about as much sense to them as Egyptian hieroglyphs. Beside the desk was a large cathode ray monitor screen sitting atop a wheeled trolley. Below the monitor was another machine containing two large reels of magnetic tape.

Motioning his visitors to be seated, Tesla said: 'You asked why the NCPE wanted me to keep quiet about the Martian transmission. I also asked that question when Troy Martell called me…'

'The Chief Administrator,' said Fort.

Tesla nodded, adding with a mirthless chuckle: 'Only I phrased it rather less politely than Mr. Lovecraft here. But, having given it some more thought, I can now see his point.'

Tesla switched on the monitor screen and the magnetic tape machine. He sat at his desk as the tape reels began to turn.

*

When the tape had ended, Lovecraft and Fort looked at each other and then at Tesla.

'My God,' said Fort. 'What was it? Some kind of experiment that went wrong? The pyramid... a machine?'

'That's what I thought, at first,' Tesla replied as he got up and crossed to one of the file cabinets. 'An experiment in energy production... yes, that's what I thought, but then, I am an engineer at heart, and one tends to approach problems from the direction that's most comfortable to oneself. But now I'm not so sure. Now... well...' He opened the file cabinet and took out a thick folder. 'These are the psychological evaluations of the crew of Rocketship X-M, conducted by Deborah Pellin, the Director of Space Medicine.'

Fort leaned forward. 'They're confidential. How come you have them?'

'I'm one of the contractors engaged by the NCPE; I helped to design the X-M,' Tesla replied. 'I worked on the spaceframe and the atomic motors, so I have access to every aspect of mission planning. I've also been working on the X-M 2, helping to improve the design in order to minimise the psychological stress of spaceflight. For that, I needed access to the crew's medical reports: I needed to know exactly how the mission affected them, physically and mentally.' Tesla tapped the file. 'What I read in here... well, let's just say that the current mental state of the X-M crew is not just the result of being shut up in a giant tin can for months on end.'

'And just what *is* the crew's current mental state?' asked Fort.

'Extreme emotional trauma,' Tesla replied, 'caused by the dreams they have been having ever since they returned from Mars.'

'Dreams?' said Lovecraft.

'That's Dr. Pellin's conclusion, and judging by the content of the dreams, I'd have to agree.'

'What are they dreaming about?' asked Fort.

Tesla opened the folder and handed several pages to Fort. 'By rights I shouldn't be showing you this. As you say, this material is confidential, but in view of recent events…'

Lovecraft leaned across, and he and Fort read the pages together.

TRANSCRIPT OF FIFTH PSYCHOLOGICAL
EVALUATION SESSION WITH
CAPTAIN THORNE SMITH, COMMANDER,
X-M EXPEDITION
RECORDED ON 8TH. OCTOBER 1924
ATTENDING PHYSICIAN: DEBORAH JANE
PELLIN, M.D., PH. D.

PELLIN: Would you tell me about the dream you keep having, Captain Smith?

SMITH: The dream…

PELLIN: Yes. It appears to be the same dream as the others are having.

SMITH: They began in space… on the return flight. We'd just entered the calculations for the trans-Earth trajectory into the astrogation panel. We'd fired up the main atomics and were accelerating away from Mars, congratulating each other on a job well done. We'd made it to Mars and discovered things no one could have imagined. We were so proud of each other… so proud of ourselves.

PELLIN: You had every reason to be. You'd voyaged further than any human beings in history…

SMITH: But too far… we were never meant to voyage so far. I understand that, now. There's no place for us out there. The gulfs of space are too deep… deeper than our poor minds can comprehend. The universe is too big for us, too old, too uncaring. The stars, the nebulae, the molecular clouds… they know and care nothing for us. The universe is unaware of us… or at least it *was*, until we made the terrible mistake of reaching out from our familiar, safe little world.

PELLIN: Why was that a mistake? Thorne… why? Was it because of the dreams?

SMITH: The dreams didn't tell us, but we reasoned it from them. From the things they showed us… or maybe the things that spoke to us through them.

PELLIN: What did they say?

SMITH: Say? They didn't *say* anything, not as such. They still don't. Images, that's all they are, but images that seem to *imply*.

PELLIN: What happens in the dreams?

SMITH: We fall… through abysses of twilight, of colours that are not colours and sounds that are not sound. But we don't fall because of gravity: we're… pushed, or pulled, I don't know. We look at our arms and legs, but they don't look right. It's as if they're distorted somehow, warped by some strange rearrangement of perspective. And the abysses through which we fall… they're not empty, but are crowded with angled masses of substance, alien-coloured… some organic, some inorganic. Some of the organic masses seem to awaken memories in the backs of our minds, but we can't form a conscious idea of what they represent.

PELLIN: What do these things, these 'masses of substance'… what do they look like?

SMITH: They're difficult to describe – impossible, really: it's as if they won't fit into our minds, or as if our minds are seeing them in an incomplete way. Our minds are not… *big* enough to comprehend them as they really are. The inorganic masses are prisms, labyrinths, clusters of cubes and planes, and Cyclopean buildings. The organic things are like groups of bubbles, octopi, centipedes, living Hindu idols and complex, animated arabesques.

PELLIN: And what's your reaction to seeing these things? How do they make you feel?

SMITH: We have the impression of menace... horror, and sometimes, when one of the organic entities appears by its motions to notice us, we feel absolute terror.

PELLIN: How do the entities move? What's their means of locomotion through these... abysses?

SMITH: I don't know: it's impossible to say. But some of them appear out of empty space, or disappear with no trace, as if they're winking in and out of existence. And while all this is happening, there are the sounds, shrieking and roaring, filling the abysses, and yet changing with the movements of the entities. I think...

PELLIN: Go on, Thorne... *what* do you think?

SMITH: I think that the abysses are part of another dimension... or an *additional* dimension at right-angles to our own three dimensions... or perhaps *between* our dimensions. And then there is another...

PELLIN: Another?

SMITH: Another entity... but this isn't like the others. It's dark, vaporous, made of whipping tendrils of smoke; it moves quickly, like the winds of a hurricane or a tornado. It moves through the abyss, parts of it appearing and disappearing, darting in every direction with such horrible rapidity that it's as if... as if it *occupies* every direction at once. And then it stops, as if its attention has been seized by something... and it turns towards a circle, faint, cloudlike, hanging in the abyss...

PELLIN: A circle?

SMITH: A world. Mars. The planet Mars as seen from this higher-dimensional vantage point. The planet has... *appeared* to it, flowering into its horrible awareness. The thing... *hungers* for it, for what it contains; it wants to consume it, like some obscene cosmic tumour. And then... and then a door opens...

PELLIN: A door?

SMITH: A portal between dimensions, a path leading from these higher spaces to our own realm of three dimensions. And the thing squirts itself towards the door and...

PELLIN: And?

SMITH: It eats the planet!

At this point, Captain Smith became too distraught to continue. A sedative was administered by Dr. Pellin, and the session was resumed an hour later.

PELLIN: How do you feel now, Thorne?

SMITH: Better, thank you. I'm sorry...

PELLIN: There's no need to apologise.

SMITH: The dreams... they're...

PELLIN: Why do you think that you and the others are experiencing them?

SMITH: Because of what's on Mars.

PELLIN: The city? Cydonia?

SMITH: No. I think it's because of the thing... the thing that ate the planet, the thing that sucked the life from it. It's still there, somewhere far underground, perhaps... perhaps at the very centre of Mars.

PELLIN: What makes you think that?

SMITH: Because the dreams... they're not really dreams. I think the thing is speaking to us.

'Speaking to them?' said Fort, handing the pages back to Tesla.

'They all say the same thing,' Tesla replied. 'And their dreams are becoming more and more... intense. Dr. Pellin thinks it's only a matter of a short while before their minds collapse entirely under the psychic stress. I'm afraid that if no way can be found to help them, the crew of Rocketship X-M will be driven incurably insane.'

'Well,' said Lovecraft, 'I suppose that puts paid to the X-M 2 expedition.'

'I'm afraid not,' Tesla sighed.

'How so?' asked Fort. 'I mean, there's no way the NCPE can send more people there.'

'The final decision isn't theirs to make. That rests with the Senate Committee on Planetary Exploration... and *their* position is that the X-M crew are simply suffering from the after effects of such a prolonged and stressful mission. They refuse to accept that the dreams could be anything more than simply dreams. I *suppose* one can see the difficulty of their position,' Tesla added doubtfully. 'The government has sunk untold millions of dollars into the X-M program. To cancel it now because of some bad dreams... well, the President wouldn't stand for it, and neither, I suspect, would the American people. The NCPE's hands are tied; they *must* launch the X-M 2 on schedule with a replacement crew... which is why I've been trying desperately to develop a method of shielding them once they arrive.'

'I can't believe they'd be so stupid,' said Lovecraft disgustedly. 'That thing... the thing that consumed Mars... I think we all know what it is, and why no human should *ever* set foot on Mars again.'

'A Great Old One,' said Fort. 'A weakly-godlike agency, an elemental force from Outside. A thing that called this universe its home when the universe was young...'

'That's my conclusion, also,' agreed Tesla.

'But which one is it?' wondered Lovecraft.

'At this point, there's no way of knowing,' Fort replied with a shake of his head. 'The Martian recording was made in the moments after it came through the portal between dimensions, before it could cohere into its true form. If we could see it now, we might be able to make an educated guess.' He gave a disgusted grunt. 'It should be left the hell alone – *Mars* should be left alone! If the thing's still there, it seems to be dormant. We should thank our lucky stars for that and leave Mars out of our plans for space exploration permanently.'

'The NCPE aren't going to do that,' Tesla replied. 'They're talking about a colony on Mars within ten years.'

'Do you think Crystalman knows all this?' said Lovecraft.

'Chances are he does,' Fort replied.

Lovecraft sighed loudly in exasperation. 'But we still don't know *why*. What's his motive for taking possession of the Falcon? What does he hope to achieve?'

'Cormack said Johnny Sanguine's ghost told him that an ancient evil will be released unless the Falcon is returned to Mars. Question is, does Crystalman know this? Is *this* his intention, and if so, why?'

Tesla glanced rapidly from Fort to Lovecraft, and then held up his hands. 'Hold on a moment! What's all this? Who's Cormack? And what does Johnny Sanguine have to do with it? And why are you talking about returning the Falcon to Mars?'

'Sorry, Dr. Tesla,' said Fort with a crooked smile. 'I guess we need to bring you up to speed on the whole Martian Falcon case…'

*

When Fort had finished, Tesla shook his head and chuckled. 'So what started as a skirmish between gangsters has developed into… this.'

'The major player is Crystalman,' said Fort. 'But Sanguine's following his own agenda, I'm pretty sure of that…'

'You don't believe his story about wanting to send the Falcon back to Mars in order to redeem his soul?' said Tesla.

'Not for a second. No, Sanguine's up to something else. He wants the Falcon, we can be sure of that…'

'So why come up with the story about needing to get it back to Mars?' asked Tesla.

'Howard wondered the same thing.' Fort fell silent, thinking. Then he said: 'It's pretty clear that Sanguine wants O'Malley to do his work for him and get the Falcon from Crystalman, which implies that Sanguine can't do it alone, not even with his vampire goons... which in turn implies that Crystalman's hideout is impregnable, or damn close. That makes sense. What if this story about taking the Falcon back to Mars is really just a way of getting it to a specific location so that Sanguine can send in his boys to snatch it?'

'It's possible,' said Lovecraft, 'but it does raise another question. Do Johnny Sanguine and Crystalman want the Falcon for the same reason?'

Fort gave a miserable sigh. 'I don't know.'

'One thing's for sure,' said Tesla. 'If Crystalman and Johnny Sanguine want the Falcon, then it follows that the artefact is extremely dangerous. So... not only must it be retrieved, it must also be destroyed.'

'Easier said than done,' grumbled Fort.

'True,' said Tesla, standing up, 'but I may have the solution to both those problems.'

'Really?' said Lovecraft. 'And what might that be?'

Tesla smiled at him, but the smile was uncertain. 'Follow me,' he said.

CHAPTER 22
The Kitab Al Azif

Furtively, as if moving through an ancient land he thought he knew well, but which had now become unfamiliar and threatening, Father Cormack O'Malley walked along the marble-floored corridors leading to the Papal Secret Archives of the Vatican. Beyond the Leonine Wall which enclosed the city-state, the midnight hum of unsleeping Rome – a white noise of diesel engines punctuated by the occasional bleat of a horn which echoed and re-echoed like some great thing stirring constantly in troubled contemplation – had gradually given way to a profound silence.

Like a tomb, O'Malley thought. *Let us pray that the tomb is not the Earth itself...*

He did not walk alone: beside him strode the pensive, bespectacled figure of Ambrogio Damiano Achille Ratti, Pope Pius XI. Neither man had spoken since their conversation in Pius's private office. It seemed as though the weight of the decision that had been made was too great to allow further conversation.

All the ages of Man were enshrined in the colossal walls that rose on each side of the two striding figures, preserved miraculously in paint and marble, and the printed words of thousands of books and manuscripts; and it seemed to O'Malley that the history of both Man and the Holy Mother Church that sought to guide him towards God were a living part of the immense chambers and interminable corridors and galleries through which the American priest and the Bishop of Rome moved.

Love and devotion to his calling stirred in O'Malley's heart, as well as pride – although he well understood that the latter emotion was an inappropriate alloy which threatened to contaminate the purity of the others, and he silently entreated God to rid him of it. His faith was as unshakeable as the walls of Saint Peter's Basilica; yet the foul thing towards which he and Pius turned their stride, here in the midnight heart of the Church, made his mind and soul tremble together.

They continued into the lower zone of the *Cortile del Belvedere* before turning right into the long wing that enclosed the lower half of Bramante's *Cortile*. At opposite ends of this wing stood two doors, one of which led to the Vatican Library, the other to the Archives. At this late hour, the place was almost deserted. They could have come during the day, of course: no one would have questioned their presence in the Archives; but the thought of performing this task in the unsullied daytime under the innocent gaze of the faithful seemed inappropriate. In any event, O'Malley's flight had got into Rome's Fiumicino Aerodrome at 9.00p.m., and he had made his way directly to the Vatican with his strange and terrible request. He had wanted to get this over and done with as soon as possible, and he thanked God that the Holy Father had agreed to it – however reluctantly.

It was indeed better to do this under the concealing blanket of night... like a thief who was about to steal that which did not and should never belong to the human race: the knowledge that had been spat into the face of Mankind by the mad Arab, Abdul Alhazred more than twelve hundred years ago.

Al Azif.

The *Necronomicon.*

'But I am not a thief,' whispered O'Malley.

Pius glanced at him. 'What was that, old friend?'

O'Malley heaved a sigh that was so heavy it made his entire body shudder, its sudden sound almost blasphemous in the silence.

'I am doing God's work. Even by looking upon those words that should never be looked upon. By reading the words of a mind driven to the edge of annihilation by its quest for forbidden knowledge. I am still doing God's work!'

'I know,' said Pius in a quiet voice. 'That is why I agreed to allow this... and that is why I chose to accompany you, for I will not allow you to endure it alone.'

Slowly, as if carrying an insupportable weight upon their shoulders, they climbed the stairs leading to the *piani nobili* containing the Manuscript Depository. They passed the small café, now deserted, where academics and researchers could take a break from their work without leaving the Archives.

The night prefect rose from his desk as Pius and O'Malley approached. 'Holy Father!' he exclaimed. 'Is there... is there some way I can be of service?'

Pius smiled warmly and hoped that the prefect didn't realise that the smile was a lie. 'No, Fernando,' he replied in his quiet, gentle voice. 'Thank you, but we can manage.'

The night prefect nodded, returned the Pope's smile and bowed. The thought of asking why he was here at midnight in the company of a priest whose name was unknown to him didn't even occur to the prefect: to do so would have been a terrible impertinence. Besides, it was not unheard of for high-ranking members of the Church to conduct research in the Archives late at night – although he could not remember an occasion when the Holy Father himself had done so. He merely assumed that he was performing his duties with the tireless devotion for which he was so well known and loved; and so he waited for the Holy Father and the unknown priest to pass into the Archives, and then returned to his desk.

Pius knew the exact location of the book; he had no need of the complex indices and cross-referenced lists to help him find it – although in his heart of hearts he wished that through some miracle of God's infinite mercy, they would find it scorched to dust instead of intact... waiting. It would have been a daunting task had they been merely curious outsiders wandering among the kilometres of steel shelves that held the tens of thousands of volumes comprising the *Archivio Segreto*. Daunting and futile, mused Pius, for the book did not lie here, out in the open, nor was access granted to the curious. *The suicidally curious*, he added to himself. The very thought made him cringe inwardly, and he silently thanked the long-departed soul of Pope Paul IV for deciding that the *Necronomicon* should be the first book to be placed upon the *Index Librorum Prohibitorum*, the Index of Prohibited Materials, in 1559.

He led O'Malley to a stout wooden cabinet standing alone at the far end of the dimly lit hall, an ancient sentinel jealously guarding its secrets. Their figures cast shadows that seemed to bow mockingly as they passed the silent ranks of books and manuscripts.

Pius withdrew a large key from a pocket of his soutane. He hesitated, holding the key in front of the lock; O'Malley sensed that his trepidation had increased. He knew what his old friend was thinking: he was about to perform an unclean act, a violation of the laws of God and the universe...

Pius turned to O'Malley. 'Cormack,' he whispered, 'are you absolutely *sure* about this? Is there nothing I can say to dissuade you?'

'You could have forbidden me, Ambrogio,' O'Malley replied. 'It would have been the easiest thing in the world to say "no", but you didn't. I've told you everything; I've explained why I need to try. If it contains anything... *anything* that might help us to find out what the Martian Falcon really is, and why Crystalman wants it...'

'All right,' said Pius. 'Very well...' Taking a deep breath of air that carried the musty scent of two thousand years of history, he inserted the key and twisted. The sound of the tumblers echoed fitfully through the chamber.

He pulled open the doors.

Inside were three shelves holding several volumes, their leather spines worn and faded with age, the tooling cracked, the letters of their titles all but masked by the relentless, merciless passage of time.

Pius and O'Malley scanned the titles, peering through the gloom at the ghostly letters:

De Vermis Mysteriis
Cultes des Ghoules
The Book of Eibon
Unaussprechlichen Kulten
Regem in Flavum
Dhol Chants
Codex Pnakotus
Kitab Al Azif

'I can't remember the last time this cabinet was opened,' said Pius, not bothering to hide the disgust in his voice. 'I can't remember the last person I knew who was so lost, so desperate, as to look to any of these... *things*... for guidance.'

'Pray that I find guidance this time, old friend,' said O'Malley.

'I will pray for you, Cormack... but not for that reason.'

Pius took a step back, tacitly giving O'Malley permission to proceed. O'Malley reached into the cabinet and carefully removed the book called the *Kitab Al Azif*, the *Necronomicon*. He took it to a small desk nearby and placed it there. It was large and heavy, its binding weathered and cracked – disfigured, as if time had *wanted* it gone from the world.

O'Malley sat on the wooden chair. 'The Wormius translation,' he said.

'Yes,' replied Pius, who now stood behind him, looking down over his shoulder.

'That is not dead which can eternal lie,' whispered O'Malley.

'And with strange aeons even death may die,' Pius said, completing the dread couplet. He made the sign of the Cross on O'Malley, and them himself.

The book was written by a mad poet of Sanaá in Yemen, Abdul Alhazred, who lived during the time of the Ommiade caliphs around the turn of the eighth century. He travelled widely during his strange life, visiting the ruins of Babylon and Memphis; he spent ten years in the Rub' al Khali, the 'Empty Quarter' in the Arabian Peninsula, during which he is said to have encountered the spirits and monsters which inhabit that cursed region. He claimed to have seen legendary Irem, the City of Pillars, and to have encountered the relics of the serpent people of Valusia, who ruled Earth before the advent of Man.

His death, it is said, was even stranger than his life. He settled in Damascus to compose his horrible opus, and it was in a crowded marketplace that, shortly after completion of the *Azif*, Alhazred was seized by an invisible entity and devoured in full sight of hundreds of horrified witnesses.

In A.D. 950, the book was translated into Greek by Theodorus Philetas of Constantinople under the title *Necronomicon*, meaning 'The Book of the Law of the Dead'. For a century it induced madness and death in those foolish enough to read it, until it was suppressed and many copies burned on the orders of the patriarch Michael in the eleventh century. In 1228, a Latin translation was made by an ancestor of the famed Danish physician and antiquary, Ole Worm. This translation was the one now held in the Secret Archives of the Vatican.

This was the book before which Father Cormack O'Malley now sat.

O'Malley took a deep breath and opened the large metal clasp. The hinge gave a muted squeak. He opened the book, the ancient leather creaking as the contents were revealed. The pages were brittle, and O'Malley detected a peculiar granularity in their surfaces, as though some hard substance akin to sand had been pressed into them. He had handled ancient books before, but had never encountered anything with this singular texture. He turned the pages with care that was decidedly not born of reverence.

O'Malley scanned the faded blackletter text, trying to avert his eyes from the blasphemous drawings that accompanied it – drawings that represented places that should never be seen, concepts that should never be entertained by sane minds, entities that should not exist…

How can such things be? O'Malley asked himself as he continued to turn the pages. *In a universe created by an all-loving God… how can they be?*

He shut his eyes tight and banished the thought, for this, he had been told, was one of the dangers of reading the *Necronomicon*, this subtle and insidious undermining of faith in the justness and order of the universe. This was the book's first line of attack.

He turned a page and came upon a passage that seized his eye and forced him to read.

> Nor is it to be thought that man is either the oldest or the last of earth's masters, or that the common bulk of life and substance walks alone. The Old Ones were, the Old Ones are, and the Old Ones shall be. Not in the spaces we know, but *between* them, They walk serene and primal, undimensioned and to us unseen. *Yog-Sothoth* knows the gate. *Yog-Sothoth* is the gate. *Yog-Sothoth* is the key and guardian of the gate. Past, present, future, all are one in *Yog-Sothoth*. He knows where the Old Ones broke through of old, and where They shall break through again. He knows where They have trod earth's fields, and where They still tread them, and why no one can behold Them as They tread. By Their smell can men sometimes know Them near, but of Their semblance can no man know, *saving only in the features of those They have begotten on mankind;* and of those are there many sorts, differing in likeness from man's truest eidolon to that shape without sight or substance which is *Them.* They walk unseen and foul in lonely places where the Words have been spoken and the Rites howled through at their Seasons. The wind gibbers with Their voices, and the earth mutters with Their consciousness. They bend the forest and crush the city, yet may not forest or city behold the hand

that smites. Kadath in the cold waste hath known Them, and what man knows Kadath? The ice desert of the South and the sunken isles of Ocean hold stones whereon Their seal is engraven, but who hath seen the deep frozen city or the sealed tower long garlanded with seaweed and barnacles? Great Cthulhu is Their cousin, yet can he spy Them only dimly. *Iä! Shub-Niggurath!* As a foulness shall ye know Them. Their hand is at your throats, yet ye see Them not; and Their habitation is even one with your guarded threshold. *Yog-Sothoth* is the key to the gate, whereby the spheres meet. Man rules now where They ruled once; They shall soon rule where man rules now. After summer is winter, and after winter summer. They wait patient and potent, for here shall They reign again.

O'Malley hesitated before turning the page. *Their semblance can no man know, saving only in the features of those They have begotten on mankind*, he thought. *That's important... somehow, I know that's important, but I don't know how I know.* He read the sentence again and again, and it was only with a considerable effort that he managed to tear his gaze from it and continue turning the pages.

Presently, he came upon a chapter whose title made him pause. The title was *The Life of the Universe*. He began to read the chapter.

These things I have seen when the breath of the Herb wanders through my veins. Take a handful of sand, glittering and golden. Cast it where you please, like a child at play by an innocent sea; count the grains, hold that vast number in your mind, and know that it is but a fraction of the worlds that contain life throughout the eternal cosmos. Some of these great beings have trod the stars and grown weary with the treading; and some have found knowledge of Them, and with it a fear that seizes the heart and robs them of the illusion of peace with which the rest soothe their sorrows. Bathing in Iumma's silken rays, the Grey Sisters burn space itself with the power of their thoughts. The Priestess sings within Schedar's emerald tresses songs only Carcosa understands. On sands charred black by the Dying Fire, the Seer gives wing to his inner eye, and divines the eye of chaos. And away in the deep gulfs, in the black vaults of the eternal night, far beyond the great globe of the shining Nucleus, the Vehm Brother wanders among unknown stars, and listens to the murmur of the trembling void.

Nor is it to be thought that the earth is the only child of our own sun to harbour life, for just as our own world is home to forms countless and varied, so does the gulf beyond swarm with living things of every shape imaginable, and some that would smite the consciousness were they to be seen with the living eyes of man. The Mi-Go live upon the farthest outpost, on the ice-world of Yuggoth which rolls in eternal darkness out on the rim. The giant worlds of gas with their crowns of ice are fathers to many moons, and the minds that inhabit those moons are as different to ours as ours are to the creatures of the ocean floors. The life of our system of worlds crowds upon us, yet we know it not; the history of that life is as a book that has never been opened, whose very existence is unsuspected by the common run of man. Yet does that life creep and think and feel; yet does it look to the stars and tremble at what blasphemes and bubbles beyond the vault of Heaven. In ages long past, the red warrior who stalks the sky with his sword and the head of a slain enemy was home to creatures not unlike ourselves. Of the history of this world, called by its people Vattan, I have seen much in dreams. It was once like the earth, with forests and oceans and great cities, and its people were cousins to the Atlans who dwelt on Earth in dim, distant epochs. Indeed, they were of the same race, the Vattanians having chosen Earth's sister world, the fourth from the Sun, as their home.

O'Malley stopped reading and turned on his chair to face Pius. 'The Atlans colonised Mars as well as Earth,' he said.

Pius nodded. 'The red warrior with a sword in one hand and the severed head of an enemy in the other: that was how the ancient Islamic astronomers described Mars. But that should not be surprising to us: after all, the Atlans came from the dark depths of space in the night of prehistory. There is no reason why they should only have colonised Earth. In those far-off epochs, Mars also was a green and habitable world.'

O'Malley nodded, turned back to the *Necronomicon* and continued reading.

Lovely was Vattan, before the god-king Haq ul'Suun smote it with the darkness of his hubris. For Haq ul'Suun sought to harness the power of the Outer Ones by means of forbidden and unnatural science. And when the Outer One came, it was as a flood of death and annihilation, a scourge from the spaces *between* that engulfed Vattan in a single day. And the very Sun itself became diseased, and trembled with its illness, and the Atlans saw what had happened to their cousins in the void, and they too trembled and began to make their plans to forsake this system of worlds forever; for no more could they dwell in peace, no more could their nights be spent in quiet slumber, for the nightmares would not let them be. The knowledge of what had been brought forth would not let them rest!

And Haq ul'Suun was punished by the very priests who had once bowed before him. With what little time remained before screaming annihilation took them, they seized their god-king and imprisoned his soul within the carven image of a great bird that was their symbol for justice, there to rage silently for all eternity, while the Outer One sated itself upon the life of Vattan, and then descended to the centre of that unhappy world, there to slumber, for its connection to the mind of Haq ul'Suun could not be broken while the mind of Haq ul'Suun lived. And should the mind of Haq ul'Suun ever be freed from its prison, the Outer One will rouse itself from its aeon-long sleep, and walk again between the worlds, destroying, feeding. And its harbinger will be Nyarlathotep, who of all the Outer Gods walks freely upon the earth, eternal corrupter of mankind, whose presence shall ye know by the Crystal Mask that covers his face.

O'Malley gasped and stopped reading. 'Crystal Mask,' he whispered. 'Is he...?'

'What is it, Cormack?' asked Pius.

O'Malley didn't answer; instead, he bent again over the book and continued reading.

Nyarlathotep, the Crawling Chaos, the Living Mist, the Dweller in Darkness, the Mighty Messenger; it is he who will awaken the sleeper at the centre of Vattan, for the sleeper is the merest fragment of his father, the amorphous blight of nethermost confusion which blasphemes and bubbles at the centre of all infinity – the boundless daemon sultan Azathoth, whose name no lips dare speak aloud, and who gnaws hungrily in inconceivable, unlighted chambers beyond time and space amidst the muffled, maddening beating of vile drums and the thin monotonous whine of accursed flutes. The sleeper at the centre of Vattan is not Azathoth himself, but his merest breath, the most fleeting glance from the idiot god at the centre of infinity, which seeped into the ordered universe at the behest of the fool Haq ul'Suun. *Iä! Yog-Sothoth! Iä! Hastur! Iä! Cthulhu!* Azathoth has breathed upon us! Azathoth has looked upon us! And his breath and his gaze are at the centre of Vattan, waiting, waiting! Do not let him emerge again! Do not free the mind of Haq ul'Suun! *Do you hear me, O'Malley?*

With a cry of terror and confusion, O'Malley jumped to his feet and backed quickly away from the table, his eyes fixed upon the book.

Pius took him by the shoulders and span him around. 'What is it? Tell me, Cormack.'

O'Malley shook his head, unable to believe what he had seen. 'My name,' he whispered, and then in a loud cry: 'My name! For the love of God, my name! Written there in the *Necronomicon!* How is it possible?'

Pius went to the table and looked at the passage O'Malley had just read. Then he turned and said: 'Come here.'

O'Malley shook his head and backed away still further. 'I can't. I won't!'

'Trust me, Cormack,' said Pius in his strong, gentle voice. 'Come and look.'

With immense reluctance, O'Malley edged towards the table. Pius pointed to the passage, which read:

> Azathoth has breathed upon us! Azathoth has looked upon us! And his breath and his gaze are at the centre of Vattan, waiting, waiting! But the world

is safe as long as the mind of Haq ul'Suun remains imprisoned, for he brought forth the breath and gaze of Azathoth, and while the mind is confined, so too shall be the breath and the gaze.

'I... I don't understand,' said O'Malley. 'That's not what I read. I swear upon my soul... that's not what I read.'

Pius regarded his friend in silence for a long moment, and then closed the book, replaced it in the cabinet and locked the doors. 'Let us discuss this in my office,' he said.

*

Ten minutes later, O'Malley was sitting on the comfortable leather couch in Pius's private office, holding a balloon glass one-third full of Delamain *Reserve de la Famille* cognac, one of the finest in the world. At any other time, he would have teased his old friend for such an indulgence – but at this moment he was more grateful for it than he could put into words.

He took a gulp of the exquisite cognac and said: 'What happened to me down there, Ambrogio?'

Pope Pius leaned back in his chair and looked at the crucifix on the wall above his large, ornate oak desk. The sounds of the city crept in through the slightly-open window, soothing in their normality.

'I have heard of this happening to people who read the book. It seems to... speak to them somehow. I don't know how or why, but I would say that it's a measure of the evil that is inherent in it.'

'Can an object be inherently evil?' asked O'Malley. 'Can a *text* be inherently evil? I mean... the very letters themselves, the ink of which they're formed, the paper on which they're printed?'

'The insidious nature of the *Necronomicon* goes beyond the words it contains,' Pius replied. 'That's why the surviving copies are kept strictly and securely under lock and key. I believe it carries evil within every fibre of every page; I believe it is suffused with it, like a sponge soaked with water. The book carries the stench of Hell, Cormack, and you have just caught a sniff of it. Before our meeting is over, we shall pray together.'

'Sanguine was telling the truth,' O'Malley muttered. 'A terrible scourge from the depths of space, he said...'

'A place *beyond* space,' Pius corrected.

'And the Martian who brought ruin upon his world, the god-king Haq ul'Suun... he was punished with eternal imprisonment within the carven image of a bird, the symbol of their justice.'

'The Martian Falcon,' said Pius. 'It would seem that in his efforts to harness the power of the Outer Gods, Haq ul'Suun opened the way to allow the merest breath, the merest glance of Azathoth to enter our universe from its domain at the centre of infinity.'

O'Malley shook his head in misery. 'I'd hoped Azathoth was nothing more than an obscene myth... can it be that the thing really exists?'

Pius sighed. 'Some believe that Azathoth is simply a name given to an abstract concept.'

'What do you mean?' asked O'Malley.

'Theoretical physics suggests that what we perceive as the three-dimensional universe is actually the surface of a sphere – a hypersphere I believe is the mathematical term – extending through an additional dimension. It's a strange concept which does not sit easily in the human mind: three-dimensional space curving back on itself through a fourth dimension... but if it's true, then the question arises of what lies at the centre of the sphere.'

'The centre of the universal hypersphere,' said O'Malley. 'The centre of infinity... Azathoth... the nuclear chaos... the idiot god.' He shook his head and buried his face in his hands. 'Blasphemy! It can't be true!'

Pius stood up and went to sit beside O'Malley. He placed a comforting hand on his shoulder. 'There is much we don't know of God's plan,' he said. 'All we can do is continue to strive towards a completion of what we believe to be His work.'

'Do you believe it?' asked O'Malley.

'Do I believe in Azathoth?' Pius paused. 'I believe in the existence of cosmic evil, as you do yourself – we have seen enough of it ourselves, after all.'

'But the forbidden texts imply that Azathoth is at the very foundation of the universe – the demiurge of the Gnostics, the malignant creator of us all.'

'That, of course, I do *not* believe,' said Pius. 'But we may be assured that cosmic evil *can* visit itself upon the earth, and that some evils are so powerful that their perceptions, their very *senses*, can take on partially independent life. It seems that that is what happened on Mars five million years ago. I believe that was what Alhazred meant when he wrote that Azathoth's gaze is at the centre of the planet.'

'And if Haq ul'Suun's soul is ever released from the Martian Falcon,' said O'Malley, 'the sympathetic ties binding it to slumber will be broken, and it will be free to emerge again to walk among the planets… and that's exactly what Crystalman wants…'

Pius nodded. 'For it would seem that Crystalman is Nyarlathotep – or at least an avatar of Nyarlathotep… the wearer of the Crystal Mask, the tormentor of mankind. I think you're right, Cormack: if Crystalman has the Martian Falcon, it must be his intention to release the soul of Haq ul'Suun, to free him from his eternal prison, and in so doing break the bonds that hold the breath and gaze of Azathoth in their own confinement at the centre of Mars.'

'The question is: how will he do it?' asked O'Malley. 'Is there a process to be followed? Something he must do to the Falcon? And if so, how long will it take?'

'I'm afraid I don't know the answers to those questions,' Pius replied. 'But the fact that it hasn't happened yet implies that it will take some time… or perhaps there is something necessary to the completion of the process, some object or component, which Crystalman does not yet have. Either way, I suspect that time is not on our side.'

'May God preserve and protect us,' said O'Malley. 'But what about Johnny Sanguine? What does *he* really want with the Falcon?'

'I think we may dismiss Johnny Sanguine as what he was – or still is: a gangster, a deluded, self-interested fool. It's my belief that he assumes the Falcon contains the power necessary to restore him to his half-life, to escape the punishment that awaits him. His evil soul is at least strong enough to remain on Earth for that long. I think it's most likely that he believes his vampiric body will be restored by the power within the Falcon.'

'Big mistake!' O'Malley muttered.

'Yes, but if he can be made to see his error, he may prove a powerful ally…'

O'Malley gave his friend an appalled glance. 'An *ally*? That fiend?'

'Sanguine lied to you when he said he had to retrieve the Falcon to redeem his soul in the eyes of the Almighty. But that lie may yet be transformed into truth before all this is over. If he can be persuaded to help you to save the Earth from the scourge of Azathoth, he may yet be redeemed… and isn't that your calling?'

O'Malley thought about this, and presently he nodded.

'Now,' said Pius, 'let us pray.'

CHAPTER 23
Johnny's Dream

'Is that really you, boss?' said Carmine.

'It's really me,' replied the ghost of Johnny Sanguine, which stood by the fireplace of his drawing room in Brooklyn.

Carmine looked the white-suited figure up and down. 'It sure as hell *looks* like you…'

Johnny gave him a broad smile and spread his arms wide, as if to say *Here I am. Believe it.*

'What happened to you? You were staked. That fucking bitch!'

'Yeah, she staked me all right – did a real number on me. But I'm still here.'

'How?' asked Carmine. 'Vampires can't come back as ghosts. It ain't natural!'

'No, it isn't. Believe me, I was as surprised as you. I don't know how it happened, but I can guess. It was the Martian Falcon.'

'The…' Carmine hesitated and shrugged. 'How?'

'There's a lot more to that bird than meets the eye. It's got something inside it. Maybe something supernatural, or maybe something to do with Martian technology. I dunno, but whatever it is, it… took hold of me somehow, grabbed my soul and kept it here. And it spoke to me.'

'It *spoke* to you?'

'Yeah, or maybe it *wasn't* the bird, or what's inside it…'

Carmine shook his head. 'Boss, you ain't making much sense. Are you sure you're okay?'

'Of course I'm not okay, numbnuts! I'm a fucking ghost! Vampires aren't supposed to be ghosts! But here I am, trapped in this world... powerless... all I can do is talk, beating my gums like a two-bit lawyer!' Johnny began to pace back and forth in front of the fireplace. 'But that statue, it... I think it's like a telephone...'

'A telephone?' said Carmine.

'Yeah, a telephone, but I don't know who or what's on the other end of the line. I keep getting... images, like dreams... yeah, dreams, only I'm not asleep...'

'Hallucinations?' said Carmine. 'Maybe we should get you to a shrink.'

'Carmine, it must take a hell of a lot of practice to get that stupid. A *shrink*? They're not hallucinations. Something is communicating with me. I need to know what it is.'

'Why?'

'Because whatever it is, I think it's powerful enough to recorporealise me.'

'Recorp what?'

'To make myself physical again. That's what I think it's telling me. These dreams... in them, the Falcon... it *opens* somehow, whatever's inside it is free... and I'm whole again – undead again, instead of just dead. We need to get that statue back, Carmine.'

'But we don't know where it is. All we know is Rusty staked you and skipped with it.'

'I know where it is. Crystalman has it.'

'Oh shit,' said Carmine. 'How the fuck are we going to get it back off of him? He's big time, Johnny...'

Johnny stopped pacing and turned to Carmine. 'Are you saying I'm not?'

'No, boss, I ain't saying that. Course not. But...'

'But nothing! He's got a place out on Long Island. I know – I've seen it, and what's under it. You wouldn't believe it, Carmine. All kinds of Dero shit he's got down there; even those grubby little fuckers are scared of him. Anyways, I followed Rusty after she staked me, followed her all the way to Crystalman. He's got the bird, and I want it back!' He paused and gave a silent sigh. 'But you're right, Carmine – or as close to right as you ever get. It's going to take a lot of muscle to go up against Crystalman – a *hell* of a lot – and I'm not sure we've got enough to do it.'

'So what's the answer?' asked Carmine.

'A truce and an alliance.'

'Who with?'

'Capone.'

'*Capone?* That diesel-powered piss pot?'

'Capone,' Johnny repeated.

Carmine looked confused, so Johnny waited patiently for the penny to drop. When it did, Carmine's face broke into a huge grin. 'You're saying we use Capone and his zombies as our foot soldiers,' he said. 'We let them go in and draw the fire while we get the Falcon.'

'While *I* get the Falcon. And when I'm done, I'll either leave them for Crystalman to take care of, or we take them out ourselves once I'm back. Whaddaya say, Carmine? Good plan?'

'Good plan, boss! But how do we get Capone and his soup-for-brains zombies in our corner? He ain't gonna be easy to convince. He may be a walking dumpster, but he ain't stupid.'

'You got that right. We're gonna need someone else in our corner first. Cormack O'Malley's already in my pocket…'

'Father O'Blivion? You don't say!'

'Yeah, he was the first one I spoke to after I went to Crystalman's place. I fed him a line about needing to get the Falcon from Crystalman so we can send it back to Mars on the new X-M ship.'

'Back to Mars? Why did you tell him that?'

'Because I needed to make sure none of those idiots smash the damn thing when they get to it. I needed to give O'Malley an objective that didn't involve destroying the Falcon, and it wasn't enough to just tell him it needs to go back to the Metropolitan Museum. No one's going to put their life on the line for *that* reason.'

'I sure as hell wouldn't,' said Carmine. 'So… O'Malley's definitely up for the caper?'

Johnny chuckled. 'Yeah. I told him that God told me it had to be done, so I could redeem my soul.'

'And he believed you?'

'He had no choice. I mean, that's what he does, right? Help souls to redeem themselves. He's famous for it. How could he pass up the opportunity to do that with a vampire? Thinks he's gonna get a big pat on the back from the Almighty when his own time comes. Fucking idiot.'

Johnny's smile faded a little as he recalled what he had told O'Malley. The Primal Mind, he had called it; the name had come to him in one of his dreams. O'Malley had assumed he was talking about God, and Johnny had let him believe it; but he very much doubted that the thing that spoke to him had anything to do with God.

'O'Malley'll be useful enough: he always was good in a fight. But the real reason I need him is because he's tight with Charlie Fort, and it's through Fort that I'll get to Capone and his stinkin' army.'

Another penny dropped. 'So that's why you stopped me and the boys from smoking them on the Expressway. Fort and the other guy.'

'That's why. Fort's working for Capone, obviously. If we can get to Fort through O'Malley, get him on our side, he can persuade diesel-dick to work with us. Now… did you do like I told you? Did you get the boys to keep an eye on Fort's apartment?'

Carmine nodded. 'The cops must've let them go pretty quick after the business on the Expressway. Fort went back there, and then the other guy showed up this morning. Then they left for LaGuardia…'

'LaGuardia?'

'Yeah. Couple of our boys tailed them and saw them buying tickets to Denver.'

'Denver, *Colorado*?' said Johnny.

'Yeah.'

Johnny began to pace slowly back and forth again. 'What the fuck are they doing in Colorado?'

CHAPTER 24
The Teleforce Projector

Tesla took Fort and Lovecraft to a far section of his vast laboratory, which contained yet more arcane equipment. Fort shook his head in bewilderment. 'What the hell does all this stuff do?'

'Tools of the trade, Mr. Fort,' Tesla replied.

'The trade being…?'

'To discover the secrets of the universe, of course. To study the behaviour and interactions of everything that exists, from the tiniest building blocks of the atom to the most gigantic and distant of the interstellar nebulae and the great galactic filaments drifting through the eternal void. That's my trade, my calling. To discover how it all works, why it all exists, what it all *means*…'

'And if it means nothing?' said Lovecraft. 'If there *is* no reason for it, no purpose, if we are nothing more than transitory entities lost in a chaos eternally incomprehensible to us?'

Tesla gave him a sidelong glance. 'Are you an existential nihilist, Mr. Lovecraft?'

'No, I would say not. I allow for the possibility of ego-created values and purpose, and for the transitory comfort they may bring to the thinking individual; but they could only ever exist on the human scale, and could never have any bearing on, or significance to, the wider cosmos. My own position is that they would be about as relevant to the cosmos at large as the philosophy of an ant would be to us. In fact, I prefer to term myself a Cosmicist…'

'I've never heard of that,' said Tesla.

Lovecraft gave a small embarrassed cough. 'A word of my own coinage, by which I mean that the cosmos of patterned energy, including what we know as matter, is of a nature absolutely impossible of realisation by the human brain; and the more we learn of it, the more we perceive this circumstance. Even allowing for the most radical conceptions of the relativist, we form so insignificant and temporary a part of it that all notions of special relationships and names and destinies expressed in human conduct must necessarily be vestigial myths.'

'Howard…' said Fort.

'But then surely you must be a pessimist,' Tesla declared.

'Indeed not!' Lovecraft rejoined. 'I am not a pessimist but an *indifferentist* – that is, I don't make the mistake of thinking that the resultant of the natural forces surrounding and governing organic life will have any connection with the wishes or tastes of any part of that organic life-process. Pessimists are just as illogical as optimists, insomuch as both envisage the aims of mankind as unified, and as having a direct relationship to the inevitable flow of terrestrial motivation and events.'

Fort sighed. 'Howard…'

'That is,' continued Lovecraft, ignoring him, 'both schools retain in a vestigial way the primitive concept of a conscious teleology, of a cosmos which gives a damn one way or the other about the especial wants and ultimate welfare of mosquitoes, rats, lice, dogs, men, horses, pterodactyls, trees, fungi, dodos or any other forms of biological energy.'

'Ha!' cried Tesla with a loud laugh. 'I could talk to you all day, Mr. Lovecraft; for while I believe you are wrong, I think you're wrong in a truly *fascinating* way. You should be a philosopher, sir, not a private detective!'

'He's neither,' said Fort loudly. 'And with all due respect, Dr. Tesla, we have to get back to New York as quick as we can to prevent someone from rendering the question of the meaning of existence moot.'

'Ah, you're quite right, of course,' said Tesla. 'Sorry, Mr. Lovecraft, but I think we shall have to continue our conversation some other time.'

'Indeed,' Lovecraft replied, shooting a frown at Fort.

'So,' said Fort, 'the solution to our problem…?'

Tesla went to a large workbench and picked up an object that looked like an old blunderbuss – albeit one made of silvery metal and festooned with switches and dials. 'This,' said the inventor, his voice suffused with pride, 'is my Teleforce Projector, the most powerful weapon ever created.'

Fort whistled. 'Looks pretty impressive. What does it fire?'

'A beam of charged particles…'

'A death ray?' said Fort.

Tesla shook his head in irritation. 'Not *rays*, Mr. Fort, *particles*. Rays are not applicable because they cannot be produced in requisite quantities and diminish rapidly in intensity with distance. All the energy of New York City – about two million horsepower – transformed into rays and projected twenty miles, could not kill a human being because, according to a well-understood law of physics, it would disperse to such an extent as to be ineffectual.'

'Right,' said Fort.

'My apparatus projects particles of microscopic dimensions, enabling it to convey to a small area at a great distance trillions of times more energy than is possible with rays of any kind. Many thousands of horsepower can thus be transmitted by a stream thinner than a hair, so that nothing can resist. The nozzle sends concentrated beams of particles through the air, of such tremendous energy that they can bring down a fleet of ten thousand enemy aircraft, at a distance of two hundred miles from a defending nation's border, and can cause entire armies to drop dead in their tracks.'

'Astonishing!' enthused Lovecraft. 'I would have thought that a device of this power would have to be many times larger than the instrument you're holding.'

'You're quite right, Mr. Lovecraft – at least, that was true initially. The prototype was indeed much larger; in fact, you stopped to admire it in the main laboratory.'

'Your wireless magnifying transmitter?' said Lovecraft.

'Correct. The projection of charged particle beams is the least of which it's capable, and it only took a bit of tinkering to reduce it in size to the point where it can be wielded by a person.'

Lovecraft suspected that it had taken a lot more than a 'bit of tinkering' but said nothing.

'The non-aggressive transmission of usable energy is a much subtler problem,' continued Tesla. 'But I'm gradually finding my way towards a solution.'

'Easier to destroy than to create,' said Fort without irony. 'Makes sense.'

'True,' nodded Tesla, 'but I envisage this as a weapon of defence rather than attack. It's no exaggeration to say that the flying machine has completely demoralised the world – oh, of course their peacetime uses are many: transportation of people and cargo, exploration and so on; but one of the greatest fears besetting the people of the civilised world is the threat of aerial bombing by hostile foreign powers. The Teleforce Projector offers a means of absolute protection against this and other forms of attack.'

'The ultimate weapon,' said Lovecraft. 'The one which makes war itself obsolete.'

'Precisely!' said Tesla.

Fort glanced from Lovecraft to Tesla and shook his head. *A weapon that makes war obsolete?* he thought. *There's no such damned thing, and there never will be.* 'So how does it work?' he asked.

'Well…' Tesla hesitated. 'The technical details are a little complicated, but basically the barrel of the Projector is an open-ended vacuum tube with a gas jet seal that allows the particles to exit in a high-velocity air stream, which is produced by a miniaturised version of my Tesla Turbine located in the stock, which also contains a device capable of charging the microscopic metallic particles to in excess of fifty million volts. The beam is created and directed by means of a series of electrostatic repulsors on the inner surface of the barrel.' He handed the Projector to Fort. 'Feel the weight.'

Fort hefted the device. 'Lighter than I expected,' he said.

'It's yours, for now,' said Tesla. 'I'll show you how to activate it and how to select the various settings, how to focus the beam and so on. All I ask is that you bring it back in one piece.'

'You're loaning this to us?' said Fort. 'Why?'

'To destroy the Martian Falcon, of course,' replied Tesla.

'But the statue's made of obsidian,' Fort protested. 'All we have to do is drop the damned thing.'

Tesla smiled grimly and shook his head. 'I'm afraid that won't do it. When the X-M expedition returned from Mars, both the Falcon and the rock books were studied by the NCPE's Materials Analysis Department, which concluded that although they were fashioned from minerals common on both Mars and Earth, something had been done to them – some process, probably chemical in nature, which made them all but indestructible. We have no idea how this was achieved.'

'I didn't know that,' said Fort.

'No one did,' Tesla replied. 'It's been kept under wraps by the government. And…' He gave a small, embarrassed laugh. 'I'd appreciate it if you did the same and kept it to yourselves. The fact is, the government is trying to apply the indestructibility of the Martian artefacts to our own materials. The applications for industry are numerous to say the least: with access to those kinds of production techniques, we could construct buildings a mile high with barely a second thought.' He indicated the Teleforce Projector. 'This is the only device on Earth which has a chance of destroying the Martian Falcon.'

'Splendid,' said Lovecraft. 'Now all we have to do is find it.'

Tesla broke into a broad smile. 'I have the solution to that problem, too.'

'I didn't doubt it for a moment,' said Fort, replacing the Projector on the workbench.

'When the NCPE examined the artefacts, they noticed something else about them,' Tesla continued. 'All matter oscillates at specific frequencies, but the molecules in the Martian artefacts – the rock books and the Falcon – oscillate at a highly unusual one. It's probably a side effect of the process by which they were hardened to their state of near-indestructibility, but it's detectable within a certain range.'

'Detectable?' said Fort. 'By what?'

Tesla led them to another workbench. 'By this. I call it the AOD, short for Anomalous Oscillation Detector. It's calibrated for the oscillation of the Martian rock artefacts.' He picked up an instrument the size and shape of a large flashlight. The front of the instrument was covered with a fine mesh through which could be seen a complex and delicate-looking arrangement of electrical components. In front of the on/off switch on the handgrip was a trio of tiny lights. Tesla indicated them. 'When you switch on the detector, this light will glow red; that means you're nowhere near the source of the anomalous oscillation. When you're within about two hundred yards, the red light will go out and the yellow light will come on.' The light was accompanied by a bleeping sound. 'Get to within fifty yards and the yellow light will go out and the green light will come on.' The bleeping became more urgent. 'The lights switch between each other according to the direction in which the target lies; so if the green light is on, you know you're heading towards it and it's less than fifty yards away. If you turn away from it, the green light will go out and the yellow one will re-illuminate, so you'll know you're heading in the wrong direction. Turn back towards the target and the green light will come on again. Simple.'

'Indeed,' said Lovecraft, 'but why did you build this device? Seems like a bit of a pointless exercise, if you'll forgive me for saying so.'

'Far from it, Mr. Lovecraft,' Tesla replied. 'I designed the AOD for the X-M 2 expedition. It will enable the crew to find further artefacts when they continue the exploration of the city of Cydonia – although now there is a much more pressing need for it.'

Tesla handed the device to Fort, who switched it on and frowned. 'The green light's on.'

'That's right. I have some samples of Martian minerals here in the lab: fragments of artefacts which were brought back by the crew of the X-M. I used them to calibrate the instrument.'

'Fragments?' said Fort as he switched off the AOD. 'I thought their stuff was indestructible.'

'*Almost* indestructible,' Tesla corrected. 'Don't forget, they were subjected to a force which destroyed the Martian civilisation and ruined the planet.'

'True,' nodded Fort. He hefted the AOD and glanced at the Teleforce Projector on the other workbench. 'This stuff's going to come in very handy, Dr. Tesla. We can't thank you enough.'

'There's no need to thank me, Mr. Fort,' Tesla replied with a slight smile. 'All you need to do is find the Martian Falcon and destroy it, otherwise Earth may well suffer the same fate as Mars did five million years ago…'

CHAPTER 25
Strange Pursuit

Rusty Links ran.

At first it was with the assumption that the running would be easy.

He won't find me. No one can find a shifter who doesn't want to be found. No one!

Still wearing Bradlee's form, she checked into a motel on the outskirts of a small town that might as well have been nameless for all the attention she paid to its name. She took the room key from the desk clerk and went to her room. She went to the bathroom and stood in front of the mirror for five minutes, looking at the face of the man she had killed, then picked up the briefcase containing the rock book and left the motel. The desk clerk gave her a brief glance and then went back to the sports section of the newspaper he was reading.

She walked along what passed for a main street until she reached the centre of the town, where she found a small rental car company. Using Bradlee's ID and the money in his wallet, she hired a car and drove north out of the town.

As she drove, she caught a glimpse of something in the rear view mirror: a dark smudge that seemed to float in the air behind her, but which vanished as she blinked. She shook her head, frowned and increased her speed.

She played out the likely scenario of the next few hours in her head.

It would only be a very short while before they realised something was wrong back at Cabo Cañaveral – twenty-four hours at most. Bradlee's secretary would find the note she had left, would puzzle over the unfamiliar handwriting. Would she raise the alarm then? Probably not: if she tried, Troy Martell would respond that he had just seen Bradlee at the meeting, and nothing had seemed odd about him. Of course, when Bradlee failed to return home that evening, his wife would immediately start worrying and call the NCPE, who would reply that he had shown up for work, but had mentioned that he wasn't feeling so great. His secretary would confirm that he had left early: a sore throat.

Bradlee's wife would call the Titusville police, and her concerns would immediately be taken seriously; no 'wait forty-eight hours and call us again' bullshit. A US government employee working at the world's only fully functioning rocket complex going missing a few days after the theft of the Martian Falcon in New York would get everyone's attention – especially the folks at Cabo Cañaveral. Bradlee's office would be examined by security, who would quickly discover the ruined wall safe.

And then all hell would break loose.

She would have to ditch Bradlee's car and his form soon, but that was fine. She had known she would have to before long.

*

Crystalman stood in front of the telaug machine with his eyes closed and a slight smile playing about his lips, watching the road ahead through Rusty's eyes. Had Rusty been human, it would have been a simple matter to alter the settings on the telaug to allow Crystalman access to her mind-body interface, forcing her to do his bidding. She would have had no choice but to bring the rock book to Long Island, here to meet the unpleasant fate he had devised for her.

But Rusty wasn't human: such was her chameleon nature that the telaug could not maintain a lock for long enough to influence her physical behaviour. It was an inconvenience, to be sure, but not an insurmountable one.

Crystalman would simply have to guide her back through more subtle means. The Dark Ones would help: the air elementals over which he *did* have control. One had already appeared briefly on the back seat of her car.

Gave you a bit of a start, didn't it, Rusty? Crystalman thought. *But that's nothing compared to what's about to happen…*

*

Like most of her singular race, Rusty had always lived beyond the limits of society. There were a few shapeshifters who tried to integrate themselves into the common run of humanity and who kept their true nature hidden from those around them, but they were the exception rather than the rule. It was the general consensus that, by their very nature, shifters could not be trusted – for how *could* one trust a creature whose fundamental characteristic was deceit?

So they either kept to themselves or clung to each other for solace and companionship in the face of a world that hated and mistrusted them. Rusty Links was one of the former: she had no need of companionship or solace; all she needed were her wits and enough luck to see her through the dangerous playground of life.

She had always known that her luck couldn't last forever – luck never does. Getting involved with Johnny Sanguine had been an amusing diversion; Johnny had been fun to be with – in every sense of the phrase – and the truth was that she had felt some regret at dispatching such a diverting playmate before the game had run its natural course. But Crystalman had offered good money for the Falcon – serious money, the kind she would have been a fool to turn down. She had done occasional work for him in the past, and he had always paid well. He had never tried to stiff her or double cross her, and while she had never felt entirely safe in his presence, she had still considered him to be something of a kindred spirit.

But now the terms of their association had changed, and it was very much of her doing; she began to wonder if that association had been a mistake in the first place, maybe the most serious mistake she had ever made... maybe the last mistake she would ever make.

Yes, Rusty, thought Crystalman on the other side of the telaug machine's psychic two-way mirror. *You are quite right: it is the last mistake you will ever make. You have betrayed me, and the price of betrayal is more terrible than you can conceive.*

Rusty had always preferred the east of the country and had made it her playground for many years. For that reason, she maintained a series of apartments and identities from South Carolina all the way up to Maine. Her first stop would be Charleston; she would ditch the rental car on the outskirts of town, take on a new face and lay low in the apartment for a day or so while planning her next move. Chances were she would have to leave the country for a time, while she figured out a way to destroy the rock book, but that was okay, too. There were places in Europe she hadn't seen yet, and the Far East was a near-total mystery, ripe for exploration.

Yeah, she thought, *the Far East sounds good...*

*

It was dark by the time she reached the apartment block, which was in a nondescript, middle-class neighbourhood of Charleston. Wearing a new face, she stepped off the streetcar and walked unhurriedly to the main entrance, unlocked the door and slipped inside.

She glanced at the elevator – a wrought iron cage with only one way in and out – and decided to take the stairs to her floor. She climbed, carrying the briefcase containing the rock book and Bradlee's notes.

As she walked along the corridor towards her apartment, she found herself slowing down... automatically, instinctively. Something was wrong. She didn't know what it was, but the part of her brain whose job it was to make sure she stayed alive was telling her to get the hell out of there, and fast.

She came to a halt and listened.

The corridor was silent, which was wrong in itself. Normally at this time, there were faint sounds to be heard: a radio in one apartment, dinner conversation in another; the normal sounds of a building with people in almost every room – faint and muffled, to be sure, but *there*.

The only sound she heard was that of her own breathing.

She continued the final few paces to her door and slowly inserted the key. The sound it made seemed unnaturally loud. She turned the key and opened the door a few inches – just wide enough to allow her to reach in and switch on the hall light.

What the hell are you afraid of? she asked herself. *He doesn't know about this place… he doesn't know about any of them. No one does… only you.*

She pushed the door fully open and looked down the corridor, which led to the sitting room. Along the corridor there were doors leading to the single bedroom, the bathroom and the kitchen. All were closed, as she had left them. The silence of the corridor outside had seeped into the apartment – or maybe it was the other way round…

Slowly, she edged along the corridor, opening doors and checking rooms as she went. The apartment seemed empty and undisturbed; everything was where it should be, nothing was out of place, nothing was wrong.

Except that something *was* wrong; she was certain of it.

There was only the sitting room left. She walked the rest of the way along the corridor and entered the room.

She was glad she had left the apartment door open.

Standing at the centre of the sitting room was a man-shaped figure, entirely black, like a living, three-dimensional shadow.

'Son of a *bitch!*' she whispered.

The shadow being hissed out her name. The voice was Crystalman's. 'Russsty… Rusty, you have *betrayed* me!'

'I… I don't know what you're talking about,' she said.

205

'Don't lie to me, Rusty,' said the voice. 'I am with you everywhere you go, as close to you as your own skin. You cannot escape from me, you cannot hide from me, you cannot defeat me. You know all these things, and yet still you test me.'

'How did you know?' she asked, struggling to keep her voice steady.

'That is not your concern. All that concerns you is the fact that I am waiting for you to bring the rock book to me, and that if you don't, things will go very, *very* badly for you.'

'You don't scare me, Crystalman,' Rusty said, trying to force some strength into her voice and failing miserably. 'You think you can scare me with an air elemental?'

'Not just one,' Crystalman replied with a chuckle. 'I can summon hundreds, thousands, *millions*. I can make your world a whirling maelstrom of unending, seething darkness; I can make them torment you until your mind breaks, until your brain is emptied of all rational thought. I can drive you insane, Rusty – don't doubt it.'

Rusty started to back away from the elemental. The being took a step forward. 'Bring me the rock book,' Crystalman's voice said. 'Bring it to me, as we agreed, and I will overlook your transgression; I will pay you your fee and allow you to be on your way. It will be as if none of this happened. We shall be friends again, Rusty.'

'We were never friends, Crystalman. Do you know what the rock book is?'

'Of course I do.'

'You're going to use it to free the thing that's inside the Falcon... so that something else will be freed, something on Mars, something that will destroy the Earth...'

'You have learned much, Rusty.'

'Why?' she cried. 'Why do you want to do this? You'll be killed, too!'

'Once again, that is not your concern. Bring me the book.'

'No.'

The shadow being took another step forward. 'Bring me the book, Rusty.'

'No!'

She ran from the apartment, slamming and locking the door behind her. Once out on the dark, deserted street, she shifted into the bat-winged demon-thing and launched herself into the night, her great, membranous wings thrusting her up into the moonless sky, leaving Aldous Bradlee's shredded clothes on the street below.

She glanced down at the apartment building and saw the shadow being emerging from her sitting room window. With a curse, she beat her vast wings and flew off into the night.

*

She found them waiting for her in Raleigh, North Carolina, in Roanoke, Virginia, in Annapolis, Maryland, in Philadelphia, Pennsylvania. She knew then that she would find them in Hartford, Connecticut, in Providence, Rhode Island, in Boston, Massachusetts, in Concord, New Hampshire, in Augusta, Maine…

All of her hideaways had been compromised, somehow. None were safe now. The bat-winged demon flew in circles high in the air above the eastern states, looking down in desperation, trying to think of a way to escape, and realising with a leaden weight in its belly that there *was* no way – nowhere to hide from the gaze of Crystalman.

How did he do it? Rusty asked herself. *How does he know?*

When the sun came up, she thrust herself further into the cold, high air, flying amongst the sky beasts of the ultimate altitudes, envying them their uncomplicated lives.

What the fuck do I do now? I could be on the other side of the world and he'd still find me. I could be on the moon *and he'd find me. Somehow… somehow he's inside my head…*

She felt herself beginning to tire; it was becoming more and more of an effort to keep herself aloft, especially in the thin air of the upper atmosphere.

Got to find somewhere to lay low… got to find someone to help me… but where, and who?

And then a name popped out of her memory, like the sudden flash of a lighthouse beam.

Charles Fort.

CHAPTER 26
A Proposal

Fort and Lovecraft took the red-eye back from Denver to New York, arriving at LaGuardia at 8:00a.m. They took a cab from the aerodrome to Fort's apartment and found Cormack O'Malley asleep in one of the armchairs in the lobby, his overnight bag on the floor beside him. Fort tapped him gently on the shoulder.

'That was damned quick,' he said when the priest had roused himself. 'How did you get back so soon?'

O'Malley yawned and stretched and rubbed his eyes. 'Ambrogio loaned me his plane. Jet-assisted… goes like snot – but never mind that. I need to talk to you.'

'So I gathered. Come on up.'

As they entered the elevator, O'Malley pointed to the case Fort was carrying in addition to his travelling valise. It was about the size of a violin case. 'What's that?'

'Something Dr. Tesla loaned to us,' Fort replied. 'He calls it a Teleforce Projector. Apparently, it's the only thing that stands a chance of destroying the Martian Falcon.'

'How so?'

'The NCPE reckons the damned thing's all but indestructible – something to do with the way it was made.'

'He also gave us a device which will detect the Falcon at a distance,' added Lovecraft. 'We now have the means at our disposal to find and destroy the artefact.'

'To a certain extent,' Fort added. 'We still have to get within a couple of hundred yards of it before the gadget will start working.'

'Well, that's a start,' said O'Malley.

When they arrived at Fort's apartment, he went through to the kitchen and made some coffee for them all, and they sat in the living room.

'Well, Cormack,' said Fort as he rolled a cigarette. 'You don't look all that bad after reading the *Necronomicon*. Maybe it's not the devilish thing it's cracked up to be.'

'Trust me, Charlie, it is,' O'Malley replied without smiling. 'If I had my way, I'd hunt down every last copy of the damned thing and burn the lot of them.'

Fort gave a mirthless chuckle. 'That's been tried... more than once. Did you get anything interesting from it?'

'Did I ever! Charlie... we're in trouble, and by *we* I mean everyone, the entire planet.'

Fort sat back and lit his cigarette. 'What's the deal?'

'You know how Crystalman got his name?'

'Of course I do. He wears a quartz mask. Bit theatrical in my opinion, but each to his own, I guess.'

'This isn't funny, Charlie,' said O'Malley. 'The *Necronomicon* describes what happened on Mars five million years ago. The planet was wiped out by an aspect of Azathoth that broke through into our universe from the centre of infinity...'

Fort sat forward. 'Azathoth?'

'Oh good Lord!' cried Lovecraft. 'What do you mean "an aspect"?'

'The book describes it as the "breath" or "gaze" of Azathoth...'

'So, some aspect of the being's awareness,' Lovecraft mused. 'Not the being itself, but still hideously dangerous, like the venom of a snake. Even though it's separate from what produced it, it can still wreak untold havoc.'

O'Malley nodded. 'Exactly.'

'Where is it now?' asked Fort.

'At the centre of Mars.'

Fort and Lovecraft glanced at each other.

'That's right, lads,' said O'Malley. 'It's there, dormant – *sleeping*, I guess you could say. It's somehow tied to the mind of Haq ul'Suun –'

'Haq ul what?' said Fort.

'Haq ul'Suun, the god-king of ancient Mars. He was the ultimate ruler of the planet. He was the one who opened the way into our universe for it. According to the *Necronomicon*, he was trying to harness the power of the Outer Gods and got way more than he bargained for.'

'So he was the one in the transmission which Dr. Tesla intercepted,' said Lovecraft.

'Right,' O'Malley nodded. 'His mind, his very *soul* was imprisoned within the artefact we know as the Martian Falcon – an eternal prison, a punishment whose awfulness fully matches the nature of his transgression. But the thing he summoned, the breath and gaze of Azathoth, are sympathetically tied to his soul, so as long as his soul is imprisoned in the Falcon, they will remain dormant at the centre of Mars.'

Fort shook his head. 'Are you sure about this, Cormack? I mean, *really* sure?'

'I think the *Necronomicon* speaks the truth about this. And it gets worse...'

Fort grunted. 'What a surprise!'

'The book describes an avatar of Nyarlathotep, the Crawling Chaos, the Messenger of the Great Old Ones... as a man who wears a crystal mask...'

Fort blew a stream of cigarette smoke into the air. 'Great. That's just great.'

'According to the book, the wearer of the crystal mask, Nyarlathotep, who is Azathoth's son, will bring about the return of his father's breath and gaze, and when that time comes, the Earth, the very Solar System, will be annihilated.'

'I think I need some more coffee,' said Lovecraft. He stood up and moved through to the kitchen.

'I need a drink,' said Fort, reaching for a quart of bourbon that was standing on the table beside the sofa.

Both he and O'Malley shot glances towards the kitchen as Lovecraft gave a loud cry. 'What is it, Howard?' Fort called.

Lovecraft came back into the sitting room, followed by the ghost of Johnny Sanguine.

*

'Now do you believe me, Father?' asked Sanguine as he paced slowly up and down in front of them. 'Now do you believe I'm telling the truth about the terrible danger the Martian Falcon poses to every living thing on the planet?'

'I believe you,' O'Malley rumbled. 'I also think you're lying when you say you want it returned to Mars to redeem your soul.'

Sanguine assumed a pained expression. 'That hurts, Father. If it weren't for me, you'd know nothing about what the Falcon really is. You'd still be punching hoodlums into righteousness instead of working to save the world.'

'All right, Sanguine,' said Fort. 'We know you're on the level – at least about the Falcon being dangerous. Question is, how do we find it? If Crystalman has it, where is he, and how do we get to him?'

'I know exactly where he is,' Sanguine replied. 'But getting to him is going to be tough, *real* tough. He lives in one of the big houses out on Long Island, but he spends most of his time under it…'

'Under it?' said Lovecraft.

'Yeah. There are some Dero caverns under the house – that's where his real hideout is. He's not afraid of them; in fact, I think they're afraid of him.'

If he's an avatar of Nyarlathotep, I'm not surprised, thought Fort.

As if reading his mind, O'Malley said: 'Do you know who Crystalman really is, Sanguine?' When Sanguine hesitated, he added: 'You know he's Nyarlathotep, right? Or at least, an avatar of Nyarlathotep. The Crawling Chaos, the Messenger of the Great Old Ones, son of Azathoth…'

'Of course I do,' Sanguine replied, after recomposing himself – at least, that was how it appeared to O'Malley. 'That's why I contacted you, Father – because I know the danger we're facing.'

O'Malley looked at him long and hard, and then nodded. 'Okay.'

'So the Falcon is on Long Island, or rather, *under* Long Island,' said Fort. 'You're right: getting to it is going to be tough… so how do we do it?'

'We're going to need help,' Sanguine replied. 'Serious muscle, the kind only one man can provide… if you can still call him a man.'

Fort raised his eyebrows. 'Capone? Are you seriously suggesting we ask *him* for help?'

Sanguine smiled. 'I hated him when I was alive, but I never underestimated him. He's a hard bastard, and not just because he's made of metal; he's good in a fight, and he's got some of the best muscle in the entire country: his zombies would walk into a live atomic reactor for him – mainly because they have no choice. His foot soldiers are second only to mine, and we're going to need both.'

'An army of vampires and zombies going up against the Crawling Chaos,' said Lovecraft. 'It'll be a hell of a scrap, but it could be done.'

'Yeah,' said Fort. 'Maybe it could at that… but how are we going to convince Capone to join us? He hates you as much as you hate him, and he's still smarting from the trick you pulled with the Falcon in the first place.'

'That's where you come in,' said Sanguine.

Fort frowned at him. 'Me?'

'You're working for him. He trusts you as much as he trusts anyone outside his organisation…'

'Which is to say not much,' Fort said.

'True, but it's all we've got right now. I've already put word out on the street that you want to meet with him to discuss an important matter – something that'll get him off the hook for my murder. He's laying low; no one knows where he is, but word'll get to him all right, and when it does, he won't be able to resist.'

'Where's the meeting place?' asked Fort.

'The old Marsh warehouse on the Jersey shore.'

'Neutral territory,' said Fort.

'Exactly.'

'Excuse me,' said Lovecraft. 'Neutral territory?'

'A place where the New York gangs can meet to discuss grievances, or the terms of a truce or temporary alliance,' Fort explained. 'It's also the place where negotiations to avoid war are made.' He turned to Sanguine. 'When's the meet planned for?'

'Ten o'clock tonight.'

'And if Capone doesn't show?'

'Then I guess we'll have to go in without him,' Sanguine replied. 'You'll be there, yes?'

Fort sighed. 'Yeah, I'll be there. But I can't help thinking this plan to go head to head with Crystalman is a stupid idea.'

O'Malley looked at him askance. 'What do you mean, Charlie? It's our only option.'

'Oh sure, I understand that,' Fort said, 'but attacking his place head on, even with an army of vampires and zombies... I can't see that working.'

'So what do you suggest?' asked Sanguine.

Fort was silent for several moments, thinking. Finally, he said: 'Crystalman's HQ is under his house on Long Island, in the caverns he took back from the Dero, right?'

'Right,' Sanguine nodded.

'And to stand a chance against him, we need the element of surprise. And we'll need to come from a direction he's not expecting.'

'That would be preferable,' Sanguine said slowly. 'What are you getting at?'

'Just this: if we can find a way in that's less obvious than forcing our way into the house, we'll stand a much better chance of finding the Falcon.'

O'Malley chuckled. 'I know what you're thinking, Charlie. The old IRT tunnels.'

'Of course!' said Lovecraft, clicking his fingers. 'The Interborough Rapid Transit system. The entire project was abandoned in the 1890s when the excavations revealed some Dero caverns. They built the upway system instead. The surveyors concluded that the Dero hadn't used the caverns for years, but the IRT Company's planners decided it wasn't worth the risk to continue.'

'That's right,' said Fort. 'No one wants anything to do with those nasty little bastards. If anything had happened to anyone down there, the IRT would have been sued into oblivion. The tunnels were sealed off, but they're still there. If we could get into them and then get into the Dero caverns...'

'We could get to Crystalman's hideout,' O'Malley completed. 'He wouldn't be expecting that. If we played our cards right, we could get straight in and out without him even noticing!'

'Well,' Fort chuckled, 'I wouldn't go *that* far, Cormack. He'll notice us, all right... but if we can maintain the element of surprise for long enough, it might increase our chances of getting out alive.'

'Sounds like a plan,' said Lovecraft, 'of sorts.'

'So you're all in,' said Sanguine.

'Yeah,' said Fort, 'we're in.'

Sanguine smiled. 'Then I'll see you later.'

And with that, he vanished from the room.

CHAPTER 27
A Dame in Trouble

Fort, Lovecraft and O'Malley spent the rest of that day at the Public Records Office going over the original plans of the abandoned subway system. The Interborough Rapid Transit Company had made a lot of headway before the first of the Dero caverns had been discovered, and additional tunnels had been excavated before the second, third and fourth caverns had been revealed by the boring machines – including one connecting Manhattan with Long Island beneath the East River.

'The closest station is on Park Avenue and East 57th Street,' said Fort, pointing out the location on a large surveyor's drawing.

'That's no good,' said O'Malley. 'It's a good hundred-mile-walk from there to where we need to be. It'll take us days – if the Dero don't make mincemeat of us first!'

'You're right,' sighed Fort.

'What about Manorville?' said Lovecraft. 'That's where they broke into the Long Island caverns.'

Fort examined the drawing. 'You're right, Howard. An exploratory shaft was sunk there; we could drive out to Long Island and get in that way.'

'Yes,' nodded O'Malley. 'Good idea, Mr. Lovecraft!'

'Shouldn't we notify the police?' said Lovecraft. 'I'm sure that once we explain the problem to them, they'll be more than happy to provide some backup.'

'A nice idea, but a naive one, I'm afraid' O'Malley replied. 'For one thing, there's no way that New York's finest would consider joining forces with two mob gangs; even if they believed our story, they'd probably arrest the lot of us and go after Crystalman themselves... and I for one would rather that didn't happen.'

Lovecraft nodded. 'I suppose you're right, Father.'

Fort checked his watch. It was a little after five p.m. 'Well, boys, looks like we've got all we're going to get here. What say we grab a bite and then head back to my place? Then we'll head out to Jersey.'

'Sounds good,' said O'Malley.

They took a cab from the Public Records Office to a small mom and pop restaurant a block from Fort's apartment, where they ate dinner.

They returned to the apartment to the sound of the telephone ringing. Fort picked up the receiver.

'Charlie!' cried the voice of Penny Malone. 'Where in blazes have you been? I've been calling you for the last two hours!'

Fort told her and then said: 'What's up, Penny? You sound flustered.'

'Flustered isn't the word for it, Charlie. I've got someone here who needs to speak to you right now, and I mean *right now*.'

'Okay, okay, calm down. Are you at the office?'

'Yeah.'

'Okay, I'll be right there. Who is it who wants to see me?'

'A lady by the name of Rusty Links.'

'Rusty... Jesus Christ!'

'What is it, Charles?' asked Lovecraft.

'Rusty Links is at my office with Penny right now.'

'Jesus, Mary and Joseph,' said O'Malley.

Fort said into the phone: 'All right, Penny, we'll be there in ten minutes.'

'Try and make it five, Charlie,' said Penny. 'She's scared, *really* scared. She says Crystalman is after her.'

'Five it is,' said Fort, and slammed down the receiver without waiting for a reply. To Lovecraft and O'Malley, he said: 'Let's go, right now. Links says Crystalman's after her, and if that's true, I don't want Penny anywhere near her. Come on!' He grabbed the case containing the Teleforce Projector and the Anomalous Oscillation Detector.

'You're taking that?' said O'Malley.

'Damn straight,' Fort replied. 'If things turn nasty, this'll be more use than a gun.'

*

Fort was true to his word. They hailed a cab outside his apartment building, gave the driver the address of his office, and Fort offered him twenty dollars if he'd get them there in five minutes.

'Consider it done, boss,' said the driver as he floored the gas pedal.

When they got to his office, they found Penny sitting at her desk and Rusty Links in one of the visitors' armchairs across the room.

Jeez, what a fine-looking dame, thought Fort as Rusty stood up and ran to him.

'Mr. Fort!' she cried. 'I need your help. I got your address from the phone book. You're the only one I can turn to…'

'All right, Miss Links,' said Fort as he guided her back to the chair. 'Have a seat.' Over his shoulder, he said: 'Cormack, take Penny home.'

'What are you talking about, Charlie?' Penny demanded. 'I'm staying right here.'

'No you're not, hon. Howard and I need to discuss some things with Miss Links here.' He glanced down at Rusty, who was sitting on the edge of the chair, wringing her hands and looking up at him with wide doe-eyes. 'She's involved with some very dangerous people, and I don't want you anywhere near her.'

'But Charlie!'

'I'm serious, Penny!' Fort said loudly. 'Cormack…'

'Charlie's right, Miss Malone,' said O'Malley, placing a hand gently on her shoulder.

'Your parents live on Staten Island, don't they,' said Fort.

'Uh huh.'

'All right. Cormack, take her there, and then get back here quick as you can.'

'Will do.'

Penny gave Fort an accusing look as O'Malley led her out of the office.

When the door had closed, Fort turned back to Rusty. 'All right, Miss Links. Suppose you tell me what the hell's going on and why you think I'm in any position to help you – assuming I want to, which in all honesty I don't.'

'Oh, you will, Mr. Fort,' said Rusty breathlessly. 'When you see what I've got and hear what I know, you'll want to help me, all right!'

'Were you the one who killed Johnny Sanguine?'

Rusty dropped her gaze to the floor.

Fort gave a brief, harsh laugh. 'Well, I guess I'd be a fool to expect you to admit it, huh? Let's try this: why did you come to me?'

'Because you're investigating the Falcon case,' Rusty replied in a quiet voice.

'And how do you know that? I haven't been mentioned in the papers. No one knows, except the cops.'

'Crystalman knows.'

'And how does *he* know?'

'I'm not sure. But you're in danger from him, too.'

'Oh, I'm well aware of that, Miss Links,' Fort replied with a quick glance at Lovecraft. 'Why is he after you? What did you do to get on his wrong side? You stole the Falcon for him, you turned it over to him – at least, I assume you did…?'

A quick nod.

'But now you've done something to rile him up, right? So, what is it?'

Rusty hesitated, her anxious gaze flitting back and forth. Fort could practically hear the cogs turning in her head. He gave a loud sigh. 'Do you want my help or not? If you do, you're going to have to level with me and tell me everything. If not, you can leave right now.'

Evidently, Rusty reached a decision. She reached down and pulled Aldous Bradlee's briefcase from under the armchair, where she had placed it on her arrival. She handed it to Fort. 'It's all in there,' she said. 'The reason he's after me…'

Fort took the briefcase, put it on Penny's desk and opened it. He looked at the contents, and then at Rusty. 'Is this what I think it is?' he asked.

She nodded. 'The ninth rock book. The key to unlocking the power of the Falcon.'

Lovecraft gasped and hurried over to the desk.

'There are also some notes in there,' Rusty added, 'written by the lead archivist of the X-M program. They're worth reading.'

'So you made a little trip down to Florida and stole these, right?' said Fort. 'Did you kill anyone to get them?' Rusty didn't answer, and Fort gave her a long look. He shook his head in disgust. 'I'd like to toss you out of here and leave you to Crystalman.'

Rusty's eyes flashed at him. 'Maybe you would, but you're not that stupid – at least, I hope you're not. Read the notes.'

Fort shook his head and turned back to the briefcase. Lovecraft had picked up the rock book and was carefully turning its stone pages, muttering to himself in wonderment. 'What a piece of work!' he said. 'Such craftsmanship! Such finesse in the working of–'

'Pipe down, Howard,' said Fort as he picked up the sheaf of notes and began to read, his gaze flitting between paragraphs, grabbing the salient information before moving on. Rusty watched as his eyes flicked back and forth.

When he had finished, he put the notes down and looked at Rusty. 'Do you know what's waiting at the centre of Mars?' he asked.

'I've a fair idea. A Great Old One, summoned from Outside by Haq ul'Suun five million years ago. That's why I'm here, why Crystalman is after me. He gave me the job of getting the rock book for him, but when I figured out what its true purpose is, I

220

decided that he can never be allowed to get his hands on it. I had the idea of skipping the country, taking it with me, but somehow he knew that. He sent some air elementals after me. He spoke to me through one of them, said I'd betrayed him and told me that if I didn't bring the book to him, he'd use them to drive me insane.'

'You're right about Haq ul'Suun summoning a Great Old One,' said Fort. 'But it's not just any Great Old One. It's Azathoth.'

Rusty leaped to her feet, her eyes wide. 'That's bullshit! If Azathoth were anywhere near Earth, we wouldn't be having this conversation. I dread to think what *would* be happening...'

'Not Azathoth itself,' said Fort. 'Just a moment of its awareness, of its perception of the Earth, which entered our universe when Haq ul'Suun opened the way.'

Rusty sat down again slowly. 'Crystalman knows it,' she said. 'He knows that the rock book is the key to releasing the spirit of Haq ul'Suun from the Falcon. But that was never his real objective...'

'No,' said Fort. 'His real objective is to release the awareness of Azathoth from its sympathetic confinement.'

'Yeah, but why the hell would he do that?'

'Because Azathoth is his father,' Fort replied.

Rusty looked at him open-mouthed. 'Oh Christ.'

'That's right, Miss Links. Crystalman is an avatar of Nyarlathotep. He intends to feed the Earth and everything on it to Azathoth. Real nice company you keep, if you don't mind my saying so.' Fort glanced at the rock book which Lovecraft was still holding. 'But I'll tell you something else. This might just get you off the death penalty. You've given us the way to defeat him.'

'What do you mean, Charles?' asked Lovecraft.

'This rock book, created at the time of Haq ul'Suun's imprisonment by means of – what do the notes call it? Lithotechnology? – can reverse the process and free his mind from its confinement inside the Falcon. So all we have to do to prevent that from happening is destroy the book.'

'That's easier said than done,' Rusty replied. 'I've tried smashing it, but I can't. It's unbreakable.'

'Makes sense,' said Fort. 'Created by the same means as the Falcon.' He grinned at her. 'But we'll see how unbreakable it is.' He picked up the case he had put on the floor and laid it on Penny's desk. He opened it and took out the Teleforce Projector.

'What's that?' asked Rusty.

Fort told her. 'If anything can destroy the rock book, this can.'

Rusty went to stand beside Fort and Lovecraft. 'Are you sure?'

'Actually, no, not a hundred percent, but it's our best option right now.' He glanced around at the four walls, and then indicated the inner wall separating the office from the corridor outside. 'Howard, put the book on the floor and stand it against that wall.'

Lovecraft nodded and did as Fort asked. 'Shouldn't we take it to a more secluded location and then destroy it, Charles?' he said as he rejoined Fort and Rusty at the desk.

'Ideally, yes, but we don't know how much time we've got. If Crystalman knows where Miss Links is, his elementals could be on their way here right now. We've got to destroy the thing while we have the chance.' He indicated the door to his office. 'Okay, the two of you take cover in there; it's my guess there's going to be some shrapnel flying around.'

Lovecraft opened the door and he and Rusty stood in Fort's office on either side of the door. Fort glanced at them and shook his head. 'Not enough. Get behind the wall and hunker down.'

Lovecraft and Rusty disappeared from view behind the wall. 'Good luck, Charles,' said Lovecraft.

Fort switched on the Teleforce Projector and took careful aim at the rock book. His finger closed on the trigger.

At that moment, the corridor door burst open and John Carter, Dave Wiseman and several uniformed policemen surged into the room. All had their weapons drawn.

'Drop it, Charlie!' shouted Carter.

'What the hell!' cried Fort.

'Do it, or we'll drop you.'

Fort lowered the Projector.

'On the desk, and hands in the air.'

Fort put the Projector on the desk and raised his hands.

'Step away.'

Fort took a couple of paces back.

'Anyone else here with you? Your buddy Mr. Lovecraft, maybe?'

'No,' said Fort. 'Just me.'

'Like hell,' said Wiseman, peering at the door to Fort's office. 'Whoever's back there, get out here, now!'

'Do as he says,' said Fort over his shoulder.

'Are you sure, Charles?' asked Lovecraft from behind the wall.

Fort sighed. 'Yes, Howard, I'm sure.'

'Well,' said Lovecraft as he edged into view. 'I suppose they'd have checked in here anyway.'

'That we would, Mr. Lovecraft,' said Carter.

As Rusty followed Lovecraft through the door, Wiseman added: 'Well well, Miss Rusty Links, I presume.' With a glance at Carter, he added: 'See, John? I told you Fort was dirty; been in it from the start, he has.'

Rusty said nothing; she merely smiled as her skin lost its flawless alabaster hue and turned bright, hellish red.

'She's shifting!' shouted Wiseman. 'John, *now!*'

Carter pointed his weapon at Rusty, and Fort realised that it wasn't a conventional service revolver. It was smaller, and the barrel was too thin. When Carter pulled the trigger, the only sound was a muted *phut!* The needle struck Rusty in the side of her neck. She dropped to the floor instantly, her skin returning to its human colour.

'What the hell is that thing?' demanded Fort.

'New tool from the eggheads in the police armoury, Charlie,' Carter replied as one of the uniformed officers hurried across to Rusty and handcuffed her. 'Pneumatic needle gun. Each needle carries an anaesthetic compound with a component that prevents shapeshifters from doing their party trick. Only lasts for a few hours, but that's more than long enough to get them squared away.'

'That's pretty impressive tech for the NYPD,' said Fort as two more policemen moved forward and cuffed Fort and Lovecraft.

'You'd be surprised at some of the tricks we've got up our sleeve, Charlie,' said Carter.

'I guess that's true. What's the deal, John?'

'You're under arrest,' said Carter.

'On what charge, for Christ's sake?'

Carter indicated the Teleforce Projector on the desk. 'Accessory to murder... but I guess now we can add possession of an unlicensed weapon.'

'God damn it, John! Are you still playing that tune?'

'What other tune would I play?' Carter pointed to Rusty's unconscious form. 'She staked Sanguine, and here she is in your office. And we also have reason to believe she's involved in the disappearance of Aldous Bradlee...'

'Who the hell's he?'

'The chief archivist at the NCPE in Florida,' said Wiseman. 'As if you didn't know.'

Wiseman glanced around the room, saw the rock book propped against the wall and picked it up. 'And what do we have here?' he asked theatrically. 'Why, it looks like a Martian artefact! I wonder if it's the one that was stolen from the NCPE. So we can add theft to the list.' He chuckled. 'Oh, you're in it, Fort – up to your eyeballs!'

'Go screw yourself, Wiseman,' muttered Fort.

Carter walked across to the desk and picked up the Teleforce Projector. 'Where'd you get this?'

'Just read me my rights,' said Fort.

Carter looked inside the case and picked up the Anomalous Oscillation Detector. 'What's this?'

Fort scowled at him. 'I said read me my rights.'

CHAPTER 28
Too Much Knowledge

There was a police wagon and two squad cars waiting outside. Fort and Lovecraft were shoved unceremoniously into the back of the wagon while two of the uniformed officers placed Rusty's sleeping form on the floor between them. Carter gave the rock book to Wiseman, who held his hand out for the case.

'You just take the book,' Carter said. 'I'll hold onto this. I want to take a look at it.'

Wiseman nodded. 'Okay, John, I'll see you back at the precinct.'

Wiseman left in one of the squad cars while the uniformed officers climbed into the other. Carter climbed into the wagon and sat on the bench seat beside Lovecraft, who gave him a morose look as the vehicle set off. 'This is so embarrassing,' he muttered. 'Arrested! Imagine! I don't know *what* my aunts would say.'

'They'd probably say you shouldn't have got yourself mixed up with Charles Fort,' Carter replied. He lit a cigarette, blew a stream of smoke into the air and looked at Fort. 'I'm sorry, Charlie. I wish this caper could have played out some other way. But you're in it deep, and I can't see a way out for you.'

'I'm sorry too, John,' said Fort. 'I expected you to be smarter than this.'

Carter smiled and blew more smoke. 'Why don't you square with me, Charlie? Things'll go easier for you and your friend here if you do.'

Fort nodded. 'All right, I will. You remember the conversation we had when you pulled us in after the Expressway?'

'Yeah. You said the Falcon had something to do with the death of the Martian civilisation.'

'That's right. Well, it's true. Howard and I went to see Tesla…'

'So he's the one who gave you that cockamamie gun and the other gadget.' Carter said.

'Yeah. It *is* a weapon – the only weapon that stands a chance of destroying the rock book.'

Carter sighed. 'And why, for the love of God, would you want to destroy the rock book?'

'Okay, this is going to sound crazy, John, but hear me out.'

Carter shrugged. 'Go ahead. I'm all ears.'

Fort laid it all out for Carter; everything they'd learned about the Martian Falcon and the ninth rock book.

Carter whistled loudly. 'Whew! You've really gone off the deep end this time, Charlie. Nyarlathotep? Azathoth? The Great Old Ones? The Outer Gods?' He laughed harshly. 'So you're going to destroy a priceless artefact to prevent a mythical bogeyman from eating the world. Jesus, is that the best you can come up with?'

Fort sighed. 'Why am I even bothering?'

'Beats the hell out of me,' Carter replied, dropping his cigarette butt and grinding it under his heel.

Rusty groaned and began to stir.

'Welcome back, Miss Links,' said Carter.

Rusty opened her eyes and looked at him, her face expressionless. Then she frowned, and a look of fear and consternation spread across her face.

'Trying to shift? Don't bother. There's a chemical compound in your system that prevents it. You just lie there and be a good girl, okay?'

'What are you going to do with the rock book, Lieutenant?' asked Lovecraft.

'Same thing I'm going to do with the gadgets in this case, Mr. Lovecraft. Bag them as evidence.'

'Is there nothing we can say to convince you of the truth?'

Carter shrugged. 'You could try telling me the truth. That might work.' He looked at the case, which he had placed on the seat beside him; then he opened it and took out the Teleforce Projector. He examined it carefully and nodded. 'Quite a popgun you've got here, boys. Looks like it could take out half a city block.'

'It was designed to end trouble, not start it,' said Lovecraft.

'Oh, I'm sure it was,' Carter chuckled.

'Tell me something, John.' said Fort. 'How did you know we'd be at my office?'

'We've got men watching your office and your apartment. They saw Miss Links here going into your office. They also saw you arriving in a cab in a hell of a hurry, and then Father O'Malley leaving with your secretary.'

'Have you picked them up, too?'

'Not yet, but we will.' Carter replaced the Projector in its case, glanced out through the barred window behind him, reached into his jacket and pulled out his service revolver. 'As soon as I take care of the business at hand.'

Fort eyed the revolver. 'What the hell are you doing?'

'You and your friends know way too much about the Falcon, Charlie. I can't have that.' He shrugged. 'Just can't have it.'

'My God,' said Lovecraft. 'Do you mean to *murder* us?'

'Self defence,' Carter replied. 'The three of you attacked me, tried to get the keys to your handcuffs off me. Three against one – I wouldn't stand a chance. Then you would have gone for my gun and put a slug in my head. I really had no choice: you're dangerous fugitives, after all. That's what my report will read.'

'Christ,' said Fort. 'You're working for Crystalman?'

'In a manner of speaking.'

'What do you mean "in a manner of speaking"? John, what the hell's going on?'

'You're the one who told Crystalman that Charles and I were going to Colorado,' said Lovecraft.

'That's right, Mr. Lovecraft.' Carter threw him a mock-sympathetic glance. 'You know, you really should have stuck to writing pulp fiction instead of living it. You might have lived a little longer.'

Fort gazed at Carter, appalled. 'Why, John? For God's sake, why?'

'Like I said, Charlie,' Carter replied, taking aim at Fort's head. 'You know way too much.'

His finger squeezed the trigger.

CHAPTER 29
Ambush

The police wagon jolted at the instant the hammer of Carter's pistol fell, throwing off his aim. The bullet missed Fort's head by less than an inch, the report sounding like a thunder blast in the confined space.

Carter cursed. Assuming they had hit a pothole in the road, he quickly took aim again, and again his aim was thrown off by another jolt, much harder this time. And then he realised, as they all did, that the wagon had not hit a hole in the road. Carter stood up and looked through the barred window. He cursed again, more vehemently this time, as the wagon was shunted to the side by another impact. He lost his footing and fell to the floor, dropping his gun.

Lovecraft reached out with his leg and kicked the weapon away from him and under the bench seat. Rusty squirmed to the side, her hands reaching blindly behind her back, searching for it. Fort stood up and was about to kick Carter in the gut, but there was another impact and he, too, went over.

The driver struggled with the steering wheel as the wagon was hit again and again. The cabin was filled with the loud, ugly sound of metal crunching against metal. Fort tried to knee Carter in the groin, but with his hands cuffed behind his back, he was at a serious disadvantage. Carter easily evaded him and punched him hard in the face. Fort's head swam. He tried to get up but Carter punched him again. Lovecraft stood up and aimed a weak kick at the detective's head, but Carter grabbed his ankle and twisted. Lovecraft howled with pain and went down.

Carter raised his fist for a knockout punch, but at that moment the driver of the wagon lost control, and the vehicle mounted the kerb and toppled onto its side, throwing Carter and the others from the floor to the wall in a mass of thrashing limbs. Carter's head hit the wall hard as the wagon slewed along the sidewalk, smashed a lamppost flat and ground to a halt.

For a few seconds the only sounds were those of panting and groans. Fort got onto his knees and spat blood. He looked at Carter, who was unconscious. The door of the driver's cab opened and the two men inside screamed in unison and fell silent.

'What the fuck's happening?' demanded Rusty of no one in particular.

'This feels oddly familiar,' said Fort, as the rear doors were ripped from their hinges, revealing two black-suited figures. Beyond them could be seen a sleek, black car, its front wings dented, the paint chipped away to reveal the steel beneath.

'Evening, fellas,' said Fort. 'Right on time… but how did you know? Were you staking out my office as well?'

The vampires stood aside to reveal Johnny Sanguine. 'No,' he said. 'I was.' His eyes dropped to Rusty, who was picking herself up. 'Hello, doll. Long time no see.'

Rusty sighed. 'Well… I guess this is it. Do me a favour and make it quick, huh Johnny? For old times' sake?'

Johnny smiled at her. 'You think I'm gonna kill you? Nah! That's all in the past. All is forgiven. I have other work to do, other debts to repay.' He glanced up and down the street and added more urgently: 'Let's go. Can't stick around here.'

'Where to?' asked Fort.

'The meeting place, of course,' Johnny replied. 'We've still got an appointment to keep – assuming Capone shows up.'

'What about O'Malley?'

'He'll be there, too. I paid him a quick visit at your secretary's parents' place.'

'Okay.' Fort nodded at Carter's unconscious form. 'First things first. He's got the keys to our cuffs in his pocket. And we'll have to take him with us.'

'Why?' asked Johnny.

'Because he's working for Crystalman. He may have been in the Dero caverns. He might be able to tell us something useful.'

One of the vampires took Carter's keys and unlocked their handcuffs. Fort grabbed the case containing the Projector and the AOD. They stepped out of the wagon and saw that traffic was stopping and people were getting out of their cars. A tram glided past, its windows filled with gawping faces.

Somewhere in the near distance a police siren blared, growing rapidly louder.

Johnny shook his head. 'No time to take him; we have to leave right now. Come on!'

Fort glanced again at Carter. 'All right,' he said, reluctantly.

'Kill him,' said Rusty.

'What?' said Fort.

She gave him a look that said *I can't believe how stupid you are.* 'Kill him! He's working for Crystalman and he has the rock book. We can't let him live. Kill the son of a bitch, while we have the chance.'

'For God's sake, Miss Links,' said Lovecraft. 'We cannot commit cold-blooded murder!'

'Even if it means saving the planet?' said Rusty.

Lovecraft looked at Fort. 'Charles, we can't. He's our enemy and a traitor to the human race, but...'

Fort balled his fists in frustration, as a police squad car rounded the nearest corner and sped towards them. 'You're right, Howard – we can't.'

Johnny nodded to his vampires and they returned to their car. 'My boys are leaving. If you want to as well, get in the car. Right now.'

Fort sighed. 'Let's go.'

They piled into the vampires' car and took off, as the police car screeched to a halt beside the overturned wagon.

CHAPTER 30
The Meet

The oil-black sea lapped against the slowly-rotting wood of the docks, like a tongue probing reluctantly at something unpalatable. Even though the night was warm, Lovecraft shivered slightly as he and Fort and Rusty got out of the car. They looked around at the sea and the garbage-strewn shore and the great black monolith of the old Marsh warehouse that reared up like a gigantic tombstone, soundless and solitary. Its windows were smashed and pitch-dark, silently declaring the emptiness within.

Good Lord, what a foul place! Lovecraft thought. *Given back to nature... a nature that never wanted it.*

'Come on,' said Johnny. 'Follow me.'

He glided off, followed by his two vampires. As they followed, Lovecraft noted that only he, Fort and Rusty made any sound as they walked across the shingle; the vampires and their ghost boss made none.

'I can't believe you didn't take the chance when you had it,' Rusty muttered.

With ice in his voice, Fort replied: 'Murder may come easily to you, Miss Links, but not to me. There's another way to get this job done that doesn't involve putting a bullet in an unconscious man.'

Rusty gave a contemptuous shake of her head. 'Why didn't you do it, Sanguine? You know what's at stake. You could have had one of your men take care of Carter.'

Johnny smiled back at her. 'I'm trying to save my soul, Rusty, not sully it even more.'

Rusty shook her head again but didn't reply.

Headlamps cut through the darkness about two hundred yards away. A taxicab screeched to a halt. A door opened and closed and the cab drove away quickly, its driver clearly wanting to get away as fast as possible. A burly figure hurried towards them.

'Cormack?' said Fort.

'That's me,' said the priest as he joined them.

'How's Penny? Is she okay?'

'She's right enough – mind you, she and her ma and pa got a nasty fright when himself showed up.' He pointed to Sanguine, who was about to enter the warehouse through a doorway whose door was nowhere to be seen. 'So they sprung you all right, those lads.'

'Yeah, and not a moment too soon. John Carter's working for Crystalman. He was about to off us when Johnny's boys ran us off the road.'

'*Carter?*' said O'Malley. 'Lord above, who would have thought it?'

'Too bad,' said Fort. 'He was the only one of that bunch I had any liking for.'

'What happened to him?'

'He was knocked unconscious. We left him there. We would have brought him along for the ride, but we had to get away quickly.'

O'Malley peered at Fort's face in the darkness, noticing his injuries for the first time. 'Did he do that?'

'Yeah. I hope to pay him back someday soon.'

'Well, we'll worry about that when the time comes.'

They followed the vampires through the doorway and into a vast, dark space, empty save for the ragged islands of detritus scattered across the floor, like a map of a place no one wanted to visit.

Fort checked his watch. 'Five before ten,' he said. 'Think he'll show?'

'I hope so,' Johnny replied. 'Like I said, it'll be a tough job without him. I hate to admit it, but the fact is we need him and his zombies.'

'Need us for what?'

They all spun around, looking for the source of the voice, which was hard to pin down in the enormous echoing space of the warehouse.

'Capone?' Johnny called. 'Where are you?'

'Need us for what, blood-sucker?'

'Come on over here, so we can see each other.'

'I can see you just fine, and that's all that matters. Why did you call this meeting?'

'Okay, Al, okay,' said Johnny. 'We've never seen eye to eye, that's for damn sure, but right now – believe me – we're on the same side. We have a common enemy. The whole *world* has a common enemy.'

After a brief hesitation, Capone's voice continued: 'So it's true, what I heard. You're a spook.'

'Yeah, it's true. I can't hurt you and you can't hurt me. In fact, I called off my boys on the Expressway.'

'Uh huh. Hey, Charlie, what you doin' here? And the librarian… and Johnny's ex, and Father O'Blivion himself! Quite a party. I'm honoured you invited me.'

'We're here because we need your help, Mr. Capone,' said Fort. 'The whole world needs your help.'

'How about that!' Another hesitation. 'No more nightwalkers out there?'

'None,' Johnny replied. 'Just us in here.'

'Well… at least you ain't lying about that. Okay boys, move in.'

A shuffling sound drifted out of the darkness, accompanied by a dozen zombies, all armed with Thompsons, all of which were trained on the small group. And then Capone himself clanked out of the shadows, the steel of his massive cybernetic frame glinting dully, his fat, cruel face peering at them.

'All right,' said Capone with a sneer. 'Start talkin'.'

Johnny glanced at Fort, who shrugged and said: 'Start talking.'

*

When Johnny had finished, Capone looked at each of them in turn, and then burst into a huge, derisive laugh. 'You expect me to swallow that load of horseshit?' he said. 'Even my cast iron guts couldn't handle that!'

'It's not horseshit, Mr. Capone,' said Fort. 'It's the truth. You've got to believe us…'

'I don't gotta do *nothin'*!'

'Listen, Mr. Capone,' said O'Malley. 'Johnny's on the level. Do you think I'd be mixed up in this if he wasn't?'

'I was wonderin' about that,' said Capone. 'You're a good man, Father – not my type at all, and sure as hell not *his* type. So what's *really* goin' on?'

'It's just as Johnny said…'

'You're gonna go up against Crystalman on his home turf to stop him from releasing what's-his-name…'

'Azathoth,' said Fort.

'Yeah, that guy, who's gonna eat the planet.'

'That's it,' said O'Malley. 'That's the truth. You have my word on that, and you and I know what that's worth, don't we, Al?'

'Yeah… yeah, I guess we do. So what's the plan?'

Johnny smiled. 'Thanks, Al.'

'Don't thank me yet, Sanguine; I ain't said yes. I just wanna know how you think you can pull this crazy scheme off.'

Johnny nodded to Fort, who said: 'We're not going to knock on Crystalman's front door, that's for sure. We're going in under his house on Long Island, through one of the Dero caverns which the IRT Company discovered back in '95. He won't know we're coming until it's too late.'

'Know that for a fact, do you?' said Capone.

'Not really, to be honest, but we're in with a fighting chance.'

'And say you get in there without being eaten or butt-fucked by the Dero… what then?'

'Then we destroy the Falcon…'

'Destroy it?' said Capone. 'Is that such a good idea? Won't destroying it set that Martian schmuck free?'

235

Fort shook his head. 'I don't think so. If that were true, there'd be no need for the rock book in the first place. All the Martians would have had to do to release the prisoners would be to break the falcons containing their minds. If we destroy the Falcon, the rock book becomes useless, and Crystalman's game's over. And I've got something up my sleeve that'll take care of it *and* the Dero, if they decide to give us a hard time.'

'Oh yeah? And what's that?'

'Something Nikola Tesla gave me. It's called a Teleforce Projector…'

'A what?'

Fort explained what the Projector was and how it worked.

'Sounds like you've got it all worked out, Charlie. But the big question is, what's in it for me?'

'Survival,' Fort replied simply. 'You get to carry on living, along with everyone and everything else on Earth.'

The zombie standing closest to Capone turned and said: 'I don't like it, boss. Sounds like a double cross to me.'

'No one asked you, pus-brain!' said Capone.

'Sorry, boss,' said the zombie.

'And not just survival, Mr. Capone,' said Lovecraft. 'You'll be off the hook for Mr. Sanguine's murder and the theft of the Martian Falcon, not to mention being part of the group which will bring Crystalman to justice. You'll be a hero in the eyes of the people *and* the authorities. I believe that will pay off a lot of your debts to society.'

'I don't owe society *nothin'*, librarian!' Capone thundered; then, in a calmer voice, he added: 'But you're right about the other stuff. This situation's bad for business; can't get a damned thing done while I'm on the lam like this. Yeah… bad for business…'

'So what do you say, Al?' said Johnny. 'Are you in?'

Capone considered for a moment and then nodded. 'Yeah, okay, I'm in.' He indicated the zombies. 'Are these twelve boys enough for you? I hope so, 'cause I don't got no more, not the way things are right now.'

'They'll be enough,' said Johnny.

'We'll need some weapons as well,' said O'Malley. 'Tommy guns, if you have them.'

'We got them,' said Capone.

'When are you moving?' asked Capone.

'Tonight,' Fort replied. 'We left Carter unconscious but not badly injured. My guess is he'll take the rock book to Crystalman as soon as he can. It could be tonight or it could be tomorrow, but it's going to be soon. We need to get to Crystalman first. With the Falcon destroyed, the rock book will be useless.'

Capone nodded. 'All right. Let's do it.'

CHAPTER 31
Conversation with a Dero

Crystalman stood in front of the telaug machine, looking through the eyes of Rusty Links, watching and listening as the meeting with Al Capone progressed. He hadn't counted on Sanguine and his vampires intercepting the police wagon. He realised that that was a mistake, but not a particularly serious one. With hindsight, it would have been better to have Carter go to Fort's office alone and kill him and the others there. But no matter: they would be coming here, and it would be here that they met their fates.

In fact, the option which had presented itself was neater than Crystalman's original plan: there would be no bodies requiring a cover story; Fort, Lovecraft, Links and O'Malley would simply vanish from the world. No one else knew their plan. No one else would ever know. As for Johnny Sanguine... what he called the Primal Mind had spoken to him; Crystalman had listened to the echoes of his dreams and was well aware of what he wanted. Well, the prize would be given to him, but not quite in the manner he was expecting...

'Vampires!' said Crystalman contemptuously. 'What a tiresome lot you are. So many worse things than you!'

He manipulated the controls of the telaug, switching the psychic connection from Rusty Links to John Carter. The detective had been Crystalman's guest in the Dero caverns some time ago – not that he remembered, of course – as had the Chief of Police. They had been placed, unconscious, in the telaug machine and their brain patterns recorded, so that they might serve as Crystalman's spies in the Police Department. Carter had no memory of being taken over by Crystalman, or of pointing his gun at Fort's head and speaking with a voice that was not his. From his point of view, he had been taking Fort and the others in – that was all – until they had been ambushed.

Carter was sitting in a hospital examination room, being attended to by a doctor.

'Mild concussion, Lieutenant,' said the doctor. 'Nothing to worry about, but I'd take it easy for the next day or so.'

'Wish I could, doc,' Carter replied, 'but that's not going to be possible.'

The doctor sighed. 'Well… try, huh?'

Crystalman watched as Carter left the hospital and drove back to the stationhouse, where Dave Wiseman was waiting for him. Once he had assured his partner that he was all right, he asked Wiseman where he had put the rock book.

'In the evidence room, like you told me to,' Wiseman replied.

'Okay, good.'

'Listen, John,' said Wiseman. 'Concussion, the doc said, right?'

'Right.'

'Why don't you call it a night? We've got things covered here; got patrol cars out looking for Fort and the others. You need some rest, and there's not a whole lot more you can do here.'

Carter sighed and tentatively rubbed his aching head. 'I guess you're right, Dave. I'll go and grab some shuteye. You'll call me if anything happens?'

'I sure will.'

'Okay.'

Carter walked along the corridor leading to the main entrance. As he approached the stairs leading to the basement containing the evidence room, Crystalman reached for one of the controls of the telaug.

'No sleep for you just yet, Lieutenant Carter,' he murmured. 'I need the rock book, and I need it now. You will take it from the evidence room and bring it to me.'

He flipped the lever that would switch the telaug from its observation mode to the more profound connection that would allow him to control Carter's actions.

Carter changed direction suddenly and took the stairs down to the basement. He walked swiftly along a corridor and entered the Evidence Room. The duty officer behind the counter looked up from some paperwork and said: 'Evening, Lieutenant. What can I do for you?'

'Evening, Hank. Dave Wiseman brought an item in here not too long ago.'

Hank nodded. 'Uh huh. The Falcon case, right?'

'Right. I need it. The Chief wants to take a look.'

'Okay, hold on.'

Hank went through into another room, and returned a few moments later with a large, brown evidence bag, which he placed on the counter.

Carter signed for it, said goodnight and left the Evidence Room.

Crystalman smiled, and said in barely more than a whisper: 'Now… bring it to me, Lieutenant Carter… bring it to me.'

He threw some more switches and watched the display screen. Presently, a face appeared – or rather, a twisted caricature of a face: bloated, pockmarked, slobbering, a landscape of malice and depravity from which stared two pitch-black, soulless eyes.

The face of a Dero.

'What you want?' grunted the apparition.

'You have visitors coming soon.'

'When you leave? When you give us back places you took?'

Crystalman sighed. 'When I'm ready, and not before.'

'You stole from us. You stole places from us. When you give back?'

'We have had this conversation before.'

The hideous face sneered at him.

'I tell you again, you have *visitors* coming *soon*.'

'Visitors?'

'People from the surface. Food for you. Playthings for you.'

The wide, flabby mouth twisted into a leering travesty of a smile. 'We like people. People taste good. People scream loud when we play.'

'I thought you'd be pleased.'

'Why they come? They not know Dero? They not know be scared?'

'Oh, they know about you. They're coming to take more things from you, more caverns, more machines. They're coming to kill you.'

The face of the Dero twitched several times and then twisted into an expression of utter, mindless rage and hatred. 'They come to take? They come to kill? *No!* They not take, not kill. *We* kill! We kill and eat! But first we play… we show them games… games to make them scream loud! Scream for long time! We eat them while they live! Ha! We eat them while they live and scream!'

The Dero lifted something into view. Crystalman peered at the screen, unsure at first of what he was looking at. It took him a few seconds to realise that it was part of a man's head. Probably some poor derelict they had snatched from the street under cover of night, as was their habit. The Dero fingered the shattered skull, scraping out the last few gobs of brain, which it shoved into its slavering mouth.

'He play long time. He scream long and loud, like music. We sex him long time, many of us.'

Crystalman grimaced behind his mask.

'We sex him hard! And he scream!'

'And you can do all that to the visitors who are coming. The visitors who are coming to kill you and take your places and your machines.'

The Dero's face suddenly became expressionless. 'When they come?'

'Tonight. They will descend from Long Island into the caverns.'

'Long… Island.'

'The island where I live, where my house stands. The island containing the caverns I took from you. Do you understand?'

The Dero nodded. 'The caverns you took from us.'

'And you will be waiting for them, yes?'

'We will wait for them.'

'And when they enter the caverns, they will be yours.'

'Ours, yes, and we play and eat and sex.'

'They are yours to do with as you please. You can spare me the details.'

The tragic remnants of a once-great race, Crystalman thought. *How the mighty can fall, when the universe decides it has no further use for them. I almost feel sorry for you and your kind. Were the Atlans to return from their great exodus into the cosmic depths, they would annihilate you without hesitation, even though you be their kin.*

'When you go?' demanded the Dero again. 'When... *you*... go?' The question had bubbled up once again in the creature's quagmire of a brain. They never tired of asking it, even though the answer was always the same.

On this occasion, however, Crystalman said something he had never said to the Dero before: 'If you kill these visitors... I will give your caverns back to you. I will leave and never return. You will never see me again.'

The Dero looked at him, its maw hanging open in stupefaction. 'True, this?'

'True,' said Crystalman.

The Dero uttered a gurgling cackle. 'Then we kill! We kill and eat and play and—'

Yes yes yes, and so on and so forth! Crystalman thought as he broke the connection with the deeper caverns.

His promise would, he was sure, spur the Dero to even greater efforts to capture Fort and the others when they entered the caverns. The promise, of course, was quite genuine. When all this was over, when the rock book had been secured and the spirit of Haq ul'Suun released from the Martian Falcon, Crystalman would have no further need for these caverns.

The Dero could have them.

He hoped that they would enjoy them in the brief span of existence remaining to them.

CHAPTER 32
The Dero Cavern

They headed out to Long Island in O'Malley's car, all the while keeping watchful eyes on the other traffic, on constant lookout for a cop car slowing or changing direction suddenly. They saw several squad cars during the journey, but none of the cops recognised them, and they passed without incident.

Manorville was a small, unprepossessing town on the eastern edge of the Pine Barrens Preserve, a 100,000-acre swathe of pine forest on the eastern side of Long Island. They had no trouble finding the exploratory shaft that had been sunk there in 1895: it was about a mile outside of town and was enclosed within a circular chain link fence topped with barbed wire and sporting a sign every hundred feet or so that said:

DANGER!
DO NOT ENTER
PENALTY FOR UNAUTHORIZED ENTRY:
$10,000 FINE AND FIVE YEARS IMPRISONMENT

As O'Malley brought the car to a halt and switched off the engine, Fort took the case from between his feet, opened it and took out the Teleforce Projector and the Anomalous Oscillation Detector. He put the AOD in his jacket pocket.

The headlamp beams of another car cut through the darkness. The gigantic limousine pulled up alongside them and Capone got out, followed by his zombies.

'Right on time,' said Fort. He turned to look at the others. 'Ready?'

'We're ready, Charles,' said Lovecraft.

'Then let's go.'

They got out of the car and approached Capone.

'How'd you get your car back?' asked Fort. 'You left it on the Expressway… totalled, as I recall.'

'Think I only got one limo?' said Capone. 'What kinda deadbeat you think I am?'

'He probably got it from his hideout, Charles,' said Lovecraft quietly.

'Gee, thanks for putting me straight, Howard,' said Fort.

Capone gestured to one of his zombies, who took three Tommy guns from the limousine and handed them to Lovecraft, O'Malley and Rusty. 'I take it you won't be needing one,' said Capone to Fort, with a nod at the Projector.

'Not likely,' Fort replied.

The zombie reached into the limousine again and withdrew a large knapsack, which he slung over his shoulder.

'What's in the bag?' asked Rusty as she checked her Tommy gun.

'Hand grenades,' said Capone. 'Thought they might come in useful.'

Fort nodded his approval and glanced at Lovecraft, who was examining his gun in the same way an archaeologist might examine a strange artefact. 'You okay there, Howard?'

'I… well, I must confess that I've never used a firearm before.'

Capone laughed. 'Nothin' to it, librarian; just point and fire, but watch out for the recoil. It'll jump around like a rat in a sack. And speakin' of rats, where's Sanguine?'

'Nice to see you, too, Al,' said a voice from the darkness. Sanguine sauntered into the island of light from the cars' headlamps.

'And your men?' said Capone.

'Oh, they're around.'

'What do you mean "around"?' asked O'Malley.

'Never mind. They're here – that's all you need to know. Now, let's get on with this.'

There was a gate in the chain link fence, which was secured with a stout padlock. Capone reached for it, but Fort stopped him. Brandishing the Projector, he said: 'I want to try this out.'

As Capone stepped aside, Fort switched on the Projector. Remembering what Tesla had shown him, he adjusted the beam to its narrowest setting, took aim at the padlock and pressed the trigger.

A glowing blue wire of energy leaped from the muzzle and struck the lock, which fizzed and crackled, and then popped like a kernel of corn in a skillet. It dropped to the ground in incandescent orange pieces.

'Not bad,' said Capone. 'Hey, Charlie, if we get outta this, I wanna buy that gizmo off of you, okay?'

Fort grinned at Capone. *Yeah, and my uncle's the King of England, you crazy metal bastard*, he thought. He pushed open the gate and walked towards the bunker-like concrete structure that stood at the centre of the enclosure. The structure was a squat cylinder about twenty feet in diameter and ten high, and was featureless save for a single steel door. Fort made short work of the lock and pushed open the door, which gave with the loud screech of long-disused hinges. From the nearby tree line, the pinnacles of the pines exploded with the dark shapes of startled birds.

O'Malley had pilfered a couple of flashlights from the maintenance room of the Visitation Rectory. He took them out and handed one to Lovecraft, who took it and glanced uncertainly at it and his awkwardly-held Tommy gun. Rusty sighed and took the flashlight from him. Capone had his own light, bolted to his left shoulder.

They played the beams around the room, which contained nothing but a ten-foot-wide circular hole in the centre of the floor.

'Looks inviting, don't it?' said Capone as he leaned over the edge of the concrete maw and looked down, his shoulder-mounted flashlight moving back and forth. 'Can't see the bottom.'

'It goes down about three hundred feet,' said Fort, walking around the edge until he reached a line of steel rungs set into the concrete. 'Inspection ladder. Come on.' Shouldering the Teleforce Projector, he sat and swung his legs over the edge, then began to descend.

Capone moved forward, but Rusty jumped in front of him. 'You last,' she said. 'You must weigh half a ton. I don't want you ripping the ladder out before the rest of us get down there.'

Capone grunted and moved aside.

One by one, they followed Fort into the depths, their flashlight beams playing across the curved wall of the shaft and picking out discoloured vertical streaks of water-stained concrete and patches of dark green lichen that glinted wetly. The only sounds were those of their breathing and the echoing clicks of their shoes on the steel rungs.

Ten minutes later, they all reached the bottom of the shaft, including Capone, who was holding several of the inspection ladder's rungs in his massive metal hands. 'They came loose,' he said. 'Might have a job getting out this way. Didn't let them drop. Didn't want to make a noise.'

'Good thinking,' said Fort. 'And don't worry about getting out. If all goes to plan and we manage to survive the night, we'll get out through Crystalman's house.'

They looked around at the cavern into which the exploratory shaft had penetrated twenty years previously. It was large – about as big as a good-sized cathedral. In fact, it reminded Fort of a cathedral, with its high, fluted walls which met in a series of misshapen arches about a hundred feet above their heads. The similarity was further strengthened by the gigantic statues which stood against the walls, some upright, some partially toppled on the uneven ground – although any resemblance to human art was fleeting at best.

The statues were grotesque representations of strange beings, perhaps gods, or perhaps the inhabitants of distant and unknown worlds. They were the nameless denizens of the night of prehistory; of the time of the Atlans, when the

Australopithecine ancestors of humanity barked and jabbered and looked uncomprehendingly at the godlike beings who had made the world their home.

'Highly stylised,' whispered Lovecraft, as he regarded the statues with their etiolated forms, their bulbous eyes and strangely-shaped heads. 'At least, one would *hope* that they're stylised.'

Fort took a small compass from his pocket and consulted it. 'We need to head east,' he said. 'Come on. This way.' He moved off across the boulder-strewn floor of the cavern, slowly sweeping the darkness ahead with the barrel of the Teleforce Projector. 'Light!' he whispered harshly. 'I need more light! Cormack! Miss Links!'

Rusty and O'Malley fell in beside him. He glanced at Rusty. 'Can you shift yet?'

She hesitated and then shook her head. 'Still nothing. Damn that Carter and his stupid little gun!'

'Odds are it's not his. He must have got it from Crystalman. God knows how many other people he's got up his sleeve.'

Rusty glanced around, her eyes darting fearfully at the walls and ceiling of the cavern.

'That's right,' said Fort. 'Keep a lookout for the Dero. That goes for the rest of you,' he added over his shoulder.

'Yeah,' Rusty replied. 'I'm watching for them… but I'm also watching for the air elementals…'

'I don't think you need to worry too much about them,' said Fort.

She glanced at him. 'Why not? They've been hounding me up the entire eastern seaboard.'

'But they left you alone once you got to New York, didn't they? Once you came to me. Crystalman called them off. He knows we're coming, and he's got us exactly where he wants us.'

'*What?* When were you planning on telling the rest of us?'

'I've only just figured it out, dummy that I am!' Fort replied disgustedly.

'Figured what out, Charles?' asked Lovecraft, who had fallen in behind them.

'I'm afraid there'll be no element of surprise, Howard. Crystalman's onto us. He knows what we're planning. He's known all along that I was involved with the Falcon case; he got that from Carter, of course. Once he knew that Rusty here was coming to see me, he called off the air elementals and let her do just that. Maybe that was a change of plan on his part, but it suited his purposes. Apart from Carter, we're the only people who know about his plan, the only people who have the slightest chance of stopping him. And now...'

'Now we're heading directly for him. And he's prepared,' said Lovecraft. 'That is rather... vexing.'

Fort came to a halt. 'I've made a mistake – a bad one. We shouldn't have come here. We should have gone after the rock book. Shit! We should have gone after the rock book!'

'And tried to raid a stationhouse full of cops?' said Rusty. 'We wouldn't have stood a chance.'

'We'd have stood more of a chance than we do here.'

'It's all my fault,' said Rusty miserably. 'Somehow... somehow Crystalman's inside my head. He knows what I'm going to do as soon as I decide to do it.'

'Don't be too hard on yourself, Miss Links,' said Lovecraft. 'After all, you were the one who told us Crystalman's plan. You also provided us with the means to defeat him... if only Lieutenant Carter hadn't arrived when he did.'

Rusty glanced back at him and smiled. 'Thank you, Mr. Lovecraft.'

'You're most welcome, madam.'

Fort gave Lovecraft a sharp glance. 'Don't get all mushy on me, Howard. This dame's still trouble with a capital T.' He fell silent, thinking.

'So why did you let me come along, if I'm so much trouble?' said Rusty huffily.

'You know why. You're a shapeshifter. As a weapon, you're at least as powerful as this Teleforce Projector...'

'Assuming I get my ability back sometime soon.'

'Yeah... assuming that.'

'Hey, what's the hold up?' demanded Capone. 'Keep movin', ya buncha numbnuts!'

Fort turned to answer him, and then stopped, open-mouthed. Capone saw the expression on his face, and turned to look behind them, as did O'Malley.

The way back was blocked by at least fifty Dero, with more scuttling into the cavern from unseen recesses in the walls. Completely naked, their genitals dangling obscenely between their bowed, thickly-muscled legs, the creatures began to shamble towards them. Their filthy, distorted faces grinned, revealing blackened and broken teeth.

'Welcome!' they cried in their ragged, gurgling voices. *'Welcommme!'*

CHAPTER 33
Farewell, My Zombie

'Let them have it, boys!' shouted Capone.

His twelve undead soldiers turned as one, raised their submachine guns and fired. The cavern was instantly filled with the cacophony of exploding shells and the stench of cordite, but the noise was nothing compared to the insane, hate-filled, agonised shrieking of the Dero as the bullets tore into them, painting the dank air with thick, black blood.

More Dero appeared, hobbling over the ruptured bodies of their fallen comrades, screaming with rage, their wide, shapeless mouths dripping with greenish slobber. They fell upon one zombie and ripped him to shreds, hurling chunks of flesh at the others, who took no notice and continued to fire.

'Grenades!' shouted Capone. 'Grenades, you dumb fucks!'

The zombie carrying the knapsack reached in, took a grenade, pulled the pin and lobbed it at the writhing mass of Dero. Half a dozen of them were blown to bloody fragments, but that didn't stop them coming.

Rusty, O'Malley and Capone opened up with their own weapons – as did Lovecraft, but the recoil of his Tommy gun took him by surprise. He lost his footing on the rubble-strewn ground and fell flat on his back, his finger still squeezing the trigger. The bullets struck the ceiling, dislodging a large piece of masonry which plummeted to the ground, crushing another two dozen Dero.

'Not bad, librarian!' cried Capone. 'We'll make a wise guy of you yet!'

'I regret to say that is not one of my ambitions, Mr. Capone,' Lovecraft replied as he dragged himself to his feet and resumed firing.

Fort stepped forward and adjusted the Teleforce Projector to its wide-beam setting. He fired from the hip, hosing the still-advancing Dero with a glowing spray of blue death. Those it touched blew apart as if made of tissue paper, and yet others unhesitatingly advanced to take their place.

'For the love of God!' O'Malley cried. 'How many of these bastards are there?'

'More than we can handle like this!' Fort shouted back. He glanced at the power indicator gauge on the side of the Projector. The needle was at the 75% mark. He had just used a quarter of the device's electrical charge. 'Shit!' he said. 'Tesla never told us it was *this* thirsty.'

The zombie with the grenades lobbed another one and took out a half dozen more Dero. Another three of his fellows had been taken down, pummelled and dismembered, the dripping fragments of their bodies thrown into the smoke-filled air like confetti.

Dozens of Dero lay in bloody lumps on the ground, and yet they still came, howling and mewling and cursing at the interlopers; shouting at the tops of their lungs all the things they were going to do to them. Lovecraft caught snippets of this and was glad he couldn't make out the rest.

Fort glanced over his shoulder and caught sight of a small tunnel mouth in the cavern's far wall. It was in the direction they had been headed, which was a plus. 'Come on!' he yelled. 'This way!'

They all sprinted across the cavern, as yet more Dero appeared from out of side galleries to their left and right, converging on them with terrifying speed. Capone was behind the others, and several of the creatures leaped upon him, smashing his head and torso with their calloused fists. He grabbed one, threw it to the ground and stamped on its head, which exploded like a ripe watermelon. He seized another and ripped it limb from limb, then used one of its legs to beat the others to death. 'I love a good fight!' he roared. *'I'm a sucker for a good fight! Come on, the rest of you – whattaya waitin' for? I'll mash you all to a fuckin' pulp, you maggots!'*

Fort ran into the mouth of the tunnel and skidded to a halt. The tunnel contained a monorail, on top of which sat a bulbous car fashioned from a dull, pewter-hued metal. The car contained several bench seats, and the controls appeared to consist of a single lever and a number of dials. *Could we be that lucky?* he wondered as he reached into the car and pushed the lever.

Nothing whatsoever happened. He bent down to look under the car, and saw a mass of shredded wiring. *I guess not,* he thought. He peered along the tunnel, which seemed to be empty.

He heard O'Malley's voice calling out: 'Charlie! We're in trouble here!'

He ran back to the mouth of the tunnel and shouted: 'Looks clear this way!'

Capone paused in his decimation of the Dero who were unwise enough to go up against him, then turned and shouted to the zombie with the grenades: 'Hey, Milo! Toss me the sack!'

The zombie did so and then went back to work on the Dero with his machine gun. He was the only one left, and it was only a few more moments before he, too, went down under their relentless onslaught.

'So long, fellas,' said Capone as he strode swiftly into the tunnel mouth. The others were already inside. 'Run like hell,' he said, as he took out one grenade and pulled the pin.

Fort, Lovecraft, Rusty and O'Malley ran.

Capone cast a single glance at the advancing Dero, and then looked down at the eight grenades remaining in the sack. He dropped the grenade he was holding into the sack, let it fall to the ground and flicked the pin at the Dero.

Then he, too, ran like hell.

CHAPTER 34
Out of the Frying Pan...

The explosion knocked them all off their feet, except for Capone, who planted his massive piston-driven legs wide and took the force of the blast. Almost immediately, there was a deep, powerful rumbling as the roof of the tunnel behind them collapsed, cutting off the still-advancing Dero.

'That's bought us some time, I reckon,' said Capone with a wide grin.

'That it has,' said Fort as he got to his feet. 'By the way, has anyone seen Sanguine?'

'Not since the Dero appeared,' O'Malley replied. 'Can't say I'm surprised.'

'Me neither,' said Capone. 'Fuckin' night-walkin' coward! But he'll be back when the fightin's done, mark my words.'

'I don't doubt it,' muttered Fort. 'Okay, let's keep going. This is just an Atlan transit tunnel, built for the monorail.'

'Do you think there are more Dero in here?' asked Lovecraft as he peered uncertainly into the darkness ahead.

'I doubt it,' Fort replied. 'It's too narrow for them to come through in much more than single file. Doesn't suit their tactics. My guess is we'll be okay for a while. But we shouldn't hang around...'

'Then let's go,' said Capone.

As they made their way along the transit tunnel, they heard the distant shouts and grunts of the Dero echoing strangely.

The vast honeycomb network of caverns and tunnels was acting as an amplifier, so that it seemed as though the enemy were all around them – which was, in fact, the case.

Presently, the tunnel opened into a vast cylindrical chamber, the centre of which was dominated by a complex switching mechanism for the monorail cars. There were five other openings in the curved wall, containing other monorails.

They cast their flashlight beams up and could make out at least ten more levels in the gloom above them, each with its own switching mechanism anchored to the wall of the cylinder by thick metal stanchions.

'Transit hubs,' said Fort, pointing at the multiple openings in the chamber wall high above, each of which contained a monorail.

Lovecraft looked around at the five other tunnels on their level. 'But which do we choose? And is the right one even on this level? We certainly can't get up to any of the others…'

Fort checked his compass again and pointed to one of the openings. 'That one heads east, more or less. That's the direction we need to be headed.'

'YES,' said a voice that boomed and echoed through the switching chamber. They all jumped at the cacophonous sound. 'THAT IS THE DIRECTION YOU NEED TO TAKE.'

'What the *fuck*!' shouted Capone.

'Crystalman,' said Fort. 'You can hear us?'

'I CAN HEAR YOU AND SEE YOU,' the booming voice replied. 'I CAN WATCH YOUR ACTIONS AND DIVINE YOUR THOUGHTS AND INTENTIONS. YOU HAVE COME FAR. I CONGRATULATE YOU.'

'Keep you damned congratulations!' cried Fort. 'We've come to stop you, Crystalman. We know what you're planning to do, and we've come to put an end to it.'

'I KNOW. I APPLAUD YOUR EFFORTS, BUT I REGRET TO TELL YOU THAT YOU WILL FAIL. YOU KNOW THIS YOURSELVES IN YOUR HEARTS. AT THE VERY CENTRE OF YOUR CONSCIOUSNESS LAY THE SEED

OF DOUBT, WHICH HAS ALREADY FLOWERED INTO THE REALISATION THAT YOU CANNOT SUCCEED... FOR YOU KNOW WHO AND WHAT I REALLY AM.'

'Yes,' said Fort. 'You're an avatar of Nyarlathotep, the Crawling Chaos, Messenger of the Great Old Ones... the only one of them who has ever interacted directly with humanity – and then only to cause misery and strife amongst us.'

'You are the great antagonist, the being of a thousand forms,' added O'Malley. 'You have always delighted in the cultivation of madness upon the Earth... that has always been your aim, your terrible delight... so why, now, do you want to destroy it?'

'DO YOU THINK EARTH IS MY ONLY PLAYGROUND, PRIEST? DO YOU THINK THAT CRYSTALMAN IS ANYTHING MORE THAN THE MEREST FRAGMENT, THE THINNEST SHARD, THE MOST SUBTLE AND FLEETING SHADOW OF NYARLATHOTEP? HOW SMALL YOUR MINDS! HOW WEAK YOUR HEARTS!'

'You haven't answered my question,' said O'Malley. 'Why must this particular... *playground* be destroyed?'

'BECAUSE MY FATHER HAS BID IT TO BE SO. HIS GAZE AND HIS BREATH HAVE GROWN RESTLESS IN THEIR CONFINEMENT AT THE CENTRE OF THE RED PLANET; THEY GROW WEARY OF THEIR QUANTUM ENTANGLEMENT WITH THE MIND OF HAQ UL'SUUN; THEY WISH TO BE FREE TO SATE THEMSELVES ON THE EARTH, JUST AS THEY DID ON MARS FIVE MILLION YEARS AGO.'

'Is that what *you* want, Crystalman?' asked Fort. 'If that happens, your playground will be taken away; your toys will be gone...'

The voice laughed. 'I SAY AGAIN: HOW SMALL YOUR MINDS! DO YOU THINK THIS IS THE ONLY EARTH? THERE ARE COUNTLESS OTHERS IN NEIGHBOURING DIMENSIONS: AN INFINITE NUMBER OF PLAYGROUNDS, AN INFINITE NUMBER OF TINY BEINGS TO BE TORMENTED. ALL

DIFFERENT.' The voice laughed again. 'THERE IS EVEN ONE, LOVECRAFT, WHERE I AND THE REST OF MY KIN ARE THE CREATIONS OF YOUR IMAGINATION, FOR IN A UNIVERSE THAT IS INFINITE IN EXTENT AND ETERNAL IN TIME, ALL THINGS COME TO PASS. WHEN THIS EARTH IS DONE, I SHALL MOVE ON TO ANOTHER, AND ANOTHER, THROUGHOUT TIME AND SPACE, INTO ETERNITY!'

The voice of Crystalman paused, and then concluded: 'BUT NOW IT IS TIME FOR YOU TO EXIT THIS LITTLE DRAMA, FOR YOU ARE ABOUT TO BECOME THE PLAYTHINGS OF THE DERO, AND I MUST PREPARE FOR THE ARRIVAL OF LIEUTENANT CARTER, WHO IS DESCENDING TO MY CAVERNS AS WE SPEAK. FAREWELL!'

'We're too late,' said Lovecraft, his voice heavy with despair. 'Dear God, we're too late!'

'And here come the Dero,' added O'Malley, indicating the mouths of the transit tunnels all around them, from which the vile, misshapen creatures of the Inner Earth had begun to emerge, their hideous faces twisted with lopsided grins of anticipation.

Fort and the others looked up at the vast cylindrical shaft stretching into the distance far above. More Dero were emerging from the tunnel mouths along its length and scuttling down towards them, clinging to the wall like huge, hungry spiders.

Fort glanced back the way they had come. There would be no escape through that tunnel, thanks to Capone's grenades.

O'Malley looked at Fort. 'Well, Charlie, what do we do now?'

'I have no idea,' said Fort.

CHAPTER 35
Manticore

'Well, Miss Links,' said Fort, 'looks like you're going to get your comeuppance after all. Nevertheless... I'm sorry it has to be *this* way.'

He glanced at her and frowned. She was looking down at herself, a smile spreading slowly across her face. She handed him her machine gun and replied: 'We're not finished yet, Mr. Fort.'

Then she took a couple of steps towards the advancing Dero and began to take off her clothes. They halted, eyeing her, their mouths open and drooling. Fort and the others were disgusted to see their rapidly growing erections.

Rusty tossed her clothes to Lovecraft. 'Be a darling and hold onto these for me, would you? I'll need them back later.'

The drug's worn off, thought Fort. *She can feel it*.

Now completely naked, Rusty turned back to the Dero and said: 'Is this what you want?'

The creatures responded with loud, lustful grunts.

'Well, boys,' she laughed. 'Good luck getting it!' She glanced at Fort and the others. 'When I'm through changing, climb aboard.'

'Aboard what?' said Lovecraft.

'You'll see.'

The transformation was rapid, and astonishing and terrifying to behold. Rusty's beautiful naked form expanded and darkened, quickly shedding all resemblance to a human being and becoming...

'A manticore,' whispered Lovecraft. His mouth hung open in astonishment and his eyes were wide with wonder and terror. 'She's turned into a manticore!'

The great beast of Persian legend possessed the body of a lion – albeit three times the size of a normal one – and the head of a handsome, mahogany-skinned man with long, flowing black hair. From its shoulders sprouted two enormous, bat-like, membranous wings, and its thrashing tail was the segmented whip of a scorpion. The comma-shaped stinger at the tip was the size of a large watermelon.

The manticore's mouth widened in a combination of snarl and feral grin, revealing three rows of glinting white teeth like those of a shark.

Enraged that the object of their lust had become this outrageous beast, the Dero howled and surged forward.

The manticore roared in return and brought its whipping tail to bear.

'Get down!' screamed Lovecraft. 'The tail! The venom!'

They all threw themselves flat upon the ground as the barbed tip of the stinger sprayed a thick, milk-white liquid in every direction, drenching the onrushing Dero, whose bodies fizzed and bubbled and collapsed into melting puddles of gore.

'Come on!' shouted Fort as he shouldered the Teleforce Projector and climbed onto the manticore's back, securing himself with great handfuls of the creature's long, thick fur. The others followed suit; Capone climbed onto the hindquarters, whose muscles flexed and rippled as they took his weight.

The bat wings spread wide and slapped the air, and the manticore launched itself from the floor of the shaft, its handsome face straining with the effort. As it steadily ascended through the shaft, its tail swung around, spraying the Dero who were still clinging to the walls with its venom. They screamed and fell, landing amongst the others with loud, messy splats.

The manticore had reached a height of a hundred feet or so when an insistent bleeping emerged from one of Fort's pockets. Reaching with one hand, the other still clutching the creature's fur, he withdrew the Anomalous Oscillation Detector. The yellow light was on.

'Hold on, Miss Links!' he cried. 'We're within two hundred yards of the Falcon!'

The manticore paused in its ascent, its wings scything the air with great whooshing sounds. A tunnel mouth loomed directly in front of them.

'In there,' said Fort. 'That way!'

The manticore surged forward and into the tunnel, alighting on the floor and folding its wings away. Fort and the others began to climb down, but the manticore said in a powerful, inhuman voice: 'No! Stay on my back. Quicker like this, Mr. Fort. There will be more passageways. Tell me which way to go.'

Fort held the AOD in front of him, keeping an eye on the yellow light. 'All right, Miss Links. Away we go.'

With Fort and the others still on its broad back, the manticore sprang forward into the darkness.

None of them noticed that they were being followed; that they had, in fact, been followed ever since they descended through the borehole from the surface of Long Island... by a small bat.

A vampire bat.

CHAPTER 36
The Falcon and the Rock Book

The avatar of Nyarlathotep that called itself Crystalman watched as the elevator containing Lieutenant John Carter descended to the floor of the cavern in which he had his 'drawing room'. The elevator doors opened and Carter emerged, carrying the ninth rock book.

'Welcome, Lieutenant,' said Crystalman.

Carter walked towards him, his face expressionless, and handed him the rock book. Crystalman examined it in the manner of an antiques collector who had been presented with a particularly attractive *objet d'art*. 'Quaint technology,' he mused. 'Quite delightful, in its own way. Come.' He beckoned Carter to follow him as he walked across the chamber to the monorail car.

'You have done very well, Lieutenant Carter,' he continued as the car sped through the transit tunnel, towards the chamber containing the telaug machine and the Martian Falcon.

Carter said nothing – nor did Crystalman expect him to, for in this state he was voiceless unless given a voice through the telaug. It amused him, however, to converse with his slave like this, as if the man's sleeping consciousness were awake.

'And for that reason, I shall allow you to witness the beginning of the end: the process that will bring about the denouement of Earth's long history. It will be quite fascinating, I assure you. Perhaps I shall release your mind from its confinement in the moment before the end begins, so that you may see that which you have helped to unleash.'

A minute later, the monorail car swept into the chamber and slowed to a halt. Crystalman and Carter got out. Carrying the rock book, Crystalman walked across to the telaug machine and flicked a few switches. The large, asymmetrical display screen flickered to life, revealing an image of Mars.

'The Atlan penetrays are most useful,' said Crystalman. 'They can produce a real-time image of any location in the world, or in the Solar System.' He examined the ruddy-hued image of the dead planet for a moment and then smiled beneath his crystal mask. 'Soon,' he whispered.

He turned from the machine, walked to the centre of the chamber and placed the rock book on the floor. Then he went to the table on which the Martian Falcon stood, gently picked up the statuette and carried it towards the rock book.

When he had got to within five feet of the book, it sprang open, unfolding itself again and again by means of tiny metal hinges concealed within its mineral pages, until it had transformed itself into a single rectangle which covered an area of the floor about ten feet by eight.

'You see, Lieutenant?' said Crystalman over his shoulder. 'An automatic process. At the end of the punishment, the Martians would place the rock book in the near vicinity of the Bird of Justice. The book would open out automatically into the device you see now. All that was then required was for the bird to be placed at the centre of the device, and the mind of the prisoner would be released. Normally, of course, the prisoner's body would be nearby, waiting to receive the mind... but poor Haq ul'Suun's body was destroyed five million years ago. There is nowhere for his mind to go.'

He lifted the Falcon and the silently-raging mind it contained and held it before his eyes. 'I am sorry,' he said. 'Your freedom will be short-lived indeed. With no physical form to inhabit, you will fade from the universe, and with your dissolution, the quantum bonds which bind the breath and gaze of Azathoth will be broken. Let it be so!'

Crystalman walked onto the stone rectangle. As he did so, a pale, circular glow ignited at the centre. He walked to it and placed the Falcon there, then stepped back onto the floor of the chamber. 'This will take some time,' he said. 'It has been five million years since the Falcon or the rock book were required to perform their function. They are unused to this activity...' He glanced at the telaug screen. 'And yet, even now Mars trembles!'

The image on the screen showed a great gathering of red-orange clouds which began to obscure the surface of Mars, as if the distant world were experiencing a planet-wide quake which cast gargantuan plumes of dust into the thin atmosphere.

'It stirs,' said Crystalman. 'Already it stirs! Soon, it will emerge!'

He glanced at the Falcon, which had begun to take on the same glow that was now slowly pulsating at the centre of the rock book. His glance flew to Carter. 'Now, Lieutenant, let us rouse you from your own slumber, so that you may gaze upon the instrument of your own destruction, and that of your world.'

He moved across to the telaug and called up Carter's brain pattern on a small screen. His hand approached the lever that would break the machine's influence.

'Crystalman!' shouted a voice.

He turned in the direction of the voice, which came from a monorail tunnel heading deeper into the cavern system beneath Long Island.

The manticore exploded from the mouth of the tunnel and skidded to a halt. On its back were Fort, Lovecraft, O'Malley and Capone.

Crystalman laughed harshly. 'Your efforts were admirable, but you're too late! The Falcon has been reunited with the rock book. The breath and gaze of Azathoth are stirring.' He pointed to the telaug screen. 'Look! See how Mars shudders with their awakening!'

Fort unshouldered the Teleforce Projector and took aim at the rock book. 'We'll see about that!' he cried.

'Carter!' shouted Crystalman. 'Your needle gun. Shoot the manticore!'

Carter reached into his jacket and withdrew the weapon.

'Capone!' yelled Fort.

The diesel-powered gangster jumped down from the manticore as Carter took aim, and flung himself into the line of fire. The needle bounced harmlessly off his metal chest and dropped to the floor. Carter moved to the side, looking for another clear shot, but before he could do so, Capone had sprinted across the chamber, his metal feet smashing thunderously into the stone floor, and sent the detective flying against the wall. Carter slumped to the floor and lay still.

Fort took aim at the rock book and fired the Projector. The flood of incandescent energy splashed against it, making it glow even more... but it remained intact.

'Damn it!' shouted Fort.

'You've still got it set to a wide dispersal, Charles,' said Lovecraft. 'Try narrowing the beam. That may do the trick.'

'You could be right, Howard,' said Fort as he twisted the control on the side of the Projector.

At that moment, the small bat that had been following them ever since they entered the realm of the Dero fluttered into the chamber and hovered above Carter's needle gun, which lay on the floor near his unconscious body.

The bat exploded in a shower of darkness which instantly coalesced into the form of a black-suited man. The man reached for the needle gun, brought it up swiftly and fired at the manticore. The needle struck the beast in the face. The manticore staggered, its bat wings spreading as if in an effort to escape what had already happened.

The great beast fell onto its side, throwing off Fort, Lovecraft and O'Malley. The Projector flew from Fort's hands and skittered across the floor.

Capone lunged for the vampire, but he was far too fast – supernaturally fast – and in another instant he was across the chamber and seizing the Projector.

'Good evening, everyone,' said Johnny Sanguine, who appeared beside the vampire. 'This is Carmine, my right-hand man. We've been keeping an eye on you ever since Charlie and the gang came down from the surface.' He looked down at Rusty Links, in her true form once more, lying unconscious on the floor. A thin trickle of blood issued from the puncture wound below her left eye. He shook his head. 'Twice in one night. You gotta be more careful, hon.'

'Sanguine,' said Fort, dragging himself to his feet. 'Shoot the rock book. Shatter it with the Teleforce beam. Do it now!'

'Now why would I want to do that?' Johnny said.

'Haq ul'Suun's prison is weakening. He'll be free soon, and then so will Azathoth!'

Johnny laughed. 'Yeah? So what?'

'You nightwalkin' son of a bitch!' shouted Capone as he stamped towards him.

Johnny nodded at Carmine, and he fired the Projector at Capone.

The gangster screamed and fell to his knees. 'Bastard! Right in the gearbox!'

This wasn't a euphemism – not that Capone ever used them. The Teleforce beam had sliced through the complex arrangement of cogs and differentials in Capone's pelvic region, robbing him of the ability to move his legs. He toppled onto his side, cursing.

Johnny nodded to Carmine again, and the vampire aimed the Projector at the rock book.

'How long until the prison opens?' asked Johnny.

'A minute… perhaps two,' Crystalman replied. 'What are you doing, Mr. Sanguine?' They all could hear the tension in his voice.

'If Carmine here fires at the rock book, it'll shatter, won't it?' said Johnny.

Crystalman hesitated. 'No, it won't.'

Johnny smiled. 'Don't kid a kidder. I know you're lying. I'd feel it in my bones, if I had any. If the book shatters, Haq ul'Suun's mind will stay inside the Falcon, and your daddy's breath and gaze – or whatever the fuck you want to call that thing at the centre of Mars – will stay there, forever. That's right, isn't it?'

'What do you want, Mr. Sanguine?' asked Crystalman, the tension in his voice rising.

'What do *I* want?'

'Yes. You haven't ordered your man to fire yet. That means you want something. Could it be…? Ah, yes! You want to be corporeal again, don't you? You see… you're not the only one who's been keeping an eye on things.'

Johnny smiled. 'Yeah, that's what I want.'

'Well, I can give it to you, if you have your man lower the weapon.' He pointed to the telaug machine. 'This is an analogue of the punishment machines of ancient Mars. Not only can it read minds, it can *transfer* them. This is your way back to the physical world… this is what your dreams were telling you. All you need is a body for your soul to inhabit… hers, perhaps?' Crystalman indicated Rusty's unconscious form. 'It would be a fitting punishment for her, would it not… for her betrayal?'

'Yeah,' said Johnny, eyeing her. 'It would.'

'Then have your man put down the weapon,' said Crystalman, glancing at the telaug's main display, 'and we can discuss this further.'

'And what happens then?' said Fort. 'Azathoth'll be all over this planet like bad acne, and you'll be destroyed along with the rest of us, Sanguine!'

'Not if Crystalman takes me with him to one of those other Earths he mentioned.'

'Ah!' said Crystalman. 'So, you want to accompany me when I depart this world? Clever! That, too, is possible. So come! Lower the weapon, and we'll get you safely installed in Miss Links's body while the breath of Azathoth makes the journey to Earth.'

'How do I know you'll keep your end of the deal?' asked Sanguine.

'The alternative is to destroy the book and remain a ghost forever… a shadow of your former self, shall we say? Besides, I like you, Mr. Sanguine. I'd be very happy to take you along. I can give you entire worlds to control, if that's what you desire.'

Johnny nodded. 'All right. Carmine, lower the weapon.'

'Hey boss,' said Carmine. 'What about me? I mean…'

'Just lower the damned weapon!'

Crystalman laughed suddenly and pointed to the rock book and the Martian Falcon. The glow enveloping both had ceased. 'Your time is up!'

'You idiot, Sanguine,' said Fort. 'He's been playing for time, stringing you along like the sap you are! Now it's too late to stop him.'

'You're quite right, Mr. Fort,' said Crystalman, pointing to the display, which showed vast tendrils of black cloud belching from the aeon-dead volcanoes of Mars. 'The quantum bonds have been broken. The breath and gaze of Azathoth are free and heading for Earth!'

CHAPTER 37
Haq ul'Suun

'Wait,' said Johnny. 'Our deal still stands, right? You're still gonna get me into that bitch's body and take me with you when you skip the planet... right?'

'Wrong, Mr. Sanguine,' Crystalman replied icily. 'The telaug machine *is* capable of that, but I have no intention of granting your request. I needed to stall you for long enough to allow the rock book to perform its function... and now that it has... well, that's just the hand you've been dealt. You will be annihilated along with everything else on the planet.'

'You goddamned son of a bitch,' said Johnny. 'Carmine, shoot him.'

'What?' said Carmine.

'You heard me. Shoot the bastard!'

'I wouldn't do that if I were you,' said Crystalman.

'Oh yeah?' said Johnny. 'Listen, popsicle-head, if I'm gonna be destroyed, then I'm taking you with me. Carmine! *Do it!*'

Carmine fired the Teleforce Projector. The beam cut Crystalman in half. His upper torso and legs fell to the floor in twitching lumps. But if Johnny Sanguine was expecting to see blood, he was sorely disappointed.

Instead, a column of bright green light shot up from the ruin of Crystalman's body, while the mouth behind the mask cackled. 'Did you think it would be that easy? I am an avatar of

Nyarlathotep! And do you know what Nyarlathotep looks like? *Behold!*

Something stepped out of the column of green light. Something that could never have existed in any sane and ordered universe.

Something that was nightmare itself.

It was at least thirty feet tall, and stood upon three tentacle-like, prehensile legs. Its thick, cylindrical torso was covered with cilia that writhed and twitched revoltingly, while from its massive shoulders there sprouted, in place of a head, a single tentacle which whipped back and forth.

'Lord God preserve and protect us!' cried O'Malley.

The head-tentacle snapped around in his direction, as if it were the thing's primary organ of sense. The tentacle reached down towards him, and O'Malley shut his eyes and whispered a final prayer.

But the thing stopped, just as it was about to seize him… and then it turned towards the Martian Falcon.

The statuette had split down the middle, its two halves lying side by side on the smooth surface of the rock book. And from it, a thick black mist had begun to issue; a miasmal vapour that grew thicker with each passing moment.

Gradually, the black mist began to form itself into a vaguely humanoid shape: long-limbed and slender. The last parts of it to coalesce were the head and face… and when they did, the thing wore an expression of such rage and hatred that Fort, Lovecraft and O'Malley turned away in uttermost terror.

'Holy shit,' said Capone from across the chamber. 'This ain't good.'

'Haq ul'Suun,' said Johnny in awe. 'It's the spirit of Haq ul'Suun!'

At the base of Nyarlathotep's head-tentacle, a mouth opened vertically and uttered an ear-splitting screech.

'Good night, all,' said Johnny, and promptly vanished.

'Boss?' said Carmine, then: 'Fuck it – I'm outta here, too!' He dropped the Teleforce Projector, transformed himself back into the bat and flitted out of the cavern as fast as his wings would carry him.

'That's more than just a spirit,' said Fort. 'Even an *alien* spirit. We've got to get out of here.'

Nyarlathotep and the spirit of Haq ul'Suun regarded each other, squaring up like two prize fighters.

Lovecraft glanced at the still-unconscious Rusty and hurried over to her. He had lost her clothes a while ago and muttered: 'My apologies, madam,' as he picked up her naked body. 'This evening really is full of firsts,' he added to himself.

'Cormack,' said Fort as he hurried across the chamber. 'You grab Capone, I'll see to Carter.' He knelt down beside the detective and slapped his face several times. 'John. John! Wake up!'

Carter groaned incoherently as Fort put his arms under his armpits and dragged him towards the monorail car in which Crystalman and Carter had travelled from the main cavern.

O'Malley tried to do the same with Capone, but could barely budge him an inch. 'Jesus!' he wheezed. 'This fecker weighs more than my car!'

Capone slid open a panel in his stomach and flipped a lever. With a loud click, his pelvis and legs detached. 'How about now?'

O'Malley tried again. 'Better,' he said as he began to drag Capone's head and torso across the floor.

Lovecraft placed Rusty in the monorail car and then rushed back to help O'Malley with Capone, while Fort heaved Carter into the vehicle. He turned as Nyarlathotep screamed again, and watched in horrified awe as the dark spirit of Haq ul'Suun forced itself into the entity's mouth.

'It shouldn't be able to do that,' he said, more to himself than anyone else, as he threw himself into the driver's seat and slammed the control lever forward. 'Nyarlathotep is a Great Old One. What the hell *is* that thing?'

The car sped out of the cavern to the sound of Nyarlathotep's screams.

A minute later, it emerged from the tunnel into the main cavern. By this time, Carter had come to, and Rusty was also stirring. She opened her eyes and looked at Lovecraft. 'Don't tell me... you lost my clothes.'

'I'm most dreadfully sorry,' Lovecraft replied.

'Forget it. At least we're alive.'

Yeah, thought Fort. *Until Azathoth arrives.*

'What the hell's going on?' said Carter. 'Charlie? Where am I?'

'No time to explain, John,' said Fort as he helped him from the car. 'We have to get out of here.'

'Where's *here*? Last thing I remember, I was at the stationhouse, about to head home for some shuteye...'

'We're under Crystalman's house on Long Island,' Fort said as he pushed Carter towards the elevator leading to the surface.

Behind them, Lovecraft, O'Malley and Rusty were dragging Capone's upper torso across the floor. 'Nice view,' said Capone, winking at Rusty.

'Shut it, bucket brain,' she said.

The floor of the cavern began to tremble as they reached the elevator and crammed themselves inside. 'Is that an earthquake?' said Carter as Fort punched the button for the surface and the doors slid shut.

'Might as well be,' Fort replied. 'I hope this thing holds up long enough to get us out of here.'

'What's the point, Charlie?' said O'Malley. 'Crystalman's won. In a few hours, we'll all be dead – every living thing on Earth. What's the difference if we die down here or up there?'

'The spirit of Haq ul'Suun is going head to head with Nyarlathotep, and it looks like he's winning,' Fort replied. 'A ghost against a Great Old One? Should be no contest, so Haq ul'Suun's got something up his sleeve. I don't know what it is, but...'

'But what, Charles?' asked Lovecraft.

Fort didn't answer.

The elevator doors opened onto a corridor. 'Come on,' said Rusty. 'This leads to the entrance hall.'

They dragged Capone after her, along the corridor, through the entrance hall and out through the front door. 'We need a car,' said Fort, glancing around. He spotted the large garage at the side of the house. 'John, get in there and hotwire us some wheels.'

'Leave it to me,' said Carter. He ran to the garage and disappeared inside.

Seconds later, a large Duesenberg convertible emerged with the top down and Carter at the wheel. The others dragged Capone into the car and Carter floored the gas pedal.

Another few seconds and they had gained the edge of the estate. 'Stop the car, John,' said Fort. 'I want to see this.'

'See what?' asked Carter, bringing the Duesenberg to a halt.

'I don't know, but like you said, it felt like an earthquake down there, so *something's* going to happen.'

Something did indeed happen.

Crystalman's mansion was instantly vaporised by a column of blue-green light that erupted from the ground, accompanied by a cacophonous shriek that made them grimace and cover their ears. The column hurtled into the sky and was lost amongst the stars.

Silence fell.

'Charlie,' said Carter. 'Now do you want to tell me what the hell just happened?'

CHAPTER 38
Lovecraft and Fort

STRANGE ACTIVITY ON MARS

ASTRONOMERS REPORT MYSTERIOUS DARK CLOUD EMERGING FROM THE RED PLANET

POSSIBLE SIGN OF THE ANCIENT MARTIAN CIVILIZATION

DR. TESLA REPORTS DISPERSAL OF THE CLOUD

Dr. Nikola Tesla has stated that the strange dark cloud which astronomers reported issuing from the volcanoes on Mars last night appears to have dispersed.

Using the 'Teslascope', a device he designed and constructed at his laboratory in Colorado Springs, he observed the phenomenon from start to finish, and has concluded that it was most likely the result of seismic activity deep within the planet.

'I observed the cloud passing across the face of Mars for approximately seventeen minutes,' he stated, 'after which it became more and more diffuse and finally faded completely from view. My opinion is that it has dispersed into the interplanetary æther, and poses no threat to Earth.'

When asked whether it might somehow be related to the mysterious transmission which he recently received from the Red Planet, Dr. Tesla refused to comment.

Fort read the newspaper report and then passed the paper to Lovecraft. They were sitting in a booth in the drugstore on the corner of Clinton Street and Atlantic Avenue, along with Rusty Links and Cormack O'Malley.

'We gonna get any zombies in here today, fellas?' asked Hans from the kitchen.

'Not today, Hans,' Fort replied as he looked at the menu.

'Well, Charles,' said Lovecraft as he finished reading the report. 'It looks like the Earth is safe from the attentions of Azathoth, although I'm still not sure how.'

'The clue was in Haq ul'Suun's power,' Fort replied. 'Five million years ago, when he opened the portal to the space between dimensions, he was in momentary contact with the breath and gaze of Azathoth. The same quantum bond that kept Azathoth's awareness imprisoned at the centre of Mars imbued the Martian's spirit with the Great Old One's power – or at least a tiny fraction of its power. That was what allowed his spirit to go up against Nyarlathotep on equal terms.'

'Know that for a fact, do you, Charlie?' asked O'Malley.

Fort smiled. 'No, not really, but when you've been in this game as long as I have, you can make educated guesses.' He tapped the newspaper with his index finger. 'Nyarlathotep *did* win: Azathoth's awareness *was* released from Mars... but we're all still here, and Tesla reports that the darkness that emerged from the planet has dissipated harmlessly into space, following the destruction of Crystalman's house by that column of light.'

'What the hell *was* that?' asked Rusty.

'Nyarlathotep leaving our dimension, or being *forced* to leave by Haq ul'Suun,' Fort replied. 'Nyarlathotep is the offspring of Azathoth; the bond between them must be even more powerful than the quantum bond… so with Nyarlathotep gone from this dimension, there was nothing to anchor Azathoth's awareness here. It was drawn back into the space between dimensions, where it belongs.'

'And with the Great Old One's awareness gone,' added Lovecraft, 'the crew of Rocketship X-M should now be free of their nightmares. Their sanity is no longer under threat.'

Fort nodded. 'Haq ul'Suun must have been aware of Crystalman's plans from the beginning, and refused to allow the Earth to die in the same way as Mars had all those millions of years ago. He took the chance to atone for his hubris.'

'Speaking of atonement,' said O'Malley, 'that little bastard Johnny Sanguine got away scot-free after all his mischief. I still can't believe I was taken in by the little gobshite.'

'Don't be too hard on yourself, Cormack,' said Fort with a smile. 'You weren't *completely* taken in – just enough to set us all on the right track to winding up this caper. Although,' he added with a frown, 'it was more by luck than judgement that we came through.'

'I suppose so,' O'Malley nodded. 'So… what now?'

'Well, John Carter bought everything we told him, which is just as well since it's the truth, and he was there. I'm kind of glad he wasn't responsible for his actions – I do quite like the guy. Capone's off the hook and is shopping around for a new pair of legs. And Howard and I are off the hook, too.' He looked at Rusty. 'As for you… you helped us out a lot under Long Island. But you still murdered Sanguine, and I'm willing to bet you murdered that archivist at the NCPE, Aldous Bradlee. I suppose it's too much to ask that you turn yourself in.'

'*Way* too much,' Rusty replied. 'No prison can hold me, Mr. Fort, and you don't have what it takes to bring me in, so why don't you just drop the subject, huh?'

Fort shook his head. 'You're bad news, sister.'

'Bad news for anyone who tries to mess with me…'

'And bad news for some who don't.'

Rusty stood up from the table and smiled down at them. 'So long, fellas. Maybe we'll cross paths again, someday.'

Fort looked at her as she sauntered out of the drugstore. 'I sure as hell hope not,' he said.

*

'I wonder if it's true,' mused Lovecraft as he and Fort entered the building containing Fort's office.

'What's that, Howard?'

'What Crystalman said about there being a dimension in which the Great Old Ones are my literary creations. It hardly seems plausible, but…'

'But in a universe containing infinite dimensions, all things that *can* happen *do* happen. I wish to God I lived in *that* dimension! Anyway,' he continued as they climbed the stairs to the second floor, 'I've got a surprise for you.'

'Really? What's that?'

'Well, you did great for your first case, so…'

Fort was then silent until they arrived at the outer door to his office. Lovecraft looked at the sign on the frosted glass of the door. It read:

Lovecraft & Fort
PRIVATE INVESTIGATORS

'I had it done this morning, while we were out,' said Fort. He looked again at the sign. 'What the…? God *damn* it! They got the names the wrong way round! It should say Fort & Lovecraft!'

Lovecraft pondered for a moment, and then said: 'Oh, I don't know… Lovecraft & Fort has more of a ring to it, don't you think?'

Fort sighed and opened the door to the office. 'Whatever,' he said.

LOVECRAFT & FORT
PRIVATE INVESTIGATORS
WILL RETURN IN

Dial M for Mi-Go